THE LAST
BEST HOPE

ED McBAIN

THE LAST BEST HOPE

WARNER BOOKS

A Time Warner Company

Warner Books, Inc., 1271 Avenue of the Americas, New York, NY 10020
Visit our Web site at http://warnerbooks.com

 A Time Warner Company

Printed in the United States of America
First Printing: March 1998
10 9 8 7 6 5 4 3 2 1

Library of Congress Cataloging-in-Publication Data

McBain, Ed
    The last best Hope / Ed McBain.
       p.   cm.
    ISBN 0–446–51990–1
    I. Title.
    PS3515.U585L37   1998
    813'.54—dc21   97–51212
                                                      CIP

Book design by Giorgetta McRee

This is for my wife
DRAGICA DIMITRIJEVIĆ-HUNTER

THE LAST
BEST HOPE

Occasionally, Florida could be glorious in January.

When Matthew moved down here from Chicago, more years ago than he could remember, Joanna was a little girl, and there were oranges on the tree in front of the house. He would pick them for breakfast, and Susan would squeeze them for juice while Joanna swam in the pool out back. There were cardinals in the trees and the air was balmy and the sky was blue and life was sweet and lazy and Florida was all that it should be.

That was a long time ago.

Susan and he were now divorced and Joanna was fifteen and away from Florida most of the time because she was at a boarding school in Massachusetts. Rumor had it that Susan might remarry. Matthew hoped so. Once upon a time, he'd loved her.

★   ★   ★

In Florida, whenever the winter months turned a bit brisker than the Chamber of Commerce liked to admit, you heard people in antiquated winter coats and earmuffs telling you it was much worse up north, right?

Right, Matthew thought.

But you hadn't moved to Florida so it could be much worse up north. You *knew* it was much worse up north. You came down here because you expected it to be much *better.* Forty-two degrees and windy was not a hell of a lot better. And frankly, up north was not a hell of a lot worse.

Forgive me, he thought.

I'm very cranky since I got shot.

Twice.

That was almost a year ago . . . well, it would be a year this March. The first bullet hit him in the left shoulder. The second one hit him in the chest. There'd been searing pain and then a feeling of complete helplessness, his shoulder leaking, his shirt wet with blood, legs going weak, arms flapping, mouth gasping for air, everything swimming out of focus as if he were the hero in a cheap detective novel, everything getting darker and darker and somebody screamed. *Me,* he thought. I was the somebody screaming. People who make movies should tell a person that getting shot is so painful it causes you to scream aloud.

But, listen, that was last March.

Shot or not, there was no reason for Matthew or anyone else in Calusa, Florida, to be cranky this January. This year, January was the dream month every transplanted north-erner wished for. This was Florida weather the way it was supposed to be. This was weather that could make Califor-nia people turn purple with envy.

This was Paradise.

★   ★   ★

The woman sitting opposite Matthew in the corner office at Summerville and Hope was dressed for the seasonably mild weather in a white cotton, single-breasted suit and white flats. He couldn't quite place her accent, but he didn't think she was a native Floridian, despite the sun-washed blond hair and glorious tan. Legs crossed, cotton skirt riding high, blue eyes wide in a quite beautiful face, she told him she wanted a divorce.

He took down the vital statistics.

Jill Lawton.

Thirty-four years old . . .

When a woman was thirty-four, she gave you her age without hesitation. Thirty-four was a good age for a woman. Matthew himself was thirty-nine and he hoped he would ever and always remain that age, because it was not a bad age for a man to be, well beyond the callow cusp of thirty-seven, yet not quite into that barren landscape of the forties. He could understand Jack Benny completely, although he had read someplace recently that many people didn't know who Jack Benny was. Or even Alfred Hitchcock. Then again, some people didn't know who the vice president of the United States was. Sometimes he shook his head in amazement.

Jill Lawton, thirty-four years old and living in a house she and her husband had once shared on Whisper Key until he went up north a year ago, presumably to explore job opportunities.

"When's the last time you spoke to him?"

"Nine months ago."

"Had he found work by then?"

"Well, freelance. But nothing steady. He didn't want me

3

to come up until he'd found a really good position some-where."

"What sort of work does he do?"

"He's a graphic designer."

"Any idea where he might be now?"

"None," she said. "He was still up there last time I heard."

"From him?"

"What?"

"Heard. From him?"

"No. No, no. A friend told me she'd run into him. He was with another woman."

"When was this?"

"In July."

"So the last time you heard from him personally . . ."

"Was in April. Toward the end of April, actually."

"Can you tell me what he said?"

"He said he had to get out of the apartment he was in . . ."

"Where was that?"

"I can give you the address and phone number, but he's been gone from there a long time. Some friends of ours were letting him use it while they were in Europe. But they were coming back on the first of May, and he had to get out by then."

"Did he say where he was going?"

"Yes, a small hotel. Until he could find another apart-ment. Then he wanted me to come up and stay with him."

"Had he found a steady position by then?"

"No, but he said he didn't want us to be apart any longer."

"Which hotel was this?"

"A place called the Harrod. But I called there when I hadn't heard from him, and they had no record of him ever having been there."

"There's a possibility, you know . . ."

"Yes."

". . . that something might have happened to him."

"Yes, I know. But when I *still* didn't hear from him, I called Missing Persons up there and they checked all the hospitals, the jails, whatever it is they do, and there was nothing on him. So I don't think he's dead or anything. He's just gone. But someone told me there's such a thing as the Enoch Arden Law . . ."

"Yes."

"And I'm wondering if that might apply here."

Every law student is taught the Enoch Arden Law, but unless he goes into marital law, he generally forgets its provisions. *Enoch Arden* was a novel written by Alfred Lord Tennyson, and its plot dealt with a shipwrecked man who returns home after many years to find his wife married to another man who has effectively become a father to Enoch's children. Observing their happiness, Enoch decides not to intrude, and disappears in the night.

Matthew explained that under the Enoch Arden Law, a spouse could petition the court for dissolution of the marriage if a husband or wife is missing for five successive years, and a diligent search has uncovered no evidence that he or she is still alive . . .

"Well, I'm sure he's still alive. I just thought . . ."

"The petition would have to assume he's dead."

"I see."

In which case, he went on to explain, the court would require that notice of the petition be published in a newspaper in the English language once a week for three successive weeks, asking the missing spouse to come forward. If he or she did not, goodbye Charlie. But he further explained that a year's absence was not a long enough time to allow notice by publication. The law quite specifically stated that absences of less than five years' duration did not suffice.

"Besides, if you want alimony or support . . ."

"I certainly *do.*"

"Then we'd have to find him and serve him personally. But you know, Mrs. Lawton . . ."

"Jill," she corrected again. "Please."

"I'm not a marital lawyer. If we do locate your husband, and manage to serve him, I feel you should turn the actual negotiations over to a lawyer who specializes in marital law. There are several good ones in Calusa, and I'd be happy to recommend any one of them when the time comes. Unless, of course, you want a specialist to handle the matter from go, in which case . . ."

"No, I hear you're very good," she said.

"I have *investigators* who are good," he said.

"Can they find my husband?"

"I'm sure they can. Can you tell me his name, please?"

"Jack. Jack Lawton."

"How long have you been married, Mrs. Lawton?"

"Jill," she said. "Please. Sixteen years. I married him when I was a senior in high school. He was in the army, heading overseas. I thought he might get killed."

He didn't ask her which war, or even which police action, this might have been. Apparently, Jack Lawton survived his particular American war, whichever one it was. Matthew had survived his, too. Only to get shot minding his own business many years later. Ah well.

She had come well prepared. She showed him a color photograph of her husband, taken shortly before he did his disappearing act. It showed a man in his late thirties, Matthew guessed, wearing jeans and a short-sleeved sports shirt, standing against a huge oak tree, grinning into the camera. She said the picture had been taken at his mother's farm in Pennsylvania, the summer before Jack vanished. She gave Matthew the mother's name, address, and telephone number . . .

"But he's not there," she said.

"How do you know?"

"I talk to her all the time. My mother-in-law's a wonderful person, we get along beautifully."

"How old is your husband?"

"Thirty-seven. Three years older than I am."

"How tall is he?"

"Six-two."

"His weight?"

"A hundred and ninety." She hesitated. Then she said, "That was a year ago. I don't know what he weighs now."

"You say a friend was letting him use an apartment up there . . ."

"Yes."

"Can you give me the address and phone number?"

"Sure. But Jack moved out at the end of April. When the Holdens got home from Europe. Charlie and Lois. Holden."

"And their address?"

"It won't help you."

"It might."

"Okay," she said, and shrugged, and leafed through a

small, red, leather-bound address book. Matthew copied down the address and phone number.

"This friend of yours who ran into him," he said. "Did . . . ?"

"Claire Phillips. I'll give you *her* number, too, if you like. But all it was, she ran into him on the street."

"Where on the street?"

"I really don't know."

"We'll try to find out. It might give us a neighborhood."

"Sure," she said, and flipped through the address book again.

"How about your husband's Social Security number? Would you know that?"

"I'll have to call you."

"Any joint bank accounts?"

"Yes. But he hasn't written any checks on it since the middle of May."

"What's the name of the bank?"

"Calusa First."

"The account number?"

"I have it here," she said, and reached into her handbag, opened a wallet-sized check holder, and read off the number from the bottom of one of the checks.

"What's the last check he wrote?"

"To the telephone company. For April's bill."

"When was that?"

"Second week in May."

"Nothing between then and when your friend ran into him?"

"Nothing."

"So we know that up to July, at least, he was still up north."

"Still up north, yes."

"Nothing since?"

"Nothing. It's as if he disappeared from the face of the earth."

"We'll try to find him for you," Matthew said.

"Please," she said. "The bastard."

There were six Calusa police cars angled in against the curb when Matthew got to the scene at eleven that night. He had heard the news as a breaking story on television, had called Bloom's office at once, and was informed by a rather snotty sergeant that Bloom was already in the field. He drove the twenty-four miles from Fatback Key to North Galley on the mainland in twenty minutes and was stepping out of his car when yet another snotty sergeant—or for all he knew, the same one—stopped him and asked him where the hell he thought he was going.

Matthew told him he was there to see Detective Morris Bloom.

"And who are you?" the sergeant asked, scowling.

"Matthew Hope. Attorney," he added, mindful of the fact that the only Shakespearean line most policemen knew was "First thing we do, let's kill all the lawyers."

"Wait here," the sergeant said, and went behind the police barricade and onto a path between two shacks in a row of shanties that had probably been built some sixty years ago, when Calusa first began attracting midwesterners who bought land cheap and threw up any kind of structure on it, just to get away from the bitter cold up north.

North Galley Road was built along a narrow strip of sandy beach in a not particularly fashionable section of town, but it had the advantage of being fairly close to a truly

9

splendid beach on the other end of the Santo Spirito Causeway. Even the worst beaches in Calusa had no rivals on the planet. Matthew's partner, Frank, a transplanted New Yorker who had seen a few beaches hither and yon, readily admitted that the sand was more powdery white here than on any beach in the world. And none of Calusa's beaches matched Sandy Cove, just across the causeway, not five minutes from the much inferior beach upon which a man named Jack Lawton had been shot to death. Or so Matthew had learned from the ten o'clock news.

Bloom came up the path from the beach some five minutes after the beefy sergeant went to fetch him. A heavyset man an inch or so taller than Matthew, Bloom usually wore a woebegone expression better suited to an undertaker than a police detective. Wearing a rumpled suit, a white shirt, a blue tie, and dusty black shoes, he ambled up the path to where Matthew was leaning against the fender of his smoky-blue Acura, extended his hand, and said, "Don't tell me he's your client."

"Close," Matthew said.

"I've got a minute. But just," Bloom said. The beefy sergeant was still scowling. "Let me know when the M.E. gets here," Bloom told him. "We'll be in the coffee shop across the street."

Galley Road ran parallel to U.S. 41, otherwise known as the Tamiami Trail, familiarly and simply called "the Trail" by residents of Calusa, Sarasota, and Bradenton, the three cities that formed the so-called Calbrasa Triangle. The Calbrasa airport divided and defined Galley north and south. From sundown to the wee hours of the morning, prostitutes lined the North Trail near the airport, plying their wares in tight black skirts, shiny satin blouses, and spike-heeled pumps.

A snatch of hookers was sitting at a table in the coffee shop when Matthew and Bloom walked in at close to eleven-thirty that night. The women looked them over, decided they were both cops, and went serenely back to their coffee.

"Tell me about it," Matthew said.

"How do you know him?"

"I don't. His wife hired me to find him."

"Looks like you did," Bloom said.

They both ordered coffee from a blond waitress who looked very tired. The place itself looked tired, for that matter, one of those seedy roadside joints you find on through streets all over Florida. In season, traffic on the Trail was horrendous, and most savvy residents used Galley as a by-pass. The coffee shop did good business, but the walls needed paint, and the grill was greasy, and most items on the hand-lettered menu above the counter cost ninety-nine cents. A jukebox was playing a country-western song that urged the listener to take off his shoes and th'ow 'em on the flo. One of the hookers kept tapping her red high-heeled shoe in time to it.

"Big hole in his face, most likely a shotgun blast," Bloom said. "Was he gay?"

"Not that I know of."

"Cause it looks a lot like a homosexual murder," he said. "He's half-naked, wire hangers wrapped around his wrists and ankles. Plastic bag lying beside the body, might've been used over his head for kinky games, gerbil up his ass for all I know. Why was she looking for him, the wife?"

"She wants to divorce him."

"Now she doesn't have to," Bloom said.

★   ★   ★

11

There were two pieces of photo ID in the dead man's wallet, one a Florida driver's license and the other a Visa card. The pictures on them looked as different from each other as they did from the one Jill Lawton had showed Matthew in his office. Neither of them added up to positive identification. He called Jill—who'd already heard the news on television—and asked her to meet him and Bloom at the Henley Hospital morgue.

She got there at close to midnight, wearing jeans, sandals, and a man's white tailored shirt. By that time, Bloom had called the State Attorney's Office, and they had in turn notified the on-duty S.A., a woman named Patricia Demming, who'd been awakened at home on Fatback Key, where she'd been waiting for Matthew to return to her bed, by the way, and who was now at Henley looking radiantly beautiful at midnight without makeup but dressed in a crisp linen suit and low-heeled shoes that did nothing to diminish the splendor of her long shapely legs, oh how he did love that woman.

Henley Hospital was not the best in Calusa, but its morgue was no different from any other morgue in the world. There was a stench in any morgue that defied description unless you'd been on a battlefield where bloated corpses had been rotting in the sun for days on end. The attendant opened a stainless-steel door for them, allowing the first faint whiff of death to escape, and then led them into a stainless-steel chamber where the aroma became overpowering, as if someone had thrown an odious blanket over their heads, forcing them to reel back from the stink. Matthew thought Jill might faint. He knew Patricia wouldn't.

The ambulance had arrived some ten minutes before they

had. Lawton hadn't been shelved yet. Instead, he was lying on a stainless-steel table, awaiting autopsy. A rubber sheet covered him from head to toe. The attendant pulled it back.

Jill looked down at the corpse.

She was expecting her husband. She had *heard* this was her husband, she had been *told* this was her husband, but the look on her face was nonetheless one of total surprise.

"That isn't Jack," she said.

It wasn't Jack because Jack had a minuscule blue dot tattooed on his Adam's apple—

"A what?" Bloom asked.

"A dot," Jill told them. "To guide the machine."

"What machine?" Bloom asked.

They were all looking at the corpse's Adam's apple. There was no blue dot on it. There were speckles of dried blood and black powder from the shotgun blast that had torn away his face, but no blue dot.

"He had radiation therapy six years ago," Jill said. "To remove a precancerous growth on his vocal cords. The therapy worked. But the tattoo will be there forever."

In bed with Patricia later that night, Matthew told her that whenever a morgue attendant pulled back a sheet, he thought of the Swan story.

"What *is* the Swan story?" she asked.

"You don't know the Swan story?" he said.

"I'm sorry, I don't."

"*Everybody* knows the Swan story."

"Not me."

"The word 'Swan' tattooed on the guy's penis?"

"No," she said. "Tell it."

13

"Not right this minute," he said, and took her in his arms.

"I'm really very sleepy, Matthew," she said, and yawned.

"Okay," he said, but in retaliation he didn't tell her the Swan story.

Toots was telling Warren how she never stopped thinking about crack. Never. Every waking moment of her life, she thought about crack. Whatever else she might be doing, crack was always in the forefront of her mind. It was now four months since Warren had kidnapped her . . .

"I didn't kidnap you," he said.

"Abducted me," she said.

"Just carried you away from your apartment and took you out on a boat in the middle of the Gulf of Mexico, is all," Warren said.

"Cold turkey, however you slice it," Toots said.

She was looking good again. She'd cut her blond hair short, made her look like a female athlete, all tanned by the sun again, she really was looking good.

"Even with rehab, I think of it day and night," she said.

"You ought to tell them."

"Oh, please," she said, "what do you *think* we do there?

15

That's all I *do* is tell them, over and over again. Without telling them, I'd go totally nuts."

This was now ten minutes past ten on the morning of January twenty-second, a Wednesday. They were sitting in Warren's office, one of three private offices in their new digs, which were large enough to accommodate a good-sized waiting room as well. The third-floor layout used to belong to a chiropractor. Now the name on the entrance door read:

CHAMBERS, KILEY & LAMB

PRIVATE INVESTIGATIONS

Toots said they should have put her name first since she was a woman. "Ladies first," she said.

Guthrie said they should have put *his* name first because he was a man in his sixties. "Seniority," he said.

Warren said *his* name had to go first because otherwise it'd be considered racism. "Black, you know," he said.

Toots still felt it parsed better as Kiley, Chambers and Lamb. Even Guthrie sort of agreed, reluctantly. But Warren's name was nonetheless first on the door and the stationery. Besides, business was good, so who could argue?

Warren didn't mind her talking about dope. He figured the more she talked about it, the less she'd even *dream* of doing it again. Warren figured if she went back on crack again, *he'd* be the one who died. Warren figured maybe he loved her. Though he guessed Toots didn't realize it.

They were here to figure out where to *start* on this thing. Guthrie hadn't arrived yet, he never waltzed in till ten-thirty or so, said he needed his beauty sleep. Meanwhile, they were here waiting for him to show up, reluctant to begin without him, but eager to get started.

"What'd they get on his prints?" Toots asked.

"Nothing local or state. It'll take a while for the Feebs to get back."

"Did the wife have any idea how he could've got hold of her husband's ID?"

"Last she heard from the husband was the end of April."

"From where?"

"Up north."

"So now a dead guy turns up with his ID."

"Yeah."

"Shotgun murder, huh?"

"Yeah."

"Sounds like a redneck."

"Plenty of those down here. But Bloom's thinking a gay murder. Guy wearing only blue jeans, bound head and foot with wire hangers, gay bar named Timothy B's just up the beach."

"That doesn't necessarily spell gay. Any sign of fun-and-games torture?"

"A plastic bag, is all."

"Over his head?"

"No. Lying on the sand beside him."

"Doesn't sound gay to me. Does it sound gay to you?"

"Just frivolous," Warren said, and smiled. Toots smiled back. "Gay or whatever, Matthew wants to know why the ID switch. You want to pass a guy off as somebody else, you blow away his face with a shotgun, sure, but don't you figure he'll be printed, the corpse, and sooner or later they'll know he's not Lawton? The wife says Lawton was in the army, his prints are on file. And how about the tattoo? You've got to figure the wife's gonna notice the stiff doesn't have a blue dot on his neck, don't you? So why plant Lawton's ID on a corpse that won't pass muster?"

"Maybe the corpse had the ID before he *became* a corpse," Toots said.

"Yeah, maybe."

From the outside office, they heard the unmistakable sound of Guthrie Lamb hitting on the company receptionist. Priss always played the game right back. "Oh, you savage," they heard her say, and then the door to Warren's office opened and Guthrie himself walked in, sporting white linen slacks, white tasseled loafers, black socks, and a dark black sports shirt open at the throat.

He looked pretty damn good for a man in his late sixties, Warren thought, even if he never admitted to being older than sixty-two. White hair, but that was the only clue. In a swimsuit he looked like an elderly Schwarzenegger. Young girls in bikinis actually gave him the eye, go figure. Good investigator, too. Called himself a "famous detective," God only knew why since nobody outside of Calusa had ever heard of him. Behaved like a private eye from the fifties, which was when he'd first been licensed in New York. Maybe he'd been famous up there.

"Let the games begin," Guthrie said.

"They began without you," Toots said.

"Fill me in," Guthrie said. "Priss!" he yelled. "Can we get some coffee in here?"

Warren repeated everything Matthew had told him on the phone. He repeated what he and Toots had been talking about before his arrival. Priss Carpenter came in with coffee for everyone. She was wearing a purple mini with panty hose to match, a cream-colored blouse, cream-colored pumps. She was blacker than Warren, but a hell of a lot prettier.

"When will the Feebs get back?" Guthrie asked.

"You know them," Warren said.

"Anyway, the stiff is Bloom's business," Toots said. "Finding Lawton is ours."

"I've got a good question," Guthrie said. "If Lawton doesn't have a job, how does the wife expect to get alimony from him?"

"Maybe he's got a stash someplace."

"Which ties in with your thinking on the ID," Guthrie said.

"How do you mean?"

"Maybe he's worth more dead than alive. In fact, if somebody swiped his wallet, it could mean he's already dead."

They were all silent for a moment, sipping at their coffees. Bright morning sunlight slanted through the venetian blinds, throwing bars onto Warren's desk.

"Who lives in those shacks on the beach?" Guthrie asked.

Guthrie would have been the first to admit that he was the last of the Great Male Sexist Pigs, but by *anyone's* reckoning the broad who answered the door at 1137 North Galley Road was a dame of the highest order. Mrs. Adele Dob was a flaming buxom redhead in her forties, he guessed, her frizzed hair standing up all over her head as if she'd recently been struck by lightning. She opened the screen door to her house and stood holding it open with one bejeweled and braceleted hand and wrist, as if there were no such thing as bugs in the state of Florida. She was wearing a green caftan scooped low over the sloping milky-white tops of abundant breasts, he noticed. Her eyes were as green as the caftan, lined with green to emphasize them further. She was barefoot, her toenails painted to match her fingernails which matched the lipstick on her generous mouth, fire-engine red from tip to toe. A dame for sure.

"Mrs. Dob?" he asked.

"That's me," she said.

"May I come in?" he asked.

"What for?" she said.

"I understand you own the six houses in this row . . ."

"That's right, all six of them."

"A man was killed on the beach here last night . . ."

"Are you a cop?"

"Private investigator," he said, and showed her his Lucite-encased ID card. She looked it over, nodded, seemed singularly unimpressed, looked up at him again. He smiled. She did not return the smile. "We're trying to find out who the dead man was," he said.

"Who's we?" Dame Dob said.

"The attorney I work for."

"Is he planning to sue me?"

"No, no. Who?"

"This lawyer, whoever he is."

"Matthew Hope."

"It wasn't me who shot Corry, you know. Wasn't me who broke his head, either."

Guthrie hadn't heard about the broken head.

"Corry who?" he asked.

"God knows," she said.

"Let me buy you a cool drink," he said.

"Why?"

"Hot day?" he suggested.

She looked him over.

"Let me get my sandals," she said.

★　　★　　★

The restaurant was called Kelly's Stone Crab House, a local hangout on Sandy Cove Island. During the stone crab season, Kelly's served more damn crab claws than there were sand dollars on all the beaches in Florida. Then again, it was busy at any time of the year. At one that afternoon, when Guthrie and Adele walked in, the place was jammed with locals and tourists. Adele promptly asked for Dave Kelly, the grandly mustachioed proprietor of the eatery, who greeted her effusively and found them a table on the water. Guthrie figured old Davey here was planking her.

They both ordered icy cold beer and fried seafood platters. He liked the way she ate. It reminded him of that broad in the movie *Tom Jones,* the way she slurped and slobbered all over everything. Sitting, swilling, swallowing, the water lapping the dock, puffy white clouds drifting across a pale blue sky, the sound of music wafting from somewhere up the beach, Adele loosened up, the way all frails loosen up if you buy them a few beers.

"You know what I like about Florida?" she asked.

"Where are you from originally?"

"Cleveland. I used to look like Maureen O'Hara."

"You still do," Guthrie lied. "When did you come down?"

"Thirty years ago. How about you?"

"I've been here a while," he said. He never liked to give actual dates because then girls could figure out your age. Better they should think he was in his late forties, early fifties. "What do you like about Florida?"

"Just hangin out," she said. "Like we're doing now. In Florida, people enjoy just hangin out. I hang out here all the time. I come in for lunch occasionally, but usually I just make myself a salad or a sandwich at home. Most of the time, I come in for drinks before dinner. There's a nice hangin-out crowd here during Happy Hour. Or I come in late at night, you get kids comin home from the movies or wherever, here for a drink before heading home, that's a lot of fun."

He realized that by "kids," she didn't mean teenyboppers, she was talking about people her own age, whatever it might be, forty, forty-five. She was licking her fingers now, the way the broad in *Tom Jones* did.

"In Florida," she said, "you get the feeling nobody *works,* you know what I mean? Well, the old geezers down here actually *don't* work, they're all retired, their idea of a big night is going to the supermarket to push a cart around. Hey, Maude, looka this," she said, imitating a toothless old man, "they got a special on *laxatives* this week! You know the one about the guy in the nursing home?"

"Which one is that?" Guthrie asked. He knew about a thousand nursing-home jokes. Down here, jokes about nursing homes were very popular. That's because people in their eighties and nineties never thought of themselves as being old like the people in the jokes.

"This old guy goes down the hall, stops another old guy, says, 'How old do you think I am?' The other guy says, 'I don't know, sixty-four, sixty-five?' 'Wrong!' he says. 'I'm eighty-four!' He continues down the hall, stops another guy, says, 'How old do you think I am?' The second guy says, 'I don't know, sixty-two, sixty-three?' 'Wrong!' he says. 'I'm eighty-four!' He continues down the hall, there's this old lady sitting in a wheelchair, he says, 'How old do you think I am?' The old lady says, 'Unzip your fly.' He unzips his fly. She says, 'Put your penis in my hand.' He puts his penis in her hand. She jiggles it up and down, like she's

22

weighing it. 'You're eighty-four,' she says. The old guy's amazed. 'You can tell that just by jiggling my penis in your hand?' he says. 'No,' she says, 'you told me yesterday.'"

Guthrie burst out laughing.

"Yeah," she said, laughing with him.

"I thought it was gonna be the other one," he said.

"Which other one?"

"This old guy at a nursing home walks up to this old lady sitting in a wheelchair?"

"Yeah?"

"He says, 'Do you know who *I* am?' The old lady shakes her head. 'No,' she says. 'But if you go to the front desk, they'll tell you.'"

Adele started laughing again.

"I hate people who've already given up, don't you?" she said. "Buy themselves funeral plots side by side, set up trust funds for the kiddies, what the hell's left? Do you have any kids?"

"Two. Up north."

"You a widower?"

"Divorced."

"Once, twice?"

"Once was enough."

"I'm divorced, too. Twice," she said. She hesitated, and then said, "How old do you think I am?"

"Eighty-four," Guthrie said.

"Seriously."

"I don't know," he said. "Unzip your fly."

They both burst out laughing.

"Go ahead, take a guess," she said.

"And risk my life?"

"I'm sixty-one. That's the truth. I came down here after my first divorce, I was thirty-one."

"I'm sixty-three," Guthrie said, wondering what on earth was possessing him. "I used to be a private eye in New York, came down here in the late fifties when the place was still practically a fishing village."

"Famous detective, I'll bet," she said, and winked at him over a fried scallop.

"Oh, sure, famous."

"I'll bet," she said, and winked again. "Sixty-three, huh? You look terrific."

"I try to keep in shape," he said modestly.

"That's what Florida does for you," she said. "Ponce de León really *did* find the fountain of youth down here, you know that?"

"When the weather's like this, I can believe it."

"You want to go to a movie tonight?"

"Sure," he said.

"You like movies?"

"Some of them."

"Which ones?"

"The sexy ones."

"Me, too. What's the sexiest movie you ever saw?"

"Not counting porn flicks?"

"Do you watch porn flicks?"

"Oh, sure, all the time."

"We'll rent one some night."

"Sure," he said.

"So which one?"

"Should we rent?"

"No. The sexiest movie you ever saw. Not counting porn flicks."

"The sexiest movie? Or the sexiest *scene* in a movie?"

"Please don't say Sharon Stone spreading her legs to take your picture."

"I was about to say the scene with Michael Douglas and what's-her-name."

"Oh, wow!" Adele said.

"You remember that movie?"

"Oh, wow!"

"Fatal Attraction."

"Wow."

"Did you like that scene?"

"The sexiest scene of all time."

"Yeah," Guthrie said, nodding.

"Yeah," Adele said.

He signaled to the waitress, ordered another round of beers. They both sat looking out over the water, sipping the beer, basking in the bright afternoon sunshine.

"I hate movies that show old people kissing, don't you?" Adele said.

"Well, old people *do* kiss," Guthrie said, and quickly added, "I guess."

"I'm sure they do, but who wants to *see* them doing it?"

"Actually," Guthrie said, "in most movies, the guy kissing the girl is twenty, thirty years older than she is."

"Sometimes forty. You get a star almost seventy years old, he's kissing a twenty-two-year-old girl. Is that supposed to be *believable*?"

"It's the producer's fantasy," Guthrie said.

"Can you imagine the ego?"

"The producer's?"

"No, the *star's*. To think he's so desirable that a girl

scarcely out of her teens will find him *attractive*? At seventy?"

"Well, I'm sixty-three," Guthrie said, and thought Why am I *repeating* it? I must be losing my mind!

"Yes, but you're very attractive," Adele said.

"Well, thank you, but so's Clint Eastwood, actually."

"I would not like to kiss Clint Eastwood."

"Oh, come on."

"I mean it. I would definitely *not* like to kiss him. I even found it difficult to accept him kissing Meryl Streep, and she's got to be forty, am I right?"

"Glenn Close," Guthrie said. "That's the one who was all over Michael Douglas. I always get her mixed up with Meryl Streep."

"Me, too."

"What's your favorite movie of all time?" Guthrie asked.

"Gone with the Wind," she said at once.

"Bingo!" Guthrie said.

"You, too?"

"Me, too."

He wondered if he was still lying.

He didn't think he was still lying.

"You know what *else* I hate to see in a movie?" Adele asked.

"No, what?"

"*Teenagers* kissing. I mean, who *cares*?"

"Twelve-year-olds do."

"Sure, but I'm sixty-*one,* for Christ's sake!"

"You know what else I find *sexy*?" he asked.

"In movies?"

"No, in real life."

"What?"

"I mean down here. In Florida."

"What?"

"You're sitting by a hotel pool, and all the girls are wearing bikinis, and all at once this file clerk from the manager's office walks out and she's got on a business suit and high-heeled shoes and panty hose. I find that very sexy."

"Do you think I dress too casually?"

"No, I wasn't implying that."

"Because I'm not a file clerk in a manager's office, you know."

"I realize that."

"I just own six little houses and I rent them out. What I'm saying is I don't *have* to wear a suit and panty hose. I'm not *obliged* to wear them."

"That's what I find sexy. That the girl *has* to get dressed for work while everybody else is half-naked in the sun. It's a little like bondage, I guess. I think."

"Bondage, hmm?"

"Yeah. I think."

"Are you into bondage?"

"*Into* it? No, no. But I don't mind it every now and then."

"Me either."

"When it's for fun."

"Of course."

"Not for real. Not to hurt anybody."

"Of course not," Adele said. "I *do* get dressed up occasionally, you know."

"I'll bet you do."

"Garter belt, crotchless panties, high heels, the whole bit. Sixty-one years old, can you imagine?"

"You look forty."

"Ho ho."

"You do. I thought you were forty. When you opened the screen door."

"I don't usually do that."

"Do what?"

"Let all the flies in."

They stared at each other across the table.

"What do you want to know about the dead man?" she asked.

"Everything," he said.

The way Adele tells it, she first met Corry—

"Corry who?" Guthrie asked again.

"I told you, I don't know."

"So where'd you meet him?"

"Right here at Kelly's, the Sunday night before the murder. Davey gets a big crowd in here on Sunday nights, everybody wanting to hang onto the weekend before going to work the next morning . . ."

It's eleven o'clock at night.

She had left Galley Road at about nine-thirty, driven over the Santo Spirito Causeway to get here five minutes later, so she figures she's been in the place almost an hour and a half when Corry walks in. He looks like a Marlboro man in jeans and boots and a white T-shirt with one of the short sleeves rolled up over a package of cigarettes. Guy in his late thirties, early forties, she supposes, very muscular, very tanned, nice athletic swagger about him, altogether what Adele might have called a hunk if she were thirty years younger.

She's sitting over there with some other kids, at the big round table near the bar. One of the girls whistles at Corry and tells him to come on join them, which he does because not everybody at the table is a decrepit old lady in her six-ties. Most of the girls are in their early thirties, in fact, and the guys are around Corry's age, though they don't know his name yet. And there's this old geezer who joins them every now and then and just sits and nods all the time like a dummy while he peers down the front of the girls' blouses, his name is Avery. It's Avery, oddly enough, who causes the goddamn fight.

Corry takes a seat and orders a Stoli neat and they intro-duce themselves all around the table . . .

"Did he introduce himself as Jack Lawton?"

"Just Corry, as I recall. Kelly's is a first-name kind of place. Specially when there's eight, ten people sitting around a table."

"Go on."

"Well, we started playing a game where we had to think of sexy words. The same way we were thinking of sexy movies earlier, this was we had to think of sexy words. It was one of the girls who came up with the idea. Kelly's can get kind of wild sometimes. So . . ."

One of the guys says, "Tense," which actually is a nice kind of sexy word, and one of the girls comes up with "Damp," which she sort of pouts onto her lips, and another girl says, "Quiver," which is clean but sort of sexy, too, and Corry says, "Buttercup," which is kind of cowboy sexy, or maybe it's supposed to sound like something else, which makes Corry smarter than Adele first figured him.

A girl named Nancy, taking her cue from "damp," and getting a bit more literal, comes up with "Moist," closing her eyes and kissing the air with the word. Old Avery, who doesn't quite get the gist of the game, says in his geezer voice, "Tits," which no one thinks is either sexy *or* funny. So

29

naturally he's emboldened to say "Cock." All the girls hoot at him and Nancy tells him to go take his filthy old mind to the bathroom, which amuses him no end, the old fart.

Delighted by all this attention, and perhaps inspired by Corry's "buttercup," he ventures to say "Cunt," which brings young Craig, the guy who suggested "tense," to his feet with his fists balled, demanding that Avery apologize to all the young ladies at the table. This is like a movie now, where suddenly everybody here is a virgin and the cowboy in the white hat is defending the honor of each and every maiden. Except that Avery is dead drunk and still thinks it's a game.

Adele and Corry are the only two people there who seem to understand that you don't go challenging a seventy-two-year-old drunk who's grinning like a jackass at his own splendid witticisms. Adele says, "He's drunk, Craig," and Corry says, "Let it go, man." Craig says, "Not until he apologizes," and in response Avery says, "Cunt, cunt, cunt."

So Craig hits him.

He hits him real hard, knocking Avery off his chair and sending him rolling over backward toward the wall. He then reaches down and picks him up off the floor, his hands twisted into the front of the old man's shirt, buttons popping, and is pulling back his fist to flatten him completely, when Corry says again, very softly this time, "Let it go, man." Craig says, "Fuck you, man," and smashes his fist into Avery's face, at which very moment Corry lunges at him.

The two grapple like the street fighters they are, none of this carefully choreographed shit like a movie barroom fight, punches flying wildly, the men sweating and clinching and cursing and punching fiercely again until Craig grabs for a wine bottle on the table and wraps his fist around the neck, and pulls it off the table, red wine slosh-ing everywhere, Adele shrieking when it stains her white dress, and swings it at Corry's head, which effectively ends the fight.

Everybody hustles Craig out of there, fearful Kelly will call the police, which of course he doesn't dare do unless he wants his fine little restaurant to become a parking lot overnight. One of the girls offers to drive old Avery home. He is conscious enough to stare down the front of her blouse as she half carries him, half drags him out to her car.

"The bottle broke Corry's head," Adele tells Guthrie now. "He was bleeding and everything, he looked a total mess. What I did, I remembered one of my mother's old remedies for stopping bleeding, don't ask me where it came from. I soaked some brown paper towels from the ladies' room with vinegar Davey brought out from the kitchen, and put the towels on his head like a poultice. Then I took him home with me."

It turns out that Corry had lived in Los Angeles for a while, where first he'd had a job with the Automobile Club, working nights, answering telephone calls from motorists in distress. What he'd do, he'd take down the year and make of the car, and its location, and ask what seemed to be the trouble, and then he'd advise the distressed motorist to stay with the vehicle, there would be someone there within forty minutes, was what he did. The job had advantages in that it left him free to look for better jobs during the day.

Corry got a job with a lobster company while he was still looking for something better. Crown Lobster was the name of the company, there was just the boss, whose name was Mr. Stein, and a Chinese girl named Jenny, and himself,

Corry. Mr. Stein would come in every morning, and take off his suit jacket and put on a little white jacket with the words Crown Lobster stitched in red over the breast pocket. Then he'd sit behind his desk, and begin making his calls to Boothbay Harbor, Maine, where the live lobsters were packed in barrels of ice and air-expressed to California in time for that night's dinner.

Jenny came in dressed like Suzie Wong each morning, tight silk dresses slit up the thigh to her ass, and began calling all the Chinese restaurants in town, giving them lobster quotes and asking how many barrels they'd be needing today. The Chinese restaurants ordered mostly the jumbo lobsters, which they cut up and put in their various lobster dishes. The other restaurants, the ones Corry called, usually ordered either the twins, which were the one-pound lobsters, or else the medium-sized lobsters, which were the pound-and-a-half to two-pounders. Corry would call a place like André's, for example, which was a very high-class French restaurant, and ask to talk to Ira, which was the buyer's name, and then give him a quote on some "nice, live Maine lobsters," and the buyer would tell him how many barrels he needed, if any. The job was strictly a morning job, which was good in that it left plenty of time to look for something better.

All of which Adele found endlessly fascinating.

But it wasn't until they were in bed together, later that night, that Corry told her he'd finally abandoned the idea of finding something better and went back to doing what he really knew how to do, which was stickups.

★   ★   ★

"As it turned out," Guthrie said, "Corry and two accomplices robbed an all-night pharmacy on La Cienega Boulevard."

Matthew never knew when to believe him. He sometimes felt Guthrie told his stories merely for effect.

"Or at least *tried* to rob it," he said now. "Given his past reputation, I wouldn't be surprised he *stole* that wallet from Jack Lawton, who, for all we know, may be lying in a gutter someplace with his head busted open."

They were strolling up Lemon Avenue toward the offices of Summerville and Hope, having just had early morning coffee at a place called the Donut Ring on Parson and Fourth. It was another gorgeous January morning in Calusa, Florida. Matthew was wearing a seersucker suit, a pale blue dress shirt, and a dark blue tie. Guthrie was wearing a pink short-sleeved sports shirt, pink trousers to match, and white loafers, no socks. He looked very fashionable. By comparison, Matthew felt like an accountant.

"So he and two other guys *tried* to hold up a drugstore," he said.

"Yes," Guthrie said.

"What happened?"

"He chickened out because he saw an LAPD car pulling up outside. He was afraid one of the clerks had hit a silent alarm. So he got out of there fast, leaving the other two behind."

"Why a drugstore?"

"Apparently he'd had success with drugstores before. He hadn't had much success with liquor stores, apparently. At least he hinted this to Adele . . . Mrs. Dob . . . before he left her that night."

"What time did he leave her?"

33

"Well, she didn't say. I gather he lingered awhile."

"And showed up two nights later, dead on the beach behind her house."

"It would appear," Guthrie said.

"Corry who?"

"He didn't say."

That afternoon, Morrie Bloom called to tell Matthew that the FBI had got back with a positive ID on the prints lifted from the corpse. For whatever it was worth, the dead man's name was Ernest Corrington and he had two prior armed robbery convictions, both for liquor store holdups, the first one in Colorado, his native state, the most recent one in California. His last known address was on Veteran Avenue in Los Angeles. He had reported to his parole officer on October third, but had not mentioned that he was leaving the state. Being in Florida was a violation of parole in itself.

So was stealing Lawton's wallet, Matthew thought.

He phoned Claire Phillips up north at a little past three that afternoon, told her who he was, and asked if she could fill him in on the details of her chance meeting with Jack Lawton on the street last July.

"It wasn't actually on the *street*," she said. "It was in the *park*. There's this park near where I live, close to the river."

"And this was sometime in July?"

"Sometime after the Fourth. The week after the Fourth."

"Are you sure it was Mr. Lawton?"

"Oh, positive. I've known him and Jill since shortly after they were married. My husband and I used to live in

34

Calusa. That's where we met. I was wheeling my baby in the park. It was Jack all right."

"Can you tell me what you talked about?"

"Frankly, the conversation was a little awkward."

"Why was that, Mrs. Phillips?"

"Well . . . he was with another woman. Said she was a friend of his and Jill's."

"Did he introduce her?"

"As a matter of fact, he did. But, I mean . . . it was so obvious that this wasn't just a *friend.* I mean, he's married to Jill, what's he doing holding hands with this redhead in the park? And he slipped once, said something like *Gee,* what a coincidence, Holly and I live just a few blocks away."

"Did he say they were living *together*?"

"Well, he didn't specify, but a man says they're living a few blocks away, the assumption is together."

"That was her name? Holly?"

"Yes."

"Would you remember Holly what?"

"Simms? Something like that."

"What else did you talk about?"

"Oh, he told me he'd been looking for a job in graphic design, but that so far he hadn't had any real luck and he was considering other opportunities. He told me . . ."

"Did he say which opportunities?"

"No. He told me he was thinking of moving back to Florida if things didn't work out here. You have to understand, I didn't know that he and Jill had separated. As far as I was concerned, they were still married, and he was holding hands with another woman."

"Named Holly Simms."

"Or Simmons, something like that."

"You're sure it was Holly, though."

"Oh yes."

"And he said she was a friend of his and Jill's."

"Yes. Simpson maybe."

"What else did you talk about?"

"That was about it. I told you, it was very awkward. I'm standing there with my baby in the carriage, and he's holding hands with a redhead. I didn't know he and Jill were separated until I called her that night."

"To tell her you'd seen Jack."

"Well . . . yes. She's a good friend of mine."

"And did she say they were separated?"

"Actually, she said she hadn't heard from him since April, was what I think she said."

"How did the conversation end?"

"She thanked me for calling . . ."

"I meant with Jack."

"Oh. He said he had to be running along, something like that, it was all very awkward. He was taking Holly to the museum, I think he said. Simon? Could it have been Holly Simon? No, I'm thinking of Carly Simon. Something like that, anyway. Something with an S."

"Did he say which museum?"

"No."

"Are there any museums near you?"

"Well, no, not in the immediate neighborhood."

"Did Lawton tell you where *he* was living?"

"A few blocks away."

"Where do *you* live, Mrs. Phillips?"

"On the Oval. 1219."

"And he said he was living just a few blocks away, is that it?"

"Like *'Gee,* what a coincidence, Holly and I live just a few blocks away!' Yeah."

"I'm not too familiar with the city. Where would . . . ?"

"Silvermine Oval is all the way uptown," she said. "In the Eighty-seventh Precinct."

3

Detective/Second Grade Stephen Louis Carella was sitting at his desk looking out at the falling snow when Sergeant Murchison buzzed from the desk downstairs to say a lawyer from Florida was on the telephone. What Carella needed right now was a lawyer from Florida. What he needed was a lawyer from *anywhere*. Cotton Hawes had called ten minutes ago to say he was locked in traffic on a snowbound street and probably would not get there to relieve till maybe five-thirty, six o'clock. Bert Kling had called not five minutes after that to say that there were delays on all the westbound subway lines, so he'd decided to take the bus instead, but the way it looked out here on the street, there wasn't anything moving, so it might be a while before he got to the squadroom. The clock on the squadroom wall now read five minutes past four. Carella punched a button in the base of his phone.

"Eighty-seventh Squad, Carella," he said.

39

"Detective Carella, this is Matthew Hope. I'm an attorney here in Calusa, Florida. How's the weather up there?"

Whenever anyone called from Florida, they asked about the weather up north.

"It's snowing," Carella said.

"I'm sorry to hear that."

"Well, it snows up here," Carella said.

"I know. I'm from Chicago myself."

"How can I help you, Mr. Hope?"

"I'm not sure you can. I've been retained by a woman who's trying to locate her husband . . ."

"Have you tried Missing Persons?"

"Just got off the phone with them a few minutes ago. They suggested I call you. Well, not you personally, they didn't give me your name. They just said the Eighty-seventh Precinct."

"Why'd they do that, Mr. Hope?"

"Because the last known location of the man I'm looking for was in the vicinity of 1219 Silvermine Oval. A few blocks from that address."

"Has this man committed a crime?"

"Not that I know of. But he may have been the *victim* of a crime. His wallet was found in the possession of a dead man with a criminal record. Man named Ernest Corrington. Does that mean anything to you?"

"Nothing at all."

"How about Jack Lawton?"

"Is he the possible victim?"

"Yes."

"Never heard of him. You said Corrington was dead. How'd he die?"

"Shotgun wound."

"Mmm."

"Had an armed robbery record going back some ten years."

"What were his last known whereabouts? Before he turned up dead in Florida?"

"L.A. He reported to his parole officer on the third of October. I was wondering if you might have anything on him up there."

"Like what?"

"I don't know. What it is, you see, Lawton was last seen up there in July. Week after the Fourth. With a woman he was living with at the time. Presumably, anyway. Woman named Holly something. Last name begins with an S. But there's been nothing on him since. Okay, Corrington was killed in Florida two nights ago, carrying Lawton's ID. So sometime between October third and this past Tuesday, their paths had to've crossed. If it was down here, then that's where Lawton might be now. If he's still alive. If it was up there, then maybe Lawton's *still* up there. Do you follow me?"

"Sure. But I still don't know how I can help you."

"I don't know, either."

"I mean, would you like me to do a door-to-door canvass of the precinct?"

He meant this sarcastically, but this Hope person, basking down there in the sun, did not seem to get it.

"*Could* you?" he asked.

"Do what? A *canvass*?"

"Well . . . how big *is* this Silvermine Oval?"

"The Oval itself? Or the surrounding streets? In any case, I couldn't possibly . . ."

"Of course not. I wouldn't impose . . ."

"I mean, we don't work for the state of Florida here, Mr. Hope."

"I realize that. What I was going to suggest . . ."

"Mr. Hope . . ."

"Mr. Carella."

Both men fell silent.

"Mr. Carella," Hope said again, "if Lawton's still up there, then he's been the victim of a theft at best—and possibly something worse. In fact, he may be lying dead up there in a furnished room someplace."

"Here in the precinct, do you mean?"

"In the area of the Oval. Somewhere in that neighborhood."

"To my knowledge, we haven't had any dead bodies turn up in the Oval recently."

"By recently . . . ?"

"The past two, three months. The Oval's a pretty good neighborhood. In this precinct, it's considered silk-stocking."

"How about the rest of the precinct? Any unidentified bodies turn up in the *rest* of the precinct?"

"Unidentified bodies turn up all the time," Carella said. "But . . ."

"Recently? Say the past two, three months?"

"I suppose."

"Could you check?"

"Well . . ."

"I would really appreciate it. If it wouldn't be too much trouble. I mean, if it just means kicking up a computer or something."

Carella wasn't used to this kind of politeness. People up here didn't address each other this way. Not in his line of work, anyway. Besides, complying with Hope's request wouldn't mean marching out into the snow and dredging the streets for corpses; it really *would* be a simple matter of consulting the computer. He'd already typed up his D.D. reports for the shift, and everyone on the relief team would be late, anyway. So why not amuse himself searching for someone named Jack Lawton who may have hooked up with someone named Ernest Corrington sometime between last October and now, here in the big bad city?

"Let me have your number," he said.

He first did a precinct-wide search for any unidentified suicides, homicides or fatal accidents from October of last year to January of this year and came up with three victims, none of them named Lawton. He narrowed the search to the specific Silvermine Oval area and came up with nothing. He next ran a specific search for *identified* victims.

This was a more difficult search in that reports were not cross-filed by the names of victims, normally the persons most quickly forgotten in any given crime. The winter months were usually sparse on crimes of violence. If he'd been dealing with a June-through-September time frame, he'd be sitting here till midnight. But there hadn't been— well, for *this* precinct, anyway—too many assaults, armed robberies, rapes or murders committed here since October third, when Corrington had last reported to his . . .

Something just occurred to him.

Why search the files for a *victim* when you already had an ex-con who'd broken parole?

He immediately typed CORRINGTON, ERNEST and hit the SEARCH key.

★   ★   ★

43

The return call from the 87th Precinct did not come until the next morning at a quarter past ten. Matthew was sitting behind his corner-office desk looking out at a teeming rain that immediately put to rout any thoughts of Florida as a vacation paradise. Palm trees struggled in the wind, bending, rattling. Fronds raced along the sidewalks. Ankle-deep water rushed along the gutters. The twenty-fourth day of January—and *this*.

"A Detective Parker on four," Cynthia said.

He punched the four button and said, "Matthew Hope."

"Andy Parker," the voice said. "87th Squad."

"How are you, Mr. Parker?"

"Fine. About the inquiry you made yesterday, I'm the one answered the squeal, so Carella turned it over to me."

"Yes, I've been waiting to hear."

"Yeah, well, I just come in. What we've got, just before Christmas . . ."

Ernest Corrington, it would appear, had a penchant for getting into bar brawls. And losing them. Just before Christmas, in a somewhat upscale cocktail lounge called the Silver Pony, not too far from where a man named Jack Lawton was then renting a furnished apartment—but Detective Parker didn't get to that until later.

On the twentieth of December, then, a Friday night, the proprietor of the Silver Pony, familiarly called the Pony by residents of the neighborhood, dialed 911 to report that a fistfight was at the moment taking place in his posh little emporium. Car Adam Three from the Eight-Seven arrived at the scene some five minutes later to discover that the hubbub had boiled over onto the street outside, where three men were kicking the shit out of a man on the sidewalk while a fourth man struggled to pull them off. All five were taken into custody. The bruised and battered loser on the sidewalk was someone named Ernest Corrington. The man who'd been trying to help him was his pal, Jack Lawton.

Because the Pony was a posh establishment in an affluent neighborhood, the interrogation was handled by the precinct detectives rather than the responding blues. As was the case in most barroom disputes, all of the participants claimed they had acted in self-defense. Two detectives named Cotton Horse and Meyer Meyer—very peculiar names they had up there at the old Eight-Seven—questioned the three undisputed victors. Andy Parker himself questioned Corrington and Lawton, both of whom were at the time wearing an assortment of cuts and bruises.

It seemed that Corrington had come east from California to spend a few days partying with his good buddy Lawton before they both headed down to Florida. They'd been standing at the bar discussing something personal and private, when all at once these three drunks standing alongside them . . .

"Did they mention what the something personal and private might have been?"

"Not to me."

"To any of the other officers?"

"Not to my knowledge."

"Okay, what happened?"

"These three drunks made some comments and next thing you knew fists were flying."

"Comments about what?"

"I got no idea. Drunk comments."

Even taking into account that in every barroom altercation Parker had ever investigated, each and every participant claimed that each and every *other* participant was drunk, these two did seem relatively sober, and their story had the unmistakable ring of truth to it. Besides, it was the holiday season, and Parker didn't want to be bothered with a bull-shit assault charge. Peace on earth to men of goodwill, he figured, and took down their Social Security numbers and dates of birth for a routine computer check on outstanding warrants. Finding none, he sent them home with a warn-ing not to get into any more fights with guys who out-numbered and outweighed them.

"Sent them home *where*?"

"Lawton was renting an apartment on Crest. Corrington was staying with him."

"Have you still got the address?"

"Sure. 831 South Crest."

"Living there with some woman, was he?"

"Not to my knowledge."

"Woman named Holly something. With an S."

"Not to my knowledge."

"How about Corrington's parole violation in California?"

"Nothing kicked in. To my knowledge, there are no state computers linked to other states' computers. Unless a Cali-fornia warrant had already dropped, it wouldn't have banged here."

"And it didn't."

"Not back in December, anyway."

"How about now?"

"I checked *then*, not now. Anyway, be a little late, wouldn't it? Even assuming California already issued a warrant, the guys have already moved to Florida."

"Is that what they said? That they were *moving* down here? Or just coming down for a visit?"

"It sounded to me like it was a permanent move."

"How do you mean?"

"Well, they said they were going into business together. In Florida. Going down right after Christmas to start this new business. That's why they were so relieved we didn't turn this into a federal case."

"No charges pressed, right?"

"Well, Christmas."

"How about the other three?"

"We let them go, too. We've got enough *real* crooks in this precinct."

"So you think they came down to Florida right after Christmas, is that it?"

"Is what they said they were gonna do."

"Did they say where in Florida?"

"Just Florida."

"Not Miami, or St. Pete, or . . ."

"Just Florida. What I would guess, though, considering Corrington turned up dead in your fair city, is that perhaps that's where they were headed, wouldn't you guess?"

There was a bored and snotty air about the man, as if he had seen it all and heard it all and done it all up there in the frozen North and nothing anyone from the balmy South might say could possibly interest him. Matthew plunged ahead regardless.

"Did they say what kind of business?"

"Considering what you told Carella about the guy having a pair of robbery priors, I would guess the business might be holding up grocery stores, wouldn't you say?"

Same snotty air.

"Did they say *when* after Christmas they planned to come down here to start this robbery spree?" he asked.

When you've been in coma, you can get a little snotty yourself.

"No, they did not. But as a courtesy, this morning I called the super at the building where Lawton was renting the room. She told me he had a six-month lease, expiring on December thirty-first. He moved out on New Year's Day. His good friend Corrington was with him."

"Any woman with them?"

"I didn't ask."

"Then according to the super, they came down here to Florida on the first."

"Is what New Year's Day is."

"Anything else I should know?"

"The cocktail waitress says that just before the fight started, she saw one of the five guys flashing a piece."

"Which one?"

"Who knows? We frisked them here and nobody was strapped. So much for the reliability of eyewitnesses."

"Anything else?"

"Ain't that enough?" Parker said, and hung up.

The boat was plowing through a pretty good chop on the Gulf side of Calusa, not another boat in sight except for a few fishing trawlers way out on the horizon. Calusa was a boat town. There were some people, in fact, who said there was no sense living here—or *anywhere* in coastal Florida, for that matter—unless you owned a boat. Most boaters, though, they favored the Intracoastal rather than the Gulf, God only knew why. On the Intracoastal, you had to keep your speed down to what—twenty knots maybe? Had to pull back even from that whenever you entered a no-wake zone. Took you hours to travel what on land would've taken forty minutes.

When Jill and Jack were first married, he'd picked up a small Grady-White real cheap from a man who was moving back up north. Used to take it out on the Gulf because he enjoyed feeling free out there, instead of being locked in by the narrow canals of the Intracoastal. Scared Jill half to death when he opened her up, the little boat bouncing around out there like a go-go dancer. Later on, when the games started, they used to use the boat for weekend trips down to the Everglades, slept on board, nobody bothered you. That was a long time ago.

Miklos Panagos's boat was a sleek, white, ninety-some-odd-foot yacht worth, who knew, five, six million bucks. He was sitting on the boat's aft deck, spray flying, gulls following in case anyone decided to dump garbage, discussing money with Jack like a ribbon clerk instead of a shipping magnate with boats like this one parked in every marina around the world.

"On the other hand," Jack said, "the bottle is valued at two and a half million dollars."

"The *mystery* is valued at two and a half million," Panagos corrected, holding a finger up to his pockmarked face. He was dressed for Athens in August, which Calusa felt like today, wearing brown leather sandals, white cotton trousers, and a white cotton shirt open over a thick gold chain and crucifix. "As we both know," he said, "there is no documentation to prove . . ."

"We know he was in that prison . . ."

"Yes, we know that. And we know that's where the medicine bottles were unearthed, yes. But is it likely that this is the *very* bottle from which he drank? Who knows? That is the mystery, my friend. If it's the selfsame bottle, yes, it's worth two and a half million, perhaps more. If not, it's worthless. Thirteen of them were found, you know."

"I know. But if this is the bottle he actually . . ."

"*If.* There's still a dispute, my friend. That's what accounts for the mystery surrounding it. That's why people are willing to pay to *see* the damn thing! Incidentally, in the account of his death, the vessel was described as a *cup,* you know, not a *bottle.* It was very definitely called a cup."

"They didn't find thirteen *cups,* they found thirteen *bottles.* And this is the one he drank from. Anyway, translations vary. And besides, does it make a difference? You yourself said the *mystery* was what determined the value. We don't know for sure that the shroud of Turin is the one Jesus was actually buried in, do we? But popular belief . . ."

"Yes, popular belief . . ."

"Popular belief and mystery, yes . . ."

"Yes, exactly what we're dealing with here. The legend persists, I agree. And it is the *legend* that determines the value."

"Then we're agreed on the value of the bottle."

"Who said we weren't? I think it's worth every penny. I told that to Corry, and I tell it to you now. I am merely saying that a hundred thousand would seem quite sufficient as a deposit."

"Usually an option payment . . ."

"Ah, is this an option payment then?"

"A payment to ensure exclusivity, yes. An option. And that's usually ten percent, Mr. Panagos."

"I'm sorry, but two hundred and fifty thousand dollars would be out of the question. Corry never mentioned such an absurd figure. If he were still alive . . ." Panagos shook his head, as if missing the man deeply. As a matter of fact, he'd only met him once, when Corry first made contact in Miami.

"I don't think Corry realized what the expenses on this would be," Jack said. "In order to guarantee delivery, I have to engage the very best people . . ."

"Your recovery expenses are your own business."

That was the word he used, "recovery."

"But how can you expect me to hand over a quarter of a million dollars to a virtual stranger? You tell me you can deliver the bottle. I tell you good, I believe you. And I say a hundred thousand should be sufficient seed money. I mean no offense, Mr. Benson . . ."

That was the name Jack had given him. Charles Benson.

". . . but I don't know you from a hole in the wall. Should you vanish with my hundred thousand, well, then, my friend, to whom shall I turn?"

He opened his hands wide to the skies above and the hopefully benevolent gods.

"I'm sure you'd be able to find me," Jack said.

"Oh, I'm sure I would, believe me. But I hate fusses."

"Make it two hundred," Jack said.

"I'm sorry."

Jack could taste the money.

"One-fifty then."

"I choose not to haggle, Mr. Benson. Is our business concluded then?"

"All right, a hundred thousand," Jack said.

Panagos snapped his fingers. A barefoot, dust-colored man dressed in what appeared to be pale blue striped cotton pajamas came from below. Panagos merely nodded to him. The man went below again, and came back not a moment later with the kind of briefcase law students carried to make them look like legal eagles, all battered and brown and bulging, with a frayed leather carrying handle and a brass spring clasp holding it closed. Panagos snapped open the clasp. Jack watched him transferring paper-strapped packets of hundred-dollar bills from the bag to the tabletop.

"I'll count them out for you," he said.

"That won't be necessary," Jack said.

Panagos began counting bills out loud.

"One, two, three, four, five, six, seven, eight, nine, a thousand. One, two, three, four, five, six . . ."

And so on.

Jack suddenly remembered a movie called *The Asphalt Jungle,* which a lot of people confused with *The Blackboard Jungle,* perhaps because Louis Calhern was in both pictures. There was a scene in that movie—*The* Asphalt *Jungle,* not *The* Blackboard *Jungle*—where the character played by Marc Lawrence, who had a really pockmarked face, was counting out the money from a heist and everybody was watching him, and he wiped his forehead with a handkerchief and then apologized, saying, "Money makes me sweat."

Jack probably thought of this movie and Marc Lawrence sweating while he counted out the money because Panagos himself was both pockmarked *and* sweating as he counted out the hundred-dollar bills. So far, he had counted out four thousand dollars. That left ninety-six thousand to go.

"Would you care for something to drink?" he asked, interrupting himself.

This was only eleven o'clock in the morning. Jack didn't normally start drinking at such an early hour, but what the hell, the hundred-thou down payment called for a little celebration, though it still irked him that he'd only been able to get such a small binder on a two-and-a-half-million-dollar deal.

"I wouldn't mind a little Johnnie Black on the rocks," he said, and Panagos snapped his fingers again for the guy in the pajamas who took their drink orders and padded off to fetch Jack's Scotch and Panagos's cognac.

The Scotch tasted cool and clean and wonderfully expensive. Jack was thinking that on the second day of February, he'd have the rest of the two and a half million in his hands and he could order Johnnie Black whenever he felt like it. Panagos kept sipping his Courvoisier and counting hundred-dollar bills and sweating like a pig. Jack watched the stacks of hundreds piling up. He was sweating now, too.

". . . ninety-eight, ninety-nine, a hundred," Panagos said at last, and shoved the stacked hundred-dollar bills across the table like a croupier paying off a big hit. "One hundred thousand on the button, like you say."

As you say, Jack thought, but did not say.

"Thank you," he said instead, and began transferring the bills into a leather dispatch case Jill had given him on their eighth anniversary. That was when they were still flying solo. The games didn't begin until sometime later. Well, they'd been married in August, the games didn't start till a week before their ninth anniversary. Married for sixteen years in all, high school sweethearts. Who'd have thought?

Panagos's manservant filled their glasses again.

Panagos raised his snifter in a toast.

"To recovery of the bottle," he said.

"To recovery," Jack said.

You cheap fuck, he thought.

★   ★   ★

Seven, eight years ago.

The Sunday she first lays eyes on Jack and Jill Lawton. Celebrity auction on the lawn of the new library just off the causeway, overlooking the bay. Lawn parched, rolling away all withered and sere toward the water, hasn't rained since the middle of June. The town is about to burn itself up, sometimes Melanie wishes it would. She thinks she will drop dead from the heat. This is the hottest August she can ever remember here in Florida, and she's been living here a long time now, you better believe it. Hotter than this, it cannot possibly get.

Clayton Landers, who's chairman of the library board, is the one conducting the auction today. In a town like Calusa, August is the cruelest month, never mind Mr. Eliot. Doesn't get much hotter *anywhere* than it does in Calusa during the month of August. The smart money is out of town during August, down in Argentina skiing, or off sailing the fjords in Norway, anyplace but Calusa, where you can fry eggs on the sidewalks and melt in your panties on the lawn of the new Calusa Public Library, where Clayt is about to begin "this here celebrity auction," as he tells the folks beginning to gather on folding chairs in front of the podium still draped in red, white and blue bunting left over from the Fourth of July.

During the month of August, the people here in Calusa dream up things to keep from going crazy. There are medieval fairs here during August, and regattas, and bakeoffs, and a rodeo over in Ananburg, and "this here celebrity auction" to save the library's collection of newspapers going all the way back to 1912, put them all on microfilm so a new generation of hicks can learn all about this lovely little tank town they live in. Melanie doesn't know who first dreamt up the idea of celebrity auctions, but she is sure it was some spindly librarian in a town not unlike Calusa, lying in her narrow bed at night, figuring out how she could make a little money for her rickety library by playing on the sympathies and egos of writers all over the world.

Idea was to write a letter to them—never mind that they didn't *live* in Calusa, Florida, or Overall Patches, Tennessee, or Cow Spit, Indiana, where the auctions would actually be held—write them a letter saying you were having a celebrity auction to save the Edna Mae Oliver wing of the local library and could they please send along an autographed book, or some pages from a work in progress, or even an old tennis sock they once had worn, all for a good cause, please help us, dear celebrities. Most writers didn't think of themselves as celebrities, and most writers didn't give a rat's ass about a library in Sinkhole, Maine, but they all responded one way or another, and lo and behold, here is a pile of books Melanie is supposed to hold up one by one while Clayt describes each item to a whole bunch of otherwise sensible people sitting on hard folding chairs in the noonday sun.

The Lawtons come in a few minutes before the auction is about to start.

It is so hot today.

Jill Lawton . . .

She doesn't know who they are yet, doesn't know their names, just sees this good-looking young couple coming down the center aisle looking for seats, finding some in the third row on the right-hand side, Melanie watching them . . .

There's a certain disdain to the fact that they're both wearing tennis whites, both looking a little exhausted, a little sweaty in fact, Jill in short white shorts and a clingy white top, Jack wearing blue shorts and a paler blue top, Melanie guesses they don't belong to the fancy Clarendon Club, where only white tennis outfits are permitted on the courts, not that *she's* ever played there, either. At this time of her life—she's only nineteen—Melanie works as a clerical assistant in a doctor's office, which is how she happens to be here today. Her boss, Dr. Arthur Lauterbach, is on the library board, and he was the one who asked if she would help out with the auction, her being so pretty and all.

Actually, she *is* rather pretty now that she's a blonde again, she's always felt she looked better as a blonde. Her weight is down to a hundred and six again, and she feels healthy and tanned standing here watching Jack and Jill— whose names she still doesn't know—taking their seats among all the other people wearing shirts and ties and summer dresses, these are serious occasions, these here celebrity auctions. Melanie herself is wearing a short white cotton dress today, not too low-cut, but interesting enough, she supposes, cinched at the waist with a wide green belt to match her strappy sandals. She keeps watching Jack and Jill as they greet other people they know, and then the auction starts, and she's too busy holding up books and other items . . .

A writer in Montana has sent them one of those little white Bull Durham tobacco bags which once contained the tobacco he used for rolling his cigarettes, can you believe it? Signed it *Good Luck to the Caluse Library,* spelling it wrong. The pouch goes for seventy-five dollars, which Melanie guesses is about seventy dollars more than it was worth when it still had tobacco in it and before it was signed.

The Lawtons . . .

She hears their last name for the first time when the Stephen King book comes up for sale. This is a brown, paperbound book—not a glossy paperback, but something bigger in size with a softer cover—and it's titled *Six Stories.* Clayt tells them it's one of a private limited edition of eleven hundred copies printed by the Stinehour Press in Lunenburg, Vermont, numbered and signed by the author. He wants the bidding started at a hundred dollars, and Jack Lawton—she later learns this is his full name—raises his hand and Clayt says, "I have an opening bid from the Lawtons."

For some reason, Melanie smiles.

As she's smiling, Jill happens to glance at her.

And something electric flashes across that parched lawn.

Well, the Lawtons don't get the King book, although they bid up to three hundred dollars on it. It finally goes for nine hundred and fifty dollars, the highest figure paid for anything that day, but, hey, this is Stephen King and not some mere scribbler someplace. Later, while they're all drinking punch set up on tables down by the bay where it's no cooler than it was up closer to the library, Melanie is introduced to them by her employer, Dr. Arthur Lauterbach, who says Jack is the graphic artist who designed the letterhead for their stationery, "You know our letterhead, Mel," and she says, "Oh, *sure,* how do you do?" and takes first Jill's hand, and then Jack's, and they shake hands only briefly, and Lauterbach wanders off to greet some other doctors.

It is so hot on that lawn.

"You must really like Stephen King," Melanie says.

"Oh, we really do," Jill says.

"Sorry we couldn't bid higher," Jack says.

"Well, nine-fifty," Melanie says, and rolls her eyes.

"Are you as hot as we are?" Jill asks.

"Phew," Melanie says.

"Want to come home for a swim?" Jack suggests.

She hesitates only a moment.

Then she says, "Okay."

She learns while they sip gin-tonics by the pool behind their house on Whisper Key that Jack is thirty years old and Jill is three years younger. They've been married for almost nine years . . .

"Our anniversary is next week," Jack says.

"The twentieth," Jill says.

. . . and have been living here in Florida for the past two and a half years. They're all in swimsuits now, Jill wearing a blue bikini that matches her eyes, Jack in surfer trunks, Melanie in a borrowed black maillot. This is five, five-thirty, the sun is beginning to move closer to the horizon, but it won't be dark until seven, seven-thirty. By six or thereabouts, they're all on their third drinks and beginning to make fun of the various types you find at the innumerable charity events down here in Calusa, an exercise that leads to a sort of bonding since it makes all three of them feel enormously superior to people like Clayton Landers and Arthur Lauterbach and Samantha Nelson, who sponsored today's event. Jill does a fair imitation of Sammy, as she is known locally, getting her thick southern accent down pat, telling the assembled audience on the lawn that *this* year's celebrity auction earned the library one thousand one hunnerd and fifty dollars more than *last* year's auction, "Now how 'bout *that*?"

It is still stiflingly hot even though the sun will soon be gone. Strangers to Calusa can never understand why in the summertime it never seems to cool off at night. Even after a rain shower, the heat seems to linger. Melanie supposes the alcohol isn't helping much, raises the body heat, she supposes. She wishes she were wearing a bikini like the one Jill has on, but the maillot was the only thing Jill could find that fit her, something from a few years ago when she was thinner, "I wish I had your shape," she tells Melanie, although she herself is not what anyone would ever consider fat. Her curves are merely a bit more obvious than Melanie's. She's what Melanie's mother might call *zaftig*. Which means voluptuous, Melanie supposes. Yes, there *is* a voluptuous sort of languid look about Jill. Maybe it's the alcohol that's giving her eyes a sort of heavy-lidded appearance. Or maybe it's the heat.

Melanie will not remember later who suggests that they take off their suits and go swimming naked. It is already dark by that time, and there are no lights showing in any of the houses nearby, and besides there is foliage enough to conceal whatever the Lawtons and their nineteen-year-old guest may choose to do here in the dark. Jack strips off his trunks first—it's always the man who makes the first move in a situation like this one—and runs toward the lip of the pool with his rather large appendage flapping, Melanie notices, and then he dives in and Jill slowly removes her top and steps out of the bikini bottoms and walks quite elegantly toward the pool steps, taking her time as she descends into the water, the temperature of air and water virtually identical so that there is no shock, no puckering of her nipples, Melanie notices. She hesitates a moment, and then drains the gin and tonic, and places the glass on the round plastic table, and lowers first one strap of the black maillot, and then the other, and wriggles out of the suit and walks to the steps as proudly as Jill did not a moment ago, and comes down naked into the water.

Five minutes later, Jill kisses her full on the mouth.

That is the beginning.

4

I t was still snowing.

Which perhaps was why Carella kept thinking of Florida and the lawyer down there who'd called him on Thursday. Even so, he might not have done anything further to help this Hope person were it not for the coincidence that brought him to Silvermine that Saturday afternoon. The coincidence was a burglary two blocks north of where Jack Lawton had been renting an apartment.

Burglaries were common in the Silvermine neighborhood. This was because burglars knew that ripping off an apartment in the poorer sections of town wasn't as profitable an enterprise as going into a crib where you went home with something more than a vintage television set. The burglar who'd entered apartment 12C at 1120 Silvermine Oval had departed with, among other things, the requisite TV (two of them, in fact) *and* a sterling silver service for twelve, *and* a ladies' fourteen-carat cabochon-cut emerald ring, *and* a Picasso print worth a hundred thousand dollars, *and* a fully let-out mink coat.

Carella always wondered what a fully let-out mink was. Did they keep these little minks inside some kind of enclosure until it was time to cut them up into mink coats? And were they then let *out*? Was there such a thing as a *partially* let-out mink? He hoped no furriers would write to him to explain. Nor any animal rights protestors, either.

He also hoped it would quit snowing.

This city wasn't Cleveland and it wasn't Chicago, but it got its fair share of snow during the winter months, *more* than its fair share this winter. Seven feet in the past week, and still snowing to beat the band, as his mother was fond of saying, with Canadian winds blowing in off the River Harb and setting his hair to dancing and his ears to freezing. Carella never wore a hat.

A tall, slender man in his thirties, with the gait of a natural athlete—though it was hard to tell as he stomped his way through foot-high drifts on the way to where he'd parked the car—brown eyes squinted against needle-sharp flakes that swirled and raged, he thought again of Matthew Hope down there in Caloopi, Florida, wherever, and wondered again where the *girl* had gone. If Lawton had been living with a girl named Holly Something in July, where had she disappeared to in December? He was approaching Crest Avenue, the street sign for which was partially obliterated by flying snow, streetlights beginning to come on at four o'clock, lamps burning in apartment windows, the city looking as snug and as safe as a scene from Dickens, oh sure, when he figured why not stop by, ask the super a few questions? What the hell, he was in the neighborhood, anyway.

831 Crest was one of those tall skinny buildings sand-wiched between two fifteen-, sixteen-story high-rises, red brick wedged between white or gray, difficult to tell in this blinding snow. He climbed the steps to the front door, searched the bell buttons for one marked SUPER, rang it, and waited, hands in his pockets, head ducked, his hair and the shoulders of his coat covered with minuscule flakes.

The door opened on a woman in her late fifties, early sixties, wearing what Carella's mother called a "candy store owner's sweater," bulky green wool cardigan with a shawl collar. She peered out at Carella, squinted past him to the eddying snow beyond, made a clucking sound of dismay, focused on him again, and said, "Yes?"

"Detective Carella," he said, "Eighty-seventh Squad," and flashed the tin. "May I come in, please?"

"What's the trouble *now*?" she asked.

He wasn't aware of any previous trouble, but it was a busy precinct. "None, ma'am," he said. "I just wanted to ask some questions about a former tenant of yours. May I come in, please?" he asked, feeling the snow gave him an advan-tage, made him look a bit like Tiny Tim albeit without a crutch. The super looked dubious, but she stepped back from the door and allowed him entrance into a small foyer carpeted with an Oriental that had seen better days in Teheran, brass mailboxes on his right, globed light over-head, door with an etched-glass panel behind the super, whose name he still didn't know.

She was somehow intimidating, a big-boned, sharp-nosed woman with graying hair cut in what ice skating en-thusiasts used to call a wedge, wearing Ben Franklin specs and the green sweater over a tweedy skirt that looked like the one the expert in the Hitchcock movie was wearing in the restaurant scene, when they're all trying to find an explanation for the havoc the birds were causing. The drunk at the bar kept lifting his glass and saying "It's the end of the world." Mrs. Bundy, that was her name, the lady telling them all about the difference between crows and blackbirds, lighting a cigarette, pontificating. Matter of fact, the super here at 831 Crest looked altogether like that lady in the movie, except for the eyeglasses. Mrs. Bundy. He'd read somewhere that the screenwriter, some New York hack, had named her after a street out there in Los Angeles, where Carella wished he could be right this very minute, either there or in Caloopi, Florida. He closed the door behind him.

"I'm sorry, ma'am," he said, "I don't know your name."

"Grace Hardy," she said, "Mrs. Grace Hardy," which was nowhere close to Bundy, some you win, some you lose. Bundy Drive. That was the name of the street out there. "Did someone complain again?" she said.

"Complain about what, Mrs. Hardy?"

"About the skateboard ramp on the roof."

"Not that I know of. Have there been complaints?"

"Not so much in the winter, cause it's too cold for them to skate up there. But when it gets warm, people on both sides start complaining about the noise. Why *are* you here, Mr. Capella?"

"Carella," he said. "I've had a call from an attorney in Florida . . ."

Always best to tell the truth until it was necessary to lie.

". . . inquiring about a man named Jack Lawton who, I understand . . ."

"Mr. Lawton, yep," she said.

"Used to live here, is that right?"

"Rented a two-room apartment on the top floor. Don't know how he could stand the skateboard noise, but the rooms up there are cheaper because of it."

"I understand he was living here with a woman . . ."

"Holly. Yep."

"Knew them both, did you?"

"Why? Did they do something?"

"Not that I know of."

Still the truth. No reason to lie. Not yet.

"I know about the trouble at the Pony, you know," Mrs. Hardy said, narrowing her eyes shrewdly.

"Well, that was just a minor altercation," Carella said, using a big word for a small lie; the brawl had been something better than minor. No sense ever being completely honest with the citizenry, though, because you never knew when they were going to back off. Minute they thought they might be getting somebody in trouble, they began wondering if they'd be considered miserable rat finks. Basic American trait, courtesy of the MAFIA, acronym for Murderous Affiliation of Fucking Idiotic Assholes. So, hey, he didn't want Mrs. Hardy here to think he was trying to get Lawton and his Holly in trouble with the law. Which he wasn't, anyway. Besides, there was no sense making a mountain out of a bar brawl.

"Lawyer down there is trying to find him for his wife," he said, hoping this wouldn't trigger what he called the Fink Factor, but that depended on how well she'd known the two up there on the top floor, and how much faith she put in the institution of marriage.

"I thought *Holly* was his wife," she said.

"Did she *say* she was his wife?"

"Well, no, I just assumed. I knew she went by a different

65

name, but I thought that was for professional reasons. She's an actress, you know."

"I didn't know that."

"Oh, sure. She told me she'd been in movies and everything."

"Oh? Which movies?"

"Well, she didn't say."

Which meant she'd been waiting tables.

"When did they move in?" he asked.

"First of July. Mr. and Mrs. Lawton both . . . well, I *thought* she was Mrs. Lawton."

"And they moved out in January?"

"New Year's Day. *He* did."

"What do you mean?"

"She left earlier. Went down to Florida."

"Didn't happen to say *where* in Florida, did she?"

"St. Pete, I think."

"When was this?"

"Around Thanksgiving. Just after Thanksgiving."

"The twenty-ninth? The thirtieth?"

"It was a Sunday."

"Then it had to be December first."

"Are you some kind of mystic?"

"No, we had eight liquor store holdups on Thanksgiving Day. November twenty-eighth. Never forget it. You say you thought she was using a professional name . . ."

"A stage name. Is what I thought."

"What was the name, would you remember?"

"Of course. Holly Sinclair."

"Did you ever meet a man named Ernest Corrington?"

"Muscles all over him?"

"I wouldn't know."

66

"I thought you were a mystic."

"Only when it comes to what day Thanksgiving was. Did he *say* his name was Corrington?"

"*Ernest* Corrington, was what he said. He moved in with them a month or so before Mrs. Lawton left . . . well, I *thought* she was Mrs. Lawton, anyway."

Carella was thinking that a month or so before December first would've been November first or thereabouts. Which meant that Corrington had left L.A. shortly after his October third visit to his parole officer.

"Stayed with them till the lease expired at the end of the year," she said. "Mr. Lawton had a six-month lease. Moved in on the first of July, out on the last day of December. Corrington was with him. Both men came down carrying heavy suitcases."

Carella was making a mental timetable. Like trains and buses, detection never worked without a timetable. The way it seemed to be shaping up, Lawton and his girlfriend had rented the apartment on July 1, and had run into Claire Phillips wheeling her baby buggy in Silvermine Park sometime around July 7. Ernest Corrington had reported to his L.A. parole officer on October third, and was in the East sometime before the first of November, a month before Holly went down to St. Pete's. Three weeks after that, both men got into a fight at the Silver Pony because some drunks commented on a conversation that was personal and private.

"Did she say *where* in St. Pete?" he asked.

"Well, matter of fact, she did," Mrs. Hardy said, God bless her. "She was planning to stay with a woman named Lucille Schwartz. Let me get you the address."

★   ★   ★

Warren and Toots acted immediately on the information a police detective up north had given Matthew on the telephone, checked the St. Pete phone directory, and found a solitary listing for a woman named Lucille Schwartz. In this business, it was always wisest to have a woman call another woman. Man called from Calusa, you began wondering if he was a rapist or a burglar. Woman called, it was time for a nice little chat. Toots first confirmed that she was in fact speaking to Miss Lucille Schwartz . . .

"It's *Mrs.,*" the woman said.

"Mrs. Schwartz, do you know a young woman named Holly Sinclair?"

"Yes, of course I do. Though, I must tell you, that wasn't the name she was born with."

"I'm sorry?" Toots said.

"She changed it when she went into show business. That isn't her *real* name."

"I see," Toots said. "What *is* her real . . . ?"

"Said her own name wasn't good enough for an actress. I told her how about Sigourney Weaver? Is *that* good enough for an actress? *Sigourney?* Or Gwyneth Paltrow? How about *her? Paltrow?* Or even *Gwyneth,* my God! She wouldn't listen. Came down here in December, told me she'd been using the name Holly Sinclair up north, planned to use it from now on."

"What was her real . . . ?"

"Or how about Winona Ryder? *Winona?* Jesus!"

"How do you happen to know her, Mrs. Schwartz?"

"How do I happen to *know* her?"

"Yes, how do you . . . ?"

"She's my *daughter,* what do you mean how do I happen to *know* her?"

"I didn't realize . . ."

"Who'd you *think* she was?"

"Well, no one said . . . it just never occurred to me. She wouldn't happen to be there with you *now,* would she?"

"No, I'm sorry, she's not. She left for Calusa more'n a week ago."

Toots's ears went up like a coyote's.

"Would you know where she's *staying* here in Calusa?" she asked.

"Why, certainly. With Peter. Her no-good boyfriend. Is this about an acting job?"

"Peter who?" Toots asked.

The units on the ground-floor level of 6412 Pelican Way were shaded by a walkway that hugged the side of the building and provided access to the second-floor units, the deck above doubling as a roof below. The place had the ramshackle look of a hot-bed motel, perhaps because it had been converted from one some thirty years ago. Cinder block walls painted a lime green, windows covered with screens and aluminum louvers. Peter Donofrio lived in unit twenty-seven, on the second floor, toward the street side. Guthrie and Warren climbed the steps and came down the walkway to a metal screen door frame painted white, solid lower panel, tattered screen on the upper half. The wooden door beyond it was painted a flaking pumpkin color. Little round bell button set in the door frame to the right. Guthrie pressed it. Far in the distance, Sunday morning church bells tolled the hour. Ten A.M. Awed by the religious coincidence of it all, Guthrie pressed the button again. This time, no church bells bonged. There was merely the sound of the insistent buzzer somewhere in the apartment.

"Yo?" a voice called.

"Mr. Donofrio?"

"Who is it?"

"Guthrie Lamb."

Neither of the two men was strapped, but neither did they know any private detectives who carried guns. Nor were they expecting a fusillade through the door, despite what Guthrie had learned about Donofrio from the Calusa P.D. The wooden door suddenly opened, startling them. They peered through the screen at an unshaven man some five feet eight inches tall, they guessed, wearing blue walking shorts and a white tank top undershirt, black hair curling on his chest above the scoop-necked top, uncombed black hair curling on his head, thick black eyebrows scowling over suspicious brown eyes.

"Who the fuck is Guthrie Lamb?" the man asked.

"Mr. Donofrio?"

"Who the fuck wants to know?"

Guthrie held his ID card up to the screen. The man leaned in close to it. State of Florida. Licensed private investigator. Expires December 31.

"So?"

"Are you Peter Donofrio?"

"Who's *this* guy?"

Indicating Warren with a jerk of his head. Making the question sound somehow racist. Warren knew his customers inside out and backward. Could read this man's mind as if it were leaking slurs like a sieve.

"Warren Chambers," he said, and held *his* card up to the screen. *Two* private eyes now, pal, what do you make of *that*? They still didn't know if the man behind the screen door was Donofrio.

"So?" he said again.

"We're looking for your girlfriend," Guthrie said.

"Yeah? Why? What'd she do?"

"Holly Sinclair. Have you seen her lately?"

"I don't know anybody by that name."

"How about Melanie Schwartz?"

"Her neither."

"Her mother in St. Pete gave us your name and address," Guthrie said. "This isn't about your priors. We're trying to locate a man she may have known."

"So you know about the priors, huh?"

Still not opening the screen door for them. Wearing the screen door like a suit of armor and a shield.

"We know about the priors," Guthrie said. "How about opening the door and letting us in so we can sit down like human beings instead of standing here like dopes."

"Come in," the man said curtly, and swung the screen door wide. They saw for the first time that he was barefoot. They also saw what had been hidden by the solid bottom panel of the screen door. Donofrio—if this was Donofrio— was holding alongside his right leg, hanging there in his right hand, what appeared to be a very nice pistol.

"You won't need that," Guthrie said.

But his heart was pounding.

"By the way," he asked casually, "*are* you Peter Donofrio?"

"Yeah. Sit down," Donofrio said, and waved the hand with the gun in a sweeping gesture of welcome.

Both detectives looked for a place to sit, but all the chairs, as well as the floors and tabletops, were strewn with undershorts, socks, handkerchiefs, T-shirts, copies of the *Calusa Herald-Tribune* and the *New York Times,* back issues of

71

Newsweek, Playboy, Penthouse, and the *National Review,* empty cans of Coca-Cola, Sprite, and Dr Pepper, empty bottles of Budweiser, Heineken, Miller, and Coors. The path of the tornado continued into the small kitchen off the living room, where the sink and the countertops were stacked with dirty dishes, utensils and pots and pans. An open door showed an unmade bed in a room similarly littered with dirty laundry and newspapers. Donofrio saw the glances they exchanged.

"Revenge against my mother," he said, and grinned. Two teeth were missing from the front of his mouth. He looked somewhat impish, except for the very large gun in his right hand. "Who's this guy you're looking for?"

"Someone your girlfriend may have met. Holly Sinclair."

"Holly Sinclair," he said, and shook his head. "Can you believe it? What bullshit. Sit down," he said again, and this time used the gun hand to sweep assorted debris off two armchairs covered in a black fabric splashed with large pink hibiscus flowers. They sat.

"By the way," Warren said, "what kind of gun is that?"

"Meet Mr. Smith," Donofrio said at once, and waved the gun in introduction. "And his friend Mr. Wesson. .38 Chiefs Special. An excellent piece."

"Excellent," Warren agreed. "But put it away."

"Why?" Donofrio asked.

"Perhaps because it's a violation of parole?" Guthrie suggested.

"So call Tampa. I'm sure they'll believe you."

Guthrie thought about this. So did Warren. Donofrio leaned smugly against a wall table, crossing his arms over his chest, the gun pointing up at the ceiling. Behind him, there was a framed print of a flamingo that matched the color of the hibiscus on the chair covers. All the walls were painted a peach color. All the doorjambs were painted a lime green. Warren wondered who Donofrio's interior decorator was.

"You want a beer?" Donofrio asked.

"No, thanks," Warren said.

"I'll have one," Guthrie said.

Donofrio went into the kitchen and opened the fridge door. Guthrie was glad he couldn't see into it. Donofrio came back with a bottle of Coors and a bottle of Heineken.

"Which one you want?" he asked.

"The Heineken."

Donofrio popped both caps. He handed Guthrie the green bottle. "You want a glass?" he asked.

Guthrie glanced over at the kitchen sink.

"No, this is fine," he said.

"How'd you know about the priors?" Donofrio asked, tilting the bottle to his mouth.

"I checked a friend of mine before we came here."

"What kind of friend?"

"A Calusa cop. He ran you through the computer."

The detective he'd spoken to was a man who owed Guthrie a favor since he'd once testified falsely on his behalf, stating under oath that the man had not been drunk when his automobile crashed into the window of a liquor store on the South Trail. He and Harlow Winthrop, for that was his name, had been driving to the store to purchase a bottle or two of hooch when Harlow lost control of the car for some peculiar reason, probably because he was drunk. The car climbed the curb and smashed into the store, flinging display bottles hither and yon. Guthrie happened to be sitting in the car's passenger seat at the time of the smash-in, quite sober considering it was a Saturday night.

At the trial, it was the store owner's word against the word of the cop who'd responded and the word of Guthrie, who'd been a witness. Guthrie did not know any cop in the world who would testify against any other cop, and he himself was a private dick who needed the help of the police whenever he could get it. So it came down to two against one, and Harlow walked away from the DWI charge.

He got back to Guthrie some ten minutes after he'd placed his call earlier today. He told him that Peter Donofrio did indeed have a rap sheet here in the sunny state of Florida, for holding up a 7-Eleven when he was but a mere eighteen years old, and most recently for illegal possession of a controlled substance. He was now regularly reporting to his parole officer in Tampa. His last known address in Calusa was 6412 Pelican Way.

"Who gives a shit?" Donofrio said. "I'm clean now."

"Except for Mr. Smith and Mr. Wesson."

"My word against yours."

Guthrie thought about this again. So did Warren.

"Why'd you call the cops?" Donofrio asked. "Did this guy you're looking for do time?"

"No."

"Who is he, anyway?"

"Man named Jack Lawton," Warren said.

"Supposed to know Mel?"

"Supposed to know her, yes," Guthrie said.

"Ever meet Lawton?" Warren asked.

"No."

"He might have known her in New York."

"Or maybe L.A."

"Don't know him," Donofrio said.

"How about a man named Ernest Corrington?"

They saw recognition on his face, noticed the quick way he tilted the bottle to his lips again, avoiding having to look them in the eye.

"Did time in California," Guthrie said.

"I only did time in Florida."

"Still, you might have run into him here or there. Both his falls were for armed robbery."

"I never done a holdup in my life."

"How about the 7-Eleven?"

"I was framed on that."

"Hey, sure," Guthrie said.

"Yeah, yeah, but I really *was*. I was only eighteen, for Christ's sake. Besides, am I supposed to know every fuckin stickup artist in the United States?"

"No, just two or three of them on the Coast," Warren said. "Ever been to L.A.?"

"No. Have you?"

"Once."

"I never been. Anyway, I don't know this Corrington. And I don't know Lawton, either. So if you're finished with your beer, I got better things to do."

Like maybe rinse out some dirty underwear, Warren thought.

"Would you know anybody who knew Corrington?" he asked.

"I don't know anybody ever knew anybody named Corrington. Corrington sounds like a fucking *town* someplace."

"How about two guys who went into a drugstore with him in L.A.?"

"Went into a *drugstore*? What the fuck is that supposed to mean?"

"To knock it over," Warren said.

"But Corrington chickened out," Guthrie said.

"Left them standing there with their thumbs up their asses."

"I never *heard* such a story," Donofrio said, trying to look amazed but succeeding only in looking like a liar. So now they figured he not only knew Corrington, he also maybe knew the two guys who'd gone in with him. Or at least knew about the bungled job.

"Did you know Corrington was down here in Calusa?" Guthrie asked.

"I don't know Corrington, so how the fuck I'm supposed to know *where* he is?"

"Came down around New Year's."

"Why the fuck am I wasting time with you guys?" Donofrio asked. "You're not cops, who the fuck has to tell you *anything*?"

"Your parole officer might like to know you have a gun," Guthrie said.

"So run up to Tampa, who gives a fuck? It's still your word against mine."

"Two of us," Guthrie said. "We *both* saw the gun."

"How you like to see the gun up your ass?"

"How about the tape recorder? Shall we shove that up our asses, too?" Warren asked.

Guthrie caught on at once.

"Show it to him," he said.

Donofrio looked confused.

Warren pulled a small tape recorder from his jacket pocket. "We got every word said in this room," he told

Donofrio. A lie. They used the recorder to tape conversations with witnesses, but normally with their permission. "All that stuff about your two pals . . ."

"What two . . . ?"

"Mr. Smith and Mr. Wesson, remember? All here on tape," he said. Another lie. The recorder hadn't even been on. He held it up in his closed fist now.

"Wired," Donofrio said, and shook his head in confirmation of his firm belief that you couldn't trust nobody in this whole fuckin world. "What a cheap fuckin trick."

"Yep," Guthrie said.

"What do you want from me, anyway?"

"Where's your girlfriend?"

The way Donofrio tells it, this is the first he's hearing about Melanie's "friendship" with a man named Jack Lawton, whom she had not mentioned while she was here . . .

"Or I'da broken her fuckin head," he said.

. . . although she *did* tell him about this Corrington person, who was an armed robber taking acting classes from the same studio Melanie was going to, something called Theater Place. Apparently the guy was a pretty good actor, especially when he was playing lowlifes. It helped that he was very muscular, which made him look menacing. In an improv one day . . .

"Improvs is what they call these improvisations they do."

. . . he described in detail a bungled drugstore holdup, and the story had such a ring of truth to it that Melanie immediately knew it had actually happened. Corrington confirmed that this was true; he himself had been the third thief, the one who ran off when he spotted a cop's car outside. He also confided to her that he was on parole right now and shouldn't have been out of the state of California.

"These people in acting classes confide all sorts of personal things to their fellow students."

The reason Donofrio himself hadn't accompanied his girlfriend up north was that he himself was at present on parole, as the two detectives had generously pointed out to him. In Florida, however, and not the state of California. Although he had to admit that he and Melanie had sort of what might be called an open relationship in that each of them was more or less free to do as he or she chose to do, without fear of recrimination, so to speak.

"Though I would hate to catch her doing it," he admitted. "Or vice versa."

He scratched the stubble on his upper lip with the muzzle of the revolver. Warren hoped he wouldn't shoot himself in the nostril.

"When did she get here?" Guthrie asked.

"A week ago Friday."

Guthrie took out his wallet, looked at his pocket calendar. Today was the twenty-sixth. A week ago Friday . . .

"The seventeenth," he said.

Donofrio shrugged.

Guthrie was thinking the seventeenth was four days before Corrington got killed. Warren was thinking the same thing.

"Never mentioned anyone named Lawton, huh?" he said.

"Never."

"Someone she met up there? Went to museums with?"

"Museums? *Melanie?*"

"Well, at least once, anyway."

"No, she never mentioned anybody named Lawton."

"Was she here on the twenty-first?"

"When was that?"

"Last Tuesday."

"No."

"Where was she?"

"I don't know. She only stayed the weekend. She comes and goes. Like I said . . ."

"Yeah, yeah. So she got here on Friday . . ."

"Yeah."

"And left when? Monday?"

"Monday morning, right."

"For where?"

"I got no idea."

"You wouldn't happen to have a picture of her, would you?" Warren asked.

"Melanie? Sure. She's my girlfriend, ain't she? I got *lots* of pictures."

He went into the bedroom, came back a few moments later with the .38 tucked into his belt and a small cardboard carton in his hands.

"Most of these are old," he said, "but there might be a recent one. Melanie changed her appearance a lot, you know. A blonde one day, a redhead the next."

"What was she *this* time, Mr. Donofrio?"

"When she got here, she was a redhead."

"And on Monday? When she left?"

"A blonde. Here, sit down," he said, and with successive swipes of his hand swept laundry and bottles and reading material off the sofa and onto the floor. The sofa was covered with the same pink hibiscus pattern on a black field. It was also stained with what looked like spaghetti sauce, or ketchup, either of which somewhat blended with the decor. The men sat, one on either side of Donofrio, who took the lid off the carton as if he were opening an ancient Egyptian tomb. One by one, he lifted the photographs out of the box, alternately passing them either to Guthrie or to Warren. The gun butt was still sticking out of his belt. Warren hoped he wouldn't shoot himself in the balls.

The camera just loved Holly Sinclair *nee* Melanie Schwartz. From the time she was twelve or thirteen—it was difficult to determine since apparently she'd begun budding at a tender age—she'd posed in a variety of costumes ranging from a cute little sailor suit to a white cheerleader sweater and pleated skirt to, in one instance, what appeared to be toreador pants, short braided jacket and funny little hat. Always smiling. Hair always dark in those early photos. As she grew older, the hair changed from brunette to a brassy blond to red and then a softer shade of blond and back to brunette again. The preferred costume became swimming attire, usually bikinis, occasionally maillots; she showed off both to wonderful advantage. Little budding Melanie had blossomed into a buxom beauty. In fact, a sequence of photos showed her . . .

"Oops," Donofrio said.

. . . joyously topless on a barren strand of what the detectives assumed was a Florida beach. Donofrio hurried them through these, fussing and fluttering like his own maiden aunt, and then showed the most recent photos. These were studio head shots showing Melanie in various dramatic poses designed to demonstrate her wide range as an actress. In all of these most recent pictures, her hair was red, falling in soft waves to her shoulders. But this past Monday, she'd left here as a blonde.

"How old is she?" Warren asked.

"Twenty-six."

"Mind if we take one of these studio shots?" Guthrie asked. "We'll return it after we have some prints made."

"And one of the earlier ones," Warren said. "With the blond hair."

"Why are you looking for her?" Donofrio asked.

They told him his girl had possibly run into Lawton up there in the frozen North, not mentioning she'd been living with him at 831 Crest in a section known as Silvermine, not mentioning that the man who'd moved in with them shortly before she came down to Florida had been blown away with a shotgun this past Tuesday, telling him only that their job was to find Lawton for the man's wife. This was their only interest in Melanie. If she had known Lawton even peripherally, then perhaps she might know where he was now.

That was the only reason they wanted photos of her. To help them in finding her. And when they found her, *if* they found her, she might help them find Lawton. That's all they wanted to do.

Find Jack Lawton.

Jill Lawton was sunning herself beside a small ameoba-shaped pool behind her Whisper Key house when Matthew got there at a little past noon that Sunday. A glass of iced tea with a lime wedge in it rested on a small, round, glass-topped table alongside her lounge chair. She looked up as he came around the corner of the house, and then put down the magazine she'd been reading and rose to greet him. She was wearing a bikini that matched the color of the lime in her tea. Long and lean and barefoot, she extended her hand in welcome.

"You're early," she said.

"Light traffic."

"Some tea?"

"Thanks, no."

"Sit down. Please," she said.

They both took chairs around a larger round table under an umbrella.

Matthew told her all about the phone conversation he'd had with a Detective Parker of the 87th Precinct this past Friday. She listened intently. When he finished, she was silent for several moments. Then she shook her head, and said, "So he knew the dead man."

"It would seem so. Mrs. Lawton, does the name Melanie Schwartz mean anything to you?"

"No. Who is she?"

"Or Holly Sinclair?"

"No. Who are they?"

"They're one and the same person. She's the woman Jack was living with up north. The one he was with that day in the park. We know she was here in Calusa last weekend."

"Then maybe Jack's here, too."

"Maybe so."

"That's really good news."

"Yes, I suppose it is."

"Well, isn't it?"

"Well, we haven't found him yet, have we?" Matthew said.

M atthew didn't know why he called Carella again first thing Monday morning. Perhaps it was the quiet authority of his title: Detective/Second Grade. Or perhaps it was the echoing dignity of his full name, Stephen Louis Carella, conjuring as it did a grandfather walking the cobbled streets of a walled Italian village somewhere in the hills. Midwestern WASP that Matthew was, this may have sounded exotic to him. Or perhaps he was merely lost, as frequently he'd been lost ever since the quiet practice of law turned into the relentless pursuit of wrongdoers. He sometimes wondered exactly when or where *that* had happened. It was certainly some time ago. Long enough ago so that he could no longer remember. But perhaps he could attribute that to the coma. Since the coma, there were many things he couldn't remember. In any event, he somehow felt lost and somewhat fearful of the future when he placed his call to Carella.

He knew he was not a cowardly man. He had been in

dangerous situations from which he had not fled. But at the same time, he knew he was a fearful man, and given the choice between fight or flight he instinctively chose to run for the hills. That was because of the cowboys.

Until the night he met the cowboys, he hadn't had a fist-fight since he was fourteen. On the night they entered his life, he was presumably wiser, and certainly bigger, and possibly stronger than when a high-school jock named Hank advised him to keep away from his cheerleader girlfriend, whose name was Bunny Kaplowitz. Until then, Matthew had always thought only the *good* guys were named Hank. What Hank said was, "Keep away from her, dig?" or jock words to that effect. He told Hank he was a moronic turd. He still remembered the words clearly and distinctly. They were etched in acid on the restoration Dr. Mordecai Simon put into his mouth in the city of Chicago, where he was living at the time. No sooner had he uttered those memorable words than Hank blackened both his eyes, dislocated his jaw, and knocked out one of his molars.

The fight back then had to do with protecting one's disputed turf, a masculine prerogative in this land of the free and home of the brave, where macho males strutted about in Calvin Klein designer jeans. The turf in that long-ago instance was a nubile cheerleader. The turf on the night Matthew met the cowboys was a thirty-two-year-old woman named Dale O'Brien, whom he'd been dating at the time. The cowboys were bothering her, and Matthew tried to defend her. It took the intern in the emergency room at Good Samaritan almost a full hour to anoint him and bandage him and assure him repeatedly that nothing was broken although every bone in his body felt broken and his nose felt broken and his head felt broken from where the cowboys had incessantly pounded it against one of the tabletops in a joint appropriately named Captain Blood's.

Charlie and Jeff.

Those were the cowboys' names.

They were driving a blue pickup truck. There was a shotgun on a rack just inside the rear window.

A short while later, Matthew met the cowboys one more time. In a restaurant in Ananburg on a rainy day in August. This time he almost killed them. That was because his good friend Detective Morris Bloom had by then taught him a few things about kicking and gouging and taking out the strongest one first and letting the one still on his feet come to you, come to me, you son of a bitch, and blinding him if you had to.

He left Charlie and Jeff unconscious on the floor of that restaurant and he walked out into the rain and the sweltering heat, and he never looked back. Not that afternoon, anyway. But he'd been looking back ever since, expecting to see a blue pickup in the rearview mirror, expecting Charlie and Jeff to get him one more time, and finish him off for good this time, despite all the dirty fighting Bloom had taught him.

Charlie and Jeff were merely all the fears he'd ever known.

So on that Monday morning, the twenty-seventh day of January, at a little past nine, he dialed 377-0827 in the big bad city and waited while the phone rang once, twice, three . . .

"Eighty-seventh Squad, Carella."

"Detective Carella, this is Matthew Hope down here in Calusa, Florida?"

"Any luck?" Carella asked at once.

85

"We located her mother," Matthew said. "And also a boyfriend."

"Another boyfriend, huh? That's interesting."

"It gets more interesting. He's got a record. A two-time loser."

"For what?"

"The first time was robbery, the second time was dope."

"Think he's the one who did the guy on the beach?"

"Well, I don't know. But I'd sure like to find his girlfriend."

"*Cherchez la femme,* huh?" Carella said. "How's the weather down there?"

"Nice," Matthew said. "It's almost always nice down here."

There was a faint hesitation.

"Is something wrong?" Carella asked.

"No, no," Matthew said, and wondered what in his voice had betrayed doubt or fear or both. He suddenly wondered if Carella had ever been shot. "Actually," he said, "I'm calling because we've come to a sort of dead end down here . . ."

"In finding the girl?"

"Yes. Holly Sinclair, Melanie Schwartz, whoever."

"Have you tried the phone books? Sometimes that's the easiest way."

"I've got a team of very good investigators on it, but she seems to have vanished from sight."

"First Lawton, now her," Carella said.

"Are you familiar with something up there called Theater Place?" Matthew asked.

"No, what is it?"

"A studio, a workshop, I'm not sure. She was taking acting lessons there before she left the city."

"Let me take a look," Carella said. "Might give us a lead, huh?"

Us, Matthew thought.

"Theater *Place*?" Carella said.

"Yes."

Matthew figured he was thumbing through a telephone directory.

Sometimes that's the easiest way.

He waited.

"Yeah, here it is," Carella said. "All the way downtown. Section of the city we call Hopscotch, go ask. Want me to check it out for you?"

"Well, I really . . ."

"It's pretty quiet up here right now. All the bad guys are afraid to go out in the snow. Maybe I can run down there on my lunch hour, see what they know about her, okay? I'll call you back later."

"I really appreciate this," Matthew said.

And never got to ask if Carella had ever been shot because all at once he was gone.

"This is not my normal trade," Jack was telling her. "I do not normally *steal* things for a living."

Candace Knowles said nothing.

At ten that morning, she sat in a white wicker chair on the outdoor patio of the house he was renting, wearing green slacks, a green T-shirt, and white sandals. Her blond hair was cut in shaggy bangs on her forehead. Elsewhere, it fell sleek and long to her shoulders. Pale green eyes. No lipstick. It looked to Jack as if wicker and woman and costume had been designed by some ad agency art director. Which brought him back to the point.

"I'm a graphic designer," he said. "I was up north till recently, trying to find a good job. The field is very crowded. That's what got me seriously considering the job I'm offering you. Far as I'm concerned, it's my last best hope."

"Uh-huh," she said.

She hated boring fucking introductions. She also hated Florida. Today was going to be another boring fucking Florida day. Cut to the chase, she thought. We going to steal something or not?

"I need three people in addition to myself," Jack said. "According to the plan."

"What plan is that?" she asked.

"A plan this man I met up north was considerate enough to share with me."

"You said three plus you. Is he one of the three?"

"No."

"How come?"

"He recently passed away."

"Uh-huh," Candace said, and knew better than to ask who the man was or how he'd met his untimely demise. If the job sounded good, she'd take it. If not, she'd walk. Plenty more where this one came from. Besides, she didn't like working with amateurs. This better be good, she thought.

"The way this was described to me," Jack said, "it would be a lay-in job."

"Uh-huh."

"Do you know what a lay-in job is?"

She looked at him.

"Are we going to talk here, or what?" she asked.

"Well, *I* didn't know what a lay-in job was . . ."

"Maybe because this isn't . . ."

". . . till it was explained to me."

". . . your normal *trade*," she said, hitting the word hard.

"That's right, it isn't."

"Stealing things for a living, I mean."

"Yes, I understand your point."

"But it *is* mine," she said.

"I realize that."

"Which is why I'm here. Though you still haven't told me how you happened to get my name and phone number."

"That's another story."

"It's a story I'd like to hear."

"Well, this man who passed away gave it to me."

So now she'd have to know who he was, after all. She wasn't sure she liked this. All at once there was a stiff in the picture, and the way this Lawton person was waltzing around it, she suspected he hadn't exactly died of old age. She kept looking at Lawton, trying to get a bead on him, trying to figure out how much of this was bullshit and how much was genuine, debating whether she should walk out of here or not.

He was a guy in his mid-thirties, she guessed, well, closer to forty, the look of him. No Florida tan, just this sort of why so pale and wan fond lover appearance that pegged him as a snowbird. Out of shape for a guy his age, too, little paunchy, could've used a haircut, one of those fucking anachronistic hippies, she thought. A graphic designer, he'd said, it figured. She bit the bullet.

"Does this man who passed away have a name?"

"Ernest Corrington," he said.

She tried to place it. Corrington. Ernest. She couldn't remember any Ernests or Ernies in her life, professional or otherwise. Then it occurred to her. "Corry? Did he go by the name Corry?"

"Yes."

"Good dancer," she said, remembering. Nodding, all of it coming back to her. "Corry, yeah. Not such a good thief, though. Big guy, am I right? Six-two, six-three, something like that?"

"That's right."

"Lots of muscles?"

"Yes."

"How'd you happen to meet?"

"Ran into each other at a party."

"When was that?"

"Halloween."

"And that's when he gave you this plan, huh?"

"Well, it was shortly after that. And he didn't *give* it to me. He explained it to me. Described it to me. Gave me all the details. How do *you* happen to know him, can you tell me that?"

"We did a thing together in Houston."

"What sort of thing?"

"The same sort of thing I guess you want me to do for you here. You say this is a lay-in job . . ."

"Yes."

"So I figure you want a respectable-looking lady in a business suit to linger when the place closes, whatever the place may be, you haven't told me yet what the plan is Corry described to you."

"He told me you're very good at what you do."

"Yes, I'm terrific. Have you noticed how you dodge all my questions?"

"I'm simply trying to find out a little about you."

"You need a lay-in man, or don't you?"

"I need one."

"Okay, I'm the best in the business. If you can afford me. I get a thousand an hour, no matter what anyone else gets."

"Are you a lawyer or something?"

"Ha ha," Candace said. "You told me you need three people. I'm figuring that means me, a lookout and a wheel-man, I *still* get a thousand an hour. You can pay the others whatever you like, I usually take home, say, fifty, sixty large. What do you expect the take will be?"

"I'm assuming you're familiar with the various types of alarms we might encounter."

"That's what a lay-in man does," she said. "Takes out the alarms after everybody locks up for the night, lets the other creatures in. What kind of rigs do you expect?"

"Mickey Mouse stuff. That's why Corry chose the venue."

"Venue, huh?" she said, and rolled her eyes. "When do you plan on doing this thing, whatever it is?"

"February first. A Saturday night."

"Good, I'll still be down here. How much is the take?"

Direct question, you expect a direct answer.

"Where do you go after the season?" he said.

"Back to Texas. I have a ranch there. I raise cattle."

"Is that what good thieves do with their proceeds?"

"It's what I do with mine. Beef is my annuity."

"High in cholesterol. Very dangerous."

"So's living. How much is the take?"

"Let me tell you a story."

"So far, this whole *thing* sounds like a story," Candace said.

"In a sense it is. Tale of a cup," Jack said, and smiled.

"What the hell is that supposed to mean?" Candace asked.

"What kind of a job did you do with him?"

"I never give the details of jobs I've worked. I find that's a good way to stay out of jail."

"Have you ever been in jail?"

"Never. And I never hope to be. Not on a burglary rap and not on a murder, either. *If* this happens to involve a murder."

"You won't have to commit any murders," he said, and smiled.

"I'm not talking about a *future* murder. I'm talking about accessory *after*. I don't want to get involved in something that may have already happened, you understand?"

"You don't have to worry about anything like that."

"Sure. But you told me Corry's dead . . ."

"He is, but . . ."

"And you also told me he was alive early November, when he gave you this plan of his . . ."

"Described it to me."

"Explained it to you."

"Yes."

"In detail. My point is, that wasn't too long ago."

"It wasn't."

"What I'm saying, it all sounds kind of *sudden,* don't you think? His death and all? Would you mind my asking you a question?"

"Not at all."

"And please don't answer it with another question."

"I promise."

"Was he killed?"

"Yes."

"Mr. Lawton," she said, "if that's your name, goodbye," and rose from the wicker chair and was starting toward the path that ran around the side of the house, when he said, "Miss Knowles?"

She stopped on the path, and turned toward him, hands on her hips. Her eyes met his. "Did *you* kill him?" she asked.

"No, I didn't."

"Do you know *why* he was killed?"

"I would guess somebody thought he was me," Jack said. She kept staring at him.

"Do you want to hear this, or don't you?" he said. She waited a moment.

Then she shrugged and said, "Sure, why not?" and sat down again.

This time last year, Carella was investigating the murder of a concert pianist. Dead hooker had turned up, too, just to keep things interesting. This year, with all the snow, seemed like murder had taken a holiday. Robbery and rape, too. This kind of weather, your perps preferred staying indoors, toasting their feet by a nice warm fire, lighting their cigars with stolen hundred-dollar bills.

The Hopscotch area, normally busy and bustling at two in the afternoon, seemed desolate and grim on this twenty-seventh day of January, a blue Monday if ever he'd seen one. Hopscotch was so named because the first art gallery to open there was on Hopper Street, overlooking the Scotch Meadows Park. The neighborhood was now a thriving mélange of art galleries, coffee shops, restaurants, boutiques, stores selling antiques, drug paraphernalia, sandals, jewelry, unpainted furniture, and "collectibles," whatever they were. In recent years, a tide of resident stage companies had flooded the lofts and basements on many of the side streets and avenues, creating yet another small theater district in a city already brimming with wannabe actors, playwrights and directors.

Theater Place was just off Lincoln, in a building that had once been a church. A somewhat large and forbidding cross still topped its steeple, seemingly incompatible with a marquee over the church's red entrance doors. The thrusting three-sided structure announced THE MERRY WIVES OF WINDSOR, which he guessed was the current Theater Place production. A bona fide theater group, then, and not merely a studio or a workshop as Hope had suggested. He still wondered why he was going out of his way for the man. Maybe it was something in his manner. Maybe it was because he sounded so sincere. Carella opened one of the doors—and stepped into bedlam.

There were perhaps a dozen or more people in the room, all of them in seeming stages of hysteria, delusion, rage, ecstasy, or slobbering disorder. His eyes still wet from the cold outside, his hair windblown, he blew on his hands and stared with amazement at this odd collection of humans, and some animals, it now appeared, ranging in age from nineteen to ninety, crawling, leaping, moaning, groaning, hopping, screaming, laughing, crying—what the hell was going *on* here? Wasn't that a man in drag standing there adjusting seamed silk stockings, and putting on lipstick, and sipping from a champagne glass? Wasn't that a woman laughing maniacally as she danced alone to some secret music? Wasn't that another man who thought he was a goddamn *rooster*, strutting and preening and—oh Jesus, now he was crowing! And here were three more men, sitting and staring into imaginary mirrors, shaving with imaginary razors, one of them openly weeping.

"Heavy shoulders, Priscilla," someone said. "You're a gorilla, not a monkey."

Carella turned to see a tall, slender blond woman in her mid-sixties, he guessed, wearing a long green woolen dress, her long hair caught in a ponytail that trailed down her back, approaching a teenage girl who was crouched over, close to the floor, arms dangling, shoulders hunched. "Your movements are too jittery, Priscilla, too light. You want heavy shoulders and arms. A big jaw, Priscilla, *yes*! Now test the voice, you're a *gorilla*!" the woman said, and Carella grasped all at once that this was an acting class in progress. As Priscilla began going "Urh, urh, urh," grunting and glowering and pounding her chest, Carella sidled along the wall toward a row of folding chairs, hoping to be unobtrusive, realizing he was caught in the act when the woman asked, "Yes, may I help you?"

He stopped dead in his tracks.

"Yes?" she said again.

He fumbled for his shield, held it up like the calling card it was, apologetically mouthed the words "I'll wait," and took a seat against the wall. The man who'd been sipping champagne stopped at once, and began moving off the floor. "That's all right, Jimmy," the woman said, walking swiftly toward him. "Keep the fourth wall. This isn't *you* getting dressed for the party, it's the *character's* private moment."

As the class continued, Carella tried to make himself invisible, studying the room instead of the people in it, all of them struggling with demanding exercises. The walls of the church had been painted black, its tall windows draped

95

with black fabric. At the far end, opposite the entrance doors, there was now a good-sized stage where an altar must have been. He now realized that the folding chairs ranged along the walls had been moved back to clear the open work space for the class. He guessed there were a hundred or so of the chairs, perhaps fewer. Churches made him nervous. He was always sure the roof would fall in once God discovered a sinner like him on the premises. He was glad *this* church was now a theater of sorts, but he felt nonetheless uncomfortable, and was happy when the blond woman called a break some ten minutes later.

She walked over, smiled, sat beside him and said, "What laws are we breaking?"

"None that I know of," he said. "I'm Detective Carella, Eighty-seventh Precinct." He showed her the shield again. She looked at it, nodded slightly, raised her brows inquisitively. Her eyes were a luminous dark brown, almost black. Fine nose, high cheekbones, a tall, slender blond woman in a long green dress, sixty or so and aging gracefully.

"You are?" he asked.

"Elena Lopez," she said.

Faint Hispanic accent, he now realized.

"If we haven't broken any laws," she said, "why are you here?"

"I'm trying to learn whatever I can about a woman named Holly Sinclair. Or Melanie Schwartz, she may have been when she studied here."

"Melanie, yes."

"You remember her?"

"Oh yes. I remember *all* of my students. Not always by name, not as the years go by. Besides, actors often change their names—as Melanie did. Well, sometimes not even by appearance. Some of them go bald, others grow fat, they don't always look the same. But, yes, I remember most of them. Even the *bad* ones."

"Was Melanie a bad one?"

"No, on the contrary, I thought she had enormous potential. She wasn't willing to work hard, however. She wanted to become a star overnight. Holly *Sinclair,* don't you know?" she said, and threw one arm over her head in a sort of grand salute. "She wanted to take six months of lessons and then storm the town. I told her that was impossible."

"Is that how long she was here? Six months?"

"Less, I believe. She started late in the summer session— I run a summer session in July and August. She joined us around the fifteenth, something like that, I know we'd already been working for a few weeks. Maybe it was later, I have my records in the office if you'd like me to check later. But even *six* months? To become an actor? Impossible."

"How long *does* it take?"

"A lifetime," Elena replied. "But at least two years before you can step on a stage and assume a role. Why? Do you want to become an actor, Mr. Carella?"

"No, no. Hey."

"Don't be afraid to admit it. Most people harbor a secret desire to act."

"No, I never . . . no," he said, shaking his head unconvincingly.

"But most people aren't ready to put in the hard work. Well, Melanie, for example. America is a nation of successful amateurs, Mr. Carella, do you understand what I'm saying?"

"Not quite."

"A director is having his car washed, and he discovers a

young man who's never taken an acting lesson in his life. He puts him in a film and the young man becomes a big movie star overnight, never took an acting lesson. A lucky amateur."

"I guess so," Carella said, smiling.

"You think it's comical? The way art in America has been taken over by the amateurs? Not only in the acting profession. Writing, painting, sculpting, everything, every single art form! Well, not dancing. There are no amateur ballerinas anywhere in the world. Do you know why, Mr. Carella?"

"Tell me why," he said.

"Because they would fall down and *hurt* themselves."

Carella began laughing.

"Oh, yes, very comical," Elena said, but she was enjoying herself, too. "On the other hand, a lawyer who writes a novel can't break his leg, he can only get bad reviews. Do you know how many *lawyers* are writing novels these days? When did lawyers get to be such heroes? I personally *hate* lawyers."

Carella did not tell her that he was here on behalf of a lawyer.

"Or advertising men," she went on, gathering steam, "or doctors, or whoever decides 'Gee, *I* can write better than that,' and sits down without knowing his ass from his elbow, excuse me. Lucky amateurs. That's what I call them. Yes, laugh, go ahead," she said. "But how would you feel if amateurs began solving *crimes*? Little old women with knitting needles? Puttering around their gardens when they're not out chasing murderers? Lady private eyes? *Lawyers?*"

Carella did not tell her that he was here on behalf of a lawyer who was investigating a murder.

"Psychiatrists?" she said. "When's the last time you met a *psychiatrist* who solved a crime?"

"Never," Carella said.

"Or cats? Do you personally know any *cats* who solve crimes?"

"I'm sorry to say I do not."

"A good thing, too. Because next time someone is killed in this city, I would have to call a cat," she said, and gestured in airy dismissal. Her hands were wonderfully expressive. Carella wondered if she taught an exercise on how to use the hands.

"How about a man named Ernest Corrington?" he said. "Do you remember him?"

"Oh yes. Now *he* was wonderful. Strange, but wonderful. A very muscular man, you know."

"I know."

"Wonderful actor. I think he spent some time in prison. Over the years, I've had several actors who were once in prison."

"Bad actors," Carella said, smiling.

"*Good* ones, actually."

"That's what we call lawbreakers. Bad ac—"

"Oh. Yes, I see. But it's a fact. *Many* ex-convicts are good actors. They bring a sort of conviction to it."

"No pun intended."

"Sorry?"

"Conviction."

"Oh. Yes, I see. But I think creating a character *does* require great conviction. And so does going into a grocery store with a gun in your hand."

"You think they're one and the same thing, huh?"

"Well, of course not. Stop kidding me, Mr. Carella."

"He was here about the same time Melanie was, is that right?"

"Exactly. Melanie liked the summer session, came back in September. Corry joined the class in October sometime, that's when they met. During the fall session. Melanie quit early in December, told me she had to go back to Florida." Elena gave a huge Gallic shrug. "She'd already changed her name, I guess she figured she could become a star down there. How? You become a star here or you become a star in Hollywood, but you don't become a star in Florida. Not anywhere in Florida that *I* know of. Anyway, what good is becoming a star if you don't become an *actor* first?"

"How about Corrington? When did he leave?"

"I never saw him again after the twentieth. The Friday before Christmas. We had our last class of the fall session that Friday night. Are you looking for him, too?"

"No."

"I wouldn't be surprised if the two of them were some-where together. Although, you know, given Melanie's . . ."

"Think there was something between them?" Carella asked.

"Maybe. There certainly was a lot of heat in a scene they did from *Streetcar.* But with someone like Melanie, it's hard to say."

"In any case, he's dead," Carella said.

"What!"

"He was murdered," Carella said.

"Oh dear," Elena said, and fell silent for a moment. Then she asked, "Has something happened to Melanie, too?"

"Not that I know of. We're just trying to find her."

"Who's we?"

"Well . . . uh . . . someone I know in Florida."

100

"Has he tried any of the theater groups down there?"

"I don't think he has."

"Because one thing an actor does, wherever he is, is reach out to other actors."

"Even an actor who wants to become a star overnight?"

"*Especially* that kind of actor. Try the theater groups down there."

"Any other ideas?"

"Well . . ."

"Yes?"

"I suppose you could try the lesbian bars."

This is to be a Halloween party, and for the occasion Elena Lopez has decorated the black walls of the church with cutouts depicting goblins and witches, vampires and ghouls. The place is thronged with students and their guests, all of them dressed in costumes either rented or made by hand. Jack and Melanie have come as bride and groom, how cute, he in striped trousers and a gray morning coat, she in a white veil and an outrageously short white wedding dress cut dangerously low over her breasts, a blue garter high on her right thigh. Corry has come as a cowboy, how original, in black jeans and shirt and a black kerchief and black hat tilted low on his forehead. The tag from a cigarette pouch hangs out of one of the shirt pockets, but he isn't rolling his own, he's smoking Camels instead, looking for cancer, she supposes.

There are times when Melanie doesn't quite understand what drives her to do the things she does. She knows she came up north to be with Jack. That was a no-brainer. Jack sent for her, so she came up. Without telling Jill where she was going or why. Just left Calusa one day and that was that, took up housekeeping with Jack in a two-room apartment on the top floor of 831 Crest, skateboard ramp going day and night over their heads, enough to drive a person crazy. That was in July, too damn hot down in Calusa, anyway, much better up here. Joined Theater Place later that month, which was good, too, Elena was a wonderful teacher.

But there are times, like tonight, when Melanie thinks she actually *enjoys* living on the thin edge of danger. Like taking up with Peter down in Calusa, when she knew he had a record, and while she was actively engaged in what Jack called a triple somersault without a net—well, *that* had been going on forever, ever since that day of the auction and the moonlight swim. God that had been exciting, that night. But it sort of wears off after a while, the novelty. Which is maybe why she took up with Peter and his Mr. Smith and Mr. Wesson, he sometimes put the gun in her mouth while he was fucking her. And living *alone* with Jack is sort of dangerous, too, behind Jill's back this way, Jill can be mean as hell when she wants to, the things the three of them did together.

But tonight . . .

She wonders if she's been planning this ever since she did the scene from *Streetcar* with Corry, wonders if this is what's been in her mind from that very day, but who knows? She never really understands what causes her to do things that seem to be spur-of-the-moment inspirations but maybe aren't.

She introduces Jack to all the kids in the class, well, most of them aren't kids, some of them are in their forties, but everybody in class refers to everybody else as "the kids." There's a story going around that when Marilyn Monroe was studying at the Actors' Studio, this was when she was already a very big movie star, she called this actor she was supposed to do a scene with, and she said, "Hello? This is Marilyn? You know, from class?" Melanie wonders if this is a true story. She also wonders if one day she'll be as famous as Marilyn Monroe was.

It's maybe ten o'clock or thereabouts when she finally gets around to introducing Jack to Corry. The two of them seem to hit it off right away though they're really very different types, Jack sort of square and yuppie except when he's got that big thing of his inside her and he's lapping Jill's pussy at the same time, and Corry very hard and mean looking, the cowboy outfit is really perfect for him, talk about typecasting. Corry's not at all reticent about telling people he took two falls on the Coast, though he doesn't mention he is at the moment breaking parole, which he saves for when he knows Melanie and Jack better, a *lot* better. Jack shows the proper awe and admiration for a self-confessed armed robber, and the two throw back a few more beers, laughing like old buddies who did time together long ago and far away. Along around midnight, the party starts breaking up, and everybody comes out of the theater singing to the night, Elena calling after them in Spanish to please shut up, they'll wake the whole neighborhood.

It seems a bit *early* to be going home from a Halloween party, midnight is only just the witching hour, isn't it, and that's what Halloween is all about. So they go to a saloon near the theater, all of them still in costume, Jack and Melanie the bride and groom, and Corry their badass cowboy friend. Melanie and the boys start drinking harder stuff—Corry sticks with Stoli neat, and Jack's drinking Johnnie Black on the rocks, and Melanie's nursing a gin martini with a twist—and before you know it, it's two in the morning and the bartender is closing the joint, and they come reeling out of the bar looking for a taxi because it's Jack's suggestion that they go home and listen to some music and keep the party going, hell, it's Halloween.

She will remind Jack later that he was the one who suggested they keep the party going, in just those words.

In the taxi uptown, she's already wondering where all this is going to lead. These taxis up north are very tight, and she's sitting between the two men in her short white wedding dress with the blue garter tight on her thigh and the Pakistani cabbie babbling Urdu to his pals on the CB radio and she's wondering where this will all lead, ah yes, the mysteries of life. It's beginning to snow. Lightly at first, but by the time they get all the way uptown it's coming down pretty heavily, thick white flakes drifting out of the sky and beginning to blanket the empty streets.

The apartment they're living in is what's called a one-bedroom apartment, which means there's one bedroom and a slightly larger room with a tiny kitchen tacked onto it. She and Jack go into the bedroom as soon as they're home, asking Corry to mix himself a drink while they change out of the wedding costumes, there's some vodka in the freezer, though it isn't Stoli. They come out about five minutes later, Jack in jeans and a flannel shirt and a cardigan sweater, Melanie in a woolen caftan she bought in a shop near the theater. This is now almost three in the morning, and the heat's already off, so Jack offers Corry a sweater if he'd like one, and Corry accepts, which is sort of a male bonding kind of thing, Corry putting on Jack's sweater, saying it fits him like it was made for him.

She remembers all these things later.

They sit drinking and listening to Jack's tapes from when

he was a teenager, all the big hits from Wings and Diana Ross and KC & the Sunshine Band, Jack singing along with Elton and Kiki on "Don't Go Breaking My Heart." Corry's a little older than Jack, it turns out he's forty-two, and so his frame of reference is earlier in the seventies, when stuff like Janis Joplin's "Me and Bobby McGee" and Three Dog Night's "Joy to the World" and the Stones's "Brown Sugar" were all the rage. It's snowing very hard out there now and Corry wonders out loud if he'll be able to get a taxi home, and Jack says the subway's only two blocks away, and Melanie says, "Or you can stay over if you like. Sleep on the couch."

Corry looks at them both and says, "Why don't I stay over and we all sleep in the bed?"

She's surprised that Jack doesn't throw him out that very minute. But he doesn't. Instead, there's a long silence. The music has stopped, the snow is falling silently outside, the apartment is very still.

"You think that might appeal to you, Melanie?" Corry asks.

Again, she expects Jack to say something, but he doesn't. He just stands there, looking from one to the other of them.

"What do you think, Jack?" she says.

It isn't as if they haven't slept three in a bed before. They've been sleeping three in a bed for seven years now, be eight years this coming August. So this isn't something new. What's new is that before now it's been two women and a man, but tonight—if this happens, if she allows this to happen—it'll be two men and a woman. It'll be Jack and Corry and her. Both of them and *her.* There's no question in her mind but that she'll be the one who'll either let it happen or not let it happen. The way it was Jill back then on that

August night long ago who decided it was going to happen and made it happen by gliding up to Melanie in the water, and putting her arms around her, and pulling her in close, and kissing her on the mouth.

"Jack?" she says. "What do you think?"

"Be fun," Corry says.

Jack is thinking—and he admits this to both of them later—that Corry has spent time in prison and if he lets this happen between the three of them, the next thing you know he'll be getting fucked in the ass. He's thinking that Melanie and Jill have never shown any qualms about going at each other, it was Jill in fact who initiated their relationship seven years ago. In fact, he sometimes feels like a third wheel when they're making love, sometimes feels he's there only to lend respectability—well, *that's* a joke—to what Jill and Melanie are doing to each other. He doesn't want *that* sort of thing to develop here between him and Corry, that doesn't appeal to him in the slightest. In fact, he's tempted to lay it on the table right this minute, tell Corry, "Listen, my friend, if you've got any kind of homosexual activity in mind here, you'd better leave right now," but he still doesn't say anything. He just stands there sort of letting this thing evolve, the way he let it evolve that night seven years ago with Jill and Melanie.

For her part, she is as excited as she was that night long ago, waiting for something to happen here, wondering if she should force the issue, step right up to Corry, march right into the erection she can see bulging in his black jeans, put her hands up around the back of his neck, thrust her crotch at him, and kiss him on the mouth, force the issue the way Jill did that night in the pool. But whereas she knows that she's the one who'll make the final call, knows that without her consent nobody's going to do *anything* tonight, she senses that there's some kind of male thing happening here. Corry hasn't yet taken off Jack's sweater, and the two men are looking at each other as if silently deciding the issue between them. It's as if Corry is asking Jack's permission to dance with his wife, that sort of thing, as if Melanie is Jack's *property*. She's not married to Jack, of course, and she's certainly not his property, but she knows that's exactly what's going on here, Corry is waiting for Jack's approval before this thing can move off the dime. Once Jack agrees to it, they'll proceed to the next stage, whatever that may turn out to be. But instead of this macho bullshit infuriating her, it somehow excites her even more. It's as if she really has nothing at all to say about what will happen to her. The men will decide it, and then she'll either go along with it or not, it won't matter to them, they'll rape her if they choose to—which thought inflames her ever further.

"Jack?" she says.

Jack is wondering whether they should take an ex-con into their bed, she can see that in his eyes. But he's also ready for this, the idea is exciting to him, she can see *that* in his *pants*. What she realizes she has to do is make it seem as if they're the ones deciding this, even though she's already made the decision. In fact, she's already visualizing all sorts of combinations and permutations once they get into that damn bed, two men with huge hard-ons and a woman already so wet she's afraid she'll melt into the floor.

"Boys," she says softly, and holds out her hands to them, and takes their hands in hers. "It's very cold in here, and it's snowing out there, so why don't we all get under the covers and work it out there?"

She squeezes Jack's hand.

"Okay?" she says.

She squeezes Corry's hand.

"Okay?"

"If it's okay with Jack, it's okay with me," Corry says.

"If it's okay with Melanie, it's okay with me," Jack says.

"It's okay with me," she says, and smiles demurely.

W hat kind of a rig will this be?" Zaygo asked.

"I haven't really given it much thought," Jack said. "I figured I'd leave that up to you."

"Uh-huh," Zaygo said.

Fuckin amateur, he was thinking.

"Are we gonna be involved in any high-speed chases here?" he asked. "I mean like, will we need a cigarette?"

"What's a cigarette?" Jack asked.

Boy, Zaygo thought.

"It's this speedboat can outrun a cutter, is what it is," he said. "Long and thin and slick as baby shit. Is the Coast Guard gonna be chasin us?"

"No, I don't think so. At least, I hope not."

"This isn't a dope deal, is it? Cause I don't transport narcotics, period."

"Why is that?"

"I disapprove of substance abuse."

"I see," Jack said.

Zaygo did not look like the sort of man one imagined driving boats. In fact, he looked like perfect casting for a computer hack, short and thin with spiky black hair and rimless eyeglasses and a face riddled with acne. Jack didn't think guys in their thirties ever got acne, which is what he supposed Zaygo was, thirty-two, thirty-three, in there. When he'd told Candace Knowles what the venue would be, she was the one who suggested Zaygo as their wheel-man. Except he wouldn't be driving a car, he'd be driving a boat. "Venue" was a term Jack had picked up from the late Ernest Corrington. Corry had called the site of the failed robbery in Los Angeles "the drugstore venue." Jack sup-posed this one could be called "the museum venue." This was now three o'clock in the afternoon, and Zaygo was here and wanting to know all about the job.

"How big is the payload I'm supposed to carry?" he asked.

He was wearing rumpled blue jeans, a blue T-shirt, and white Top-Siders gone gray a century ago. His costume gave him a faintly nautical look, but it couldn't compete with the nerd image. Jack still couldn't imagine him behind the wheel of a powerboat. Good thing the payload's a small one, he thought.

"A small one," he said out loud.

Zaygo wondered what it could be. Hiring a lay-in man like Candace Knowles who didn't come cheap, hiring someone like himself who didn't get what Candace got but who didn't get paid in Oreo cookies, either. Jack would need a third man, too, as backup for when he went in. Or lookout. Whatever. So this wasn't a cheap operation here, for something small, whatever it was, unless it was a piece of jewelry.

"And you say we do the pickup back of the museum, huh?" he said.

"That's where. The dock behind the museum."

"On the water there."

"Calusa Bay. There's a dock because it used to be a private home. The museum."

"I didn't know that."

"The Ca D'Ped."

"Is that right?"

"Yes. It used to be a hacienda called Casa Don Pedro. That was when Florida was still a Spanish possession. It was renovated and refurnished as a mansion in 1927."

How very fucking interesting, Zaygo thought.

"The owner also built a hotel downtown, on the Trail. For his friends to stay in whenever they came down. It's still there. They're supposed to be renovating it."

Even *more* fucking fascinating, Zaygo thought.

"The city bought it for a museum after his death."

"The hotel?" Zaygo asked.

"No, the mansion. The Ca D'Ped."

"So is this some kind of museum piece? The payload?"

"Yes."

"What kind?"

"Oh, just a terra-cotta bottle," Jack said.

The weather in Athens at this time of year is insufferably hot. It is worse here in the prison, where substantial walls prevent the admission of even the slightest breeze. Piraeus Street, at the northern end of the prison, where the entrance gate is located, is an important thoroughfare, crossing the Street of the Marble Workers, and continuing northwestward to the Piraeus Gate itself. Whenever they visit the condemned prisoner, his companions meet at daybreak at the courthouse close by, where he was tried and condemned to death. The prison does not normally open early. Neither will it open early on this day of his execution, but they are here even before daybreak, arriving during the empty hours of the night to whisper on the courthouse steps of what the morning portends. They have learned, you see, that the ship has returned from Delos.

The ship's arrival is a matter of grave concern to them.

It means that now he can be put to death.

In ancient times, the king of Crete demanded from Athens seven young men and maidens—the so-called Seven Pair—whom he sacrificed to his monster, the flesh-eating Minotaur. Theseus set sail with the doomed seven. The people of Athens made a vow to Apollo that if the youths were saved, they would dispatch a mission to Delos, Apollo's sacred island, every year thereafter. When Theseus killed the beast, saving himself and the seven, the vow was honored, and every year since, to this very time, the ship in which Theseus sailed to Crete embarks on a mission to Delos.

This year, the stern of the ship was wreathed by the priest of Apollo, and set sail on the very day before the trial began. Its chance departure has spared his life for almost a month; by Athenian law, the city must remain "pure" during the time of the ship's absence, which means that no one may be put to death. But now the ship has returned.

From where his friends are gathered and still gathering, they can see in the near distance an armed guard standing just outside the prison gate. When they visited the prison the night before, they begged their friend to attempt escape, difficult under any circumstances for the walls are high and the only entrance is quite close to the two-story barracks, a complex of four rooms that houses on the street level the officers and guards, and on the floor above the so-called Eleven, the magistrates charged with running the prison and ordering the executions.

The prison is some hundred and twenty feet long by fifty feet wide, a good six thousand square feet overall. A long central corridor runs past five cells on one side, three cells on the other. In the cell closest to the entrance gate, a large jar is buried in the floor, brimming now with rainwater the prisoners use for bathing. There is a large courtyard at the southern end of the corridor, where multiple arrests are routinely processed.

His friends approach the gate at first light, but they are told by the guard there to come back later as the Eleven are at that very moment releasing the prisoner from his chains and giving orders that he is to die today. Not fifteen minutes later, he returns to tell them that they may come in now, and signals to the turnkey to open the gate for them.

They know the way.

He is in the first cell on the eastern side of the corridor, one in a row of three that are somewhat larger than the five opposite. Perhaps he has been given one of the larger cells because of his celebrity, though certainly there have been other important prisoners here over the years. Or perhaps the Eleven are merely making amends for the harsh penalty meted to one of their city's most distinguished citizens.

In Athens, the preferred punishments for wrongdoers are fines, exile, or death—each of which precludes long prison sentences. The condemned man's crime was "impiety." There were two counts in the indictment. The first was "corruption of the young." The second was "neglect of the gods whom the city worships." He treated the charges with contempt. So today he will die.

In Athens, a man condemned to die is given a draught of poison to drink. The poison is prepared by pounding the leaves of the hemlock plant. The man who is to administer the poison today warns the visitors that their friend is talking too much, explaining that people get overheated through excessive talking, and this can counteract the poison. For example, he tells them, wine heats the blood and is a known antidote to hemlock.

There is no wine in this cell today.

There are only old friends saying goodbye to a brave man who replies, "Never mind him. Just let him prepare his stuff so as to give two doses, or even three if need be."

Sometime in the late afternoon, he goes down the long corridor to the cell with the water jar in it and bathes there for the last time, telling his friends, "It really seems better to take a bath before drinking the poison and not give the women the trouble of washing a dead body."

Shortly after sunset, the hemlock is brought to him. And although the executioner calls it a "cup," it is in reality a small medicine bottle with a narrow neck, a flaring lip, a rounded body, and a shallow foot. There are no handles on the bottle. It is merely a cheap little terra-cotta vessel, intended to be discarded after its use as a container for the deadly hemlock.

"Well, my friend," he says to his executioner, "you're an expert in these things. What must one do?"

"Simply drink it," the man says, "and walk about till a heaviness comes over your legs. Then lie down, and it will act of itself."

He holds out the bottle.

The condemned man takes it.

He lifts it to his mouth, presses it to his lips, and drains it. He walks about and when his legs begin to feel heavy, he lies on his back, and the executioner touches his feet and his legs and pinches his foot hard and asks if he can feel it, and the dying man says no, he cannot, and the executioner feels his shins and keeps moving his hands upward.

"When the coldness reaches his heart," the executioner says, "he will be gone."

That was in 399 B.C.

In 1977, archaeologists digging in Athens unearthed the prison. In an abandoned cistern in the northwest room, they found thirteen medicine bottles, a significant concentration in light of the fact that only twenty-one such bottles were excavated at the entire site. Experts were in general agreement that these bottles—discarded immediately afterward as contaminated—were the ones that had contained the meticulously measured and individually mixed portions of hemlock ingested by condemned prisoners.

On the bottom of one of the bottles, scratched into the terra cotta, were the letters ΣOK.

This was a proper museum now, signs telling people where to park, signs showing where the entrance was, Ca D'Ped Museum of Fine Art, Calusa, Florida, ta-ra! Candace Knowles—and God protect any man, woman or child who ever called her Candy—parked her little white Porsche in a lot virtually empty at four o'clock that Monday afternoon, bright Florida sun tinting the tiled towers of the museum in the distance. She locked up, thinking she would've worn flats if she'd known the goddamn parking lot was going to be gravel, and then dropped her keys into her bag, and slung the bag over her shoulder. Usually, she packed a Browning .25-caliber automatic in the bag, but not today. Didn't want some security guard stopping her and asking what she was doing with a gun in her handbag, though in the fair state of Florida it was legal to carry one. Didn't want anyone to ask her *anything* today. Just wanted to go in there and go about her business because last time she looked today was still the twenty-seventh of January, and that meant showtime was only five days away.

She had showered and changed after leaving Lawton this morning, and she was now wearing a navy-blue cotton skirt with a boat-necked striped top, navy and lime green, strappy green sandals with a medium heel, getting scuffed all to hell from the gravel. The goddamn sandals had cost her three hundred bucks only last week. Her blond hair was caught in a ponytail at the back of her neck, held with a scarf that matched the alternate stripes in the top, and echoed the color of her eyes, covered with dark glasses now to shield them from the blinding sun and the scrutiny of whatever security guards might care to remember her come February first. There was a camera, an artist's pad, and several different-colored felt-tipped pens in the shoulder bag, the better to seemingly sketch the priceless art on the walls of the Ca D'Ped while photographing whichever alarm systems might pop out at her.

Today, she wasn't expecting much more than just familiarizing herself with the layout. She knew she'd have to go in for a dry run, maybe two or three of them, before the night of the heist, locate the boxes, determine what systems were operating here, gather the information she'd need for beating them when the time came. She was working for a thousand an hour, and the meter was running.

There were two huge entrance pillars at the head of the long gravel driveway—*more* goddamn gravel—that led to the museum itself perched on the lip of the bay to the west, the sun already beginning to dip behind it. The color on the pillars was the one favored by the Spanish settlers, a sort of pinkish peach topped with a row of earth-colored tiles. The museum was painted the same color as the pillars, its turrets and towers and roofs capped with the same earth-colored tiles. Candace negotiated the bruising little pebbles underfoot and finally, and with a sigh, climbed the wide, low, flat steps that led to the massive mahogany entrance doors, carved with what appeared to be all the little winged angels in Paradise.

She paid a five-dollar admission fee at a little booth to the left of the entrance doors. The floor underfoot was covered with huge blue tiles. Sunlight streamed into every corner of the reception hall, setting the tiles alive, causing them to look like wind-ruffled waves. She felt as if she were stepping into a cathedral flooded with pale blue water. A security guard . . .

That's *one,* she thought.

. . . directed her to a cloakroom where she was asked to check her bag. She asked the woman behind the counter if it was okay to take her camera, her sketch pad and her pens inside with her, and the woman said, "Sorry, no cameras, honey," some you win, some you lose. If a man had called her honey, she'd have told him she wasn't *his* honey or anybody *else's* honey, thanks. She rummaged in the bag for the pad and two pens, accepted a claim check from the woman, and then moved into the museum proper.

It was hard to imagine anyone ever having lived here.

The first impression was one of enormous columns and massive arches through which sunlight streamed. Beyond the arches was a landscaped interior courtyard open to the sky, more columns and arches on each of its sides. The museum's main galleries surrounded the courtyard on three sides, the reception hall forming the fourth enclosing side. There were four additional galleries on the second level of the building. Lawton did not yet know in which of the rooms the cup would be exhibited.

There was a security guard in each of the galleries.

Plus one at the front door made eight altogether.

She couldn't imagine any of them standing around here all night long, not to protect *this* stuff. She suspected they went home at night, leaving security either to an alarm system, if there was one, or a night watchman. She hoped there wasn't a night watchman. Maybe there wouldn't be. Lawton had told her that the last time the museum was broken into was never.

She chatted up one of the guards on the second floor, asking him about a couple of not very good paintings on the walls, getting him to gab before he fell asleep here leaning against the wall and watching dust motes climbing shafts of sunlight. He was a guy in his late sixties, probably came down to Florida to retire, discovered that lying on the beach all day and going to the malls at night was okay only if you had something else to do. Took a job as a security guard here in a backwater museum, didn't know squat about the paintings on the walls, informed her that there ought to be a brochure downstairs someplace, describing all the art.

Lawton had told her most of the stuff here was early

American art, supposed to be only moderately good and not exceptional in any way, no matter how much the museum hyped it. Getting the cup was something of a coup. It had gone from the Getty Museum in Malibu to the Art Institute in Chicago and from there to where Lawton and Corrington had seen it on exhibit at ISMA and learned that the next three stops on the tour were the Corcoran Gallery in D.C., the High Museum in Atlanta, and the Ca D'Ped right here in little old Calusa, coincidentally known as the Athens of Southwest Florida.

"Getting all geared up for the big exhibit?" she asked the guard.

"Which one is that?"

"The Greek stuff," she said.

"Oh yeah. What's that, anyway?" he asked.

"Very important stuff," she said. "Ancient Greek."

"Yeah?"

"Oh yes. You'll probably be getting big crowds."

"Be a change, anyway," he said.

She was trying to find out if there'd be extra security personnel, but she didn't want to push it with a direct question, no matter how stupid this jackass seemed to be. Didn't want to ask him if there was a night watchman here, either. She chatted with him for another minute or so, and then went into another of the second-floor galleries and began making a sketch of one of the paintings, a portrait of a man, a woman presumably his wife, and the ugliest little girl in all Colonial America. At the same time, she was scanning what appeared to be alarm wiring on the windows facing the street side of the room. In a little while, she moved closer to one of the windows, as if to study her sketch in the light streaming in. It was very definitely alarm wiring.

119

Her job was to neutralize the entire area on the night of the heist, so that Lawton could come in and grab the cup. Museum closed at six. She'd lay in to do her dirty work, plenty of time to do what had to be done before Lawton and his backup moved in at ten. She suspected that the wiring here was just sufficient to protect this permanent collection of second-rate art, nothing truly sophisticated, nothing too complicated to subvert.

But it might be a different story when the cup got here.

Up north, it had been exhibited in a room all by itself, in a specially wired glass cube. Lawton didn't think the cube traveled with the cup. It had been exhibited in a sort of cage at the Getty in Malibu where Corrington had seen it for the first time. He'd almost wet his pants the day they discovered that Calusa, Florida was a scheduled stop on the exhibition tour. Calusa, *Florida*? Oh dear God, will wonders never, thank you very very much, dear God.

Candace suspected that the downstairs galleries, because of all those open arches leading to the courtyard, were wired for sound and motion. If so, a Mickey Mouse museum like this one might simply have a ring of guards protecting the cup during the day, and trust to the alarm system and a watchman at night, please don't let there be a watchman. If the cube traveled south with the cup, she'd have to figure out how it was armed and how she could disarm it.

She spent another hour or so roaming around downstairs, making sketches, locating the equipment that confirmed her surmise about a sound-motion system. Then she reclaimed her bag, and walked back to where she'd parked the Porsche.

Oddly, her heart was pounding.

★   ★   ★

THE LAST BEST HOPE

The bartender was an attractive blonde wearing a pale pink T-shirt with the short sleeves deliberately cut jaggedly. In the Middle Ages, they used to call this "a dagged edge." With a d. Toots knew because once upon a time, long ago, before she came to the lovely state of Florida to become Miss Tootsie Cokehead, she used to be interested in things medieval. When she was thirteen, that is. When she was pure and innocent and lovely and timid.

The girl behind the bar looked not at all medieval. Perhaps that was because her blond hair was spiked and her upper lip was pierced with a tiny gold circlet. She was also wearing, on the biceps of her left arm, just below the dagged edge of the pink cotton sleeve, a tattoo featuring a spiderweb and a fat black spider. First Lawton with his blue dot and now the bartender. When you're in love, the whole world wears a tattoo.

Tootsie felt a little out of place here, even though in her former incarnation as a committed drug addict, oh yes indeed, she had performed a good many sexual acts with other women. *Upon* other women, that is. Performed. Do me, Toots. Oh yes. Always for money, mind you. What she'd been, you see, was a downright whore. Black hooker knocks on the hotel room door? Minister opens it, peers out at her, demands to know who she is and where she's from. Black hooker says, "Idaho. I jess d'*ho*." Yuk yuk and yes indeedy. I was just the *whore*. Nice clean white girl from Illinois, comes down to the state of Florida to enjoy the sun, finds a little bit of snow instead. In case you just arrived from Mars yesterday morning, snow is cocaine. The White Leash, mister. The Devil's Dandruff, sister. Came down here a single girl, got married to coke. Try it, my dear, won't you? Take a sniff, take a lick, have a little sip. Whammo!

Idaho.

Welcome to the club.

Never again, she thought.

Slit my wrists first.

It was strange being here in the Liquid Zipper. But the cop up north had phoned Matthew and clued him in to theater groups and lesbian bars, so here she was during the so-called Happy Hour, women looking her up and down and making it apparent they wouldn't mind a little sip of *her*, because back then to tell the truth there were times in her almost incessant drugged haze when she didn't at all mind sex with another female. Most times she faked it, of course, hell, it was just for the money, just for the White Lady, do anything for the Girl, anything at all. But still . . .

It . . .

Well . . .

It was strange being here.

Maybe because it reminded her of back then, she supposed, what she did back then, the things she did back then. Reminded her, too, that she'd thought it was cool at first, what she was doing, cool and somehow sexy, well, hell, no sex in the world was as good as cocaine, male, female, police dog, goldfish, you name it, nothing beat cocaine. She'd been very happy to be married to cocaine, thank you, till death us do part.

Never again, she thought again.

Never.

"Something to drink?" the bartender asked.

"Just some club soda," Toots said. "Wedge of lime."

Booze and drugs were linked. Start on one, you were back on the other before you knew it. The bartender popped a bottle of Perrier, poured it over ice cubes without asking. Sliced a lime, dropped in a segment. Toots looked around.

The gay and lesbian population in the state of Florida was not as large as that in New York or California, and most of it was concentrated in the Miami area, on the east coast of the state. But Calusa had its share of homosexuals, too, an odd statistic in a city not particularly noted for tolerance or progressiveness. Not for nothing had Bob Dole won the states of Ohio and Michigan in his bid for the presidency. Most of Calusa's transplants originally migrated from those two states, a fact that might account for Dole having taken the state of Florida as well.

The Liquid Zipper was one of two lesbian bars in the city, the other being Lizzie's, on the Trail and closer to Sarasota. Lizzie's had a darker reputation. The clientele here at the Liquid Zipper was less butch, tending more toward tailored suits than sandals and jeans. The zipper of the place's name was metallic and shiny-wet, half open over the vamp of a spike-heeled red satin pump realized over the bar in a cutout representation, some four feet wide and two feet tall.

"Haven't seen you here before," the bartender said.

"My first time," Toots said.

"A virgin," the bartender said, and smiled.

"Sure," Toots answered, and smiled right back. "I'm looking for someone named Melanie Schwartz, also known as Holly Sinclair, do you know her?"

"You a cop?"

"Nope."

"Why are you looking for her?"

"So you know her, huh?"

"Why are you looking for her?"

"Must be an echo in here."

"You *are* a cop, right?"

"Private," Toots said, and reached into her handbag. She pulled out her wallet, took out her ID card, handed it across the bar.

"Toots, huh?" the bartender said.

"Toots."

"Never had a Toots in here before. They let you put a nickname on your card?"

"It's not a nickname."

"Toots?"

"Toots. There's *still* an echo in here."

"That's your real name?"

"Swear to God. How about Melanie? Have you ever had a Melanie in here before?"

"That was the girl's name in *The Birds*. That movie Alfred Hitchcock wrote."

Toots did not think Alfred Hitchcock had written that movie.

"Sexy movie," the bartender said.

Toots didn't think it was sexy, either.

"We get lots of Scarletts in here," the bartender said out of the blue.

"Lots of them, huh," Toots said, and wondered what had made her think of the name Scarlett.

"Favorite in here," the bartender said.

"What made you think of it?"

"Think of what?"

"The name Scarlett."

"Well, the other girl."

"What other girl?"

"Melanie. The other girl in the movie. The one gives birth."

"Oh."

"I don't know nothin bout birfin babies, Missie Scahlett," the bartender said, doing a fairly good imitation, wiping her bar rag along the bartop in time with her slow drawl.

"How about Melanie Schwartz? Seen her in here lately?"

"Try Lizzie's," the bartender said. "I work there Tuesday nights. She was in last Tuesday."

The night Corrington was murdered, Toots thought.

Since Matthew's modest adopted city had pretensions to culture, there were no fewer than six resident theaters in the area, plus three dinner theaters, and—of course—the resplendent and world-renowned complex on Calusa Bay, the Helen Gottlieb Memorial Hall.

His partner, Frank, insisted that the Gott, as it was familiarly called, was nothing more than what would be a summer playhouse up north, catering to road shows the hicks from the Midwest were thrilled to see while they vacationed down here. Frank dismissed the fact that the venue had played host to the varied likes of Isaac Stern, and Buddy Rich, and the New York City Ballet, and second companies of *A Chorus Line* and *Annie* and any number of other Broadway hits. To Frank, Calusa was, and always would be, a tank town.

Matthew didn't call the Gott, where, because of its very touring-company nature, he knew he couldn't possibly find Melanie Schwartz. But he did call every other theater possibility on his list, and didn't hit pay dirt until he got to the very last name: the Sand and Surf Dinner Theater—"How *original!*" Frank might have exclaimed. The man he spoke to there was named Timothy Regan and he told Matthew he was resident manager of the theater. Matthew asked him if he knew anyone named Melanie Schwartz or Holly Sinclair, and the man told him Yes, he did, which almost knocked Matthew off his chair after having heard so many people telling him No, I'm sorry.

"Is she working there now?" he asked.

"No, I'm sorry, she isn't," Regan said.

"When *was* she working there?"

"Last month."

"Acting in one of your shows?"

"No," Regan said. "Waiting tables."

"You wouldn't happen to have her address, would you?" Matthew asked, and held his breath.

"Yes, I'm sure we do," Regan said. "Just hold on a minute, please."

You knew Lizzie's was playing for keeps the minute you walked in the front door. There's discreet and there's overt, and if you didn't get the feeling you were being stripped naked before you took a single step inside the door, then the place was a total failure and the big portrait of Lizzie Borden over the bar was signaling to the wrong crowd.

Toots almost backed out.

Something here spelled danger, and it wasn't merely the voracious looks that flashed like tiger eyes in a jungle night. Maybe it was the thick scent of marijuana wafting on the air. Maybe it was the incessant jangle of metal rock coming from the juke. Just the smell of pot should have sent her out of there in a hurry. It didn't.

There was something about the reformed junkie that thrived on danger. Just as the practicing addict knew that an overdose, or just plain bad shit, or a sexual encounter gone wrong, or any number of a dozen other dire extremities might await her on any deserted street or in any barren room in the empty hours of the night, so did the junkie on the wagon know that disaster was always a breath away. Take that first drink, puff that first joint, and you were done. Finished. Kaput. And yet, the proof of any former addict's stability was in looking temptation straight in the eye and then spitting in its face. There was booze aplenty here, and marijuana clouded the air, and only God knew what chemical pleasures awaited in the shadowed plush velvet booths that lined the walls like waiting cabriolets.

She took a step inside.

"Well, hello, dear," a woman said, and placed her hand on Toots's arm.

1297 Barrington was on a wilder stretch of beach toward the end of Sabal Key. Old Florida, the natives called it. Florida as it used to be. Actually, the house was a dilapidated structure on stilts in a row of similar structures, not unlike the six wooden shacks Adele Dob owned on Galley Road. Matthew got there at about seven-fifteen that night, parking the car just as the sun was dipping into the Gulf of Mexico. The house against the reddening sky looked somewhat eerie, a dark haunted spindly silhouetted thing. A single light burned on the street side. Somewhere in the distance, a record player reminisced. Aside from that, there was only the sound of sea rushing sand.

Matthew got out of the smoky-blue Acura he'd been driving forever now, or at least since Susan and he divorced, which sometimes felt like forever. A taxi wheeled around the corner, pulled to a stop on the other side of the street. A door opened. Toots Kiley stepped out and slammed the door behind her. She was smoking a cigarette. He considered that a bad sign.

"You don't need that," he said.

"Yes, I do," she said.

"I don't think so."

"Who are you? The Nicotine Police?"

"I'm your friend," he said.

"I came *that* fucking close," she said, and dropped the cigarette onto the sandy sidewalk and ground it out under the heel of her pump. "Do you know a place named Lizzie's?"

"No. Are you okay?"

"I'm okay."

"Sure?"

"Positive. I told you, Matthew. I'd slit my wrists first."

"Don't do that, either. What's Lizzie's?"

"A lesbian bar. Did you know that Lizzie Borden was a lesbian?"

"No."

"Neither did I. But some hack wrote a novel some years back in which he postulated that Lizzie killed her father and her stepmother because she got caught doing the maid. What do you think of that?"

"I think she was acquitted."

"She was."

"Who told you she was lesbian?"

"Any number of women of the same persuasion. All at Lizzie's, all intent on plying me with liquor, grass, and a modicum of crack. All of which I refused. But barely. If I hadn't got Melanie Schwartz's address in the next ten minutes or so, I'd be on the *Enterprise* by now."

"I'm glad you're not."

"I'm glad, too. The cigarette helped."

"No, it didn't."

"You're right, it didn't. How'd *you* get here?"

Matthew told her how he had got there. The sun was in the water already, the night was black. They went up the front walk to the address they'd both obtained separately from two separate sources. Closer to the front door, they heard music now. Ravel's *Bolero*. Over and over again, sounding as if the record were stuck. Only this time the record *was* stuck. Each time a phrase repeated itself, there was a faint click. *Click* and then into the riff again. *Click*. The riff. *Click*.

Matthew rang the doorbell.

No answer.

Ravel intimidated the night.

He looked at Toots. She shrugged. He rang the doorbell again. *Click* and into the same infuriating riff. He tried the doorknob. It turned under the slow pressure of his hand. He eased the door open a crack.

"Miss Schwartz?" he called. "Miss Sinclair?"

She was sitting in an easy chair alongside black metal shelves upon which rested a CD player and a pair of miniature speakers. Ravel kept clicking and riffing over and over again but Melanie Schwartz wasn't hearing the insistent rhythms, Holly Sinclair wasn't hearing anything. Her head was tilted to one side and her hands were lying at her sides, palms upward. She was wearing nothing but an ivory-colored silk slip, her legs widespread, her toes turned in, looking very much like a teenager in a Calvin Klein ad, except that the front of the slip was drenched in blood.

★   ★   ★

Morrie Bloom was telling them a few things about the previous murder.

"Not that I'm yet saying they're linked," he said.

They were still at the crime scene. It was twenty minutes to ten by Matthew's watch. Technicians were still working the house and the beach, torchlights flashing everywhere, long silver fingers probing the night, men calling to each other. The ambulance was still waiting at the curb for Melanie's body; the medical examiner wasn't yet through with her. Dome lights blinked amber and red on the roofs of the six or seven police cars parked like jackstraws at the curb. Across the street, behind the police barricades, spectators were craning for a better look at the house where bloody murder had been committed. The rents in this neighborhood were relatively cheap and so there were a lot of young people in the area, as well as young people *attracted* to the area by a bar called Sonny's some eight blocks away, which blasted rock and roll music to the night as if trying to attract aliens on Mars. There were a lot of motorcycles on the sidewalk behind the striped wooden rails of the barricades.

"First off," Bloom said, "we ran Lawton's credit card and driver's license through the Bureau. He doesn't have a record, but he used to be in the army, so his prints are on file there. And they matched some of the prints on the ID, big surprise, right? He only must've handled them ten thousand times."

"You said *some* of the prints . . ."

"Right, Matthew."

"How about the *others*?"

"A woman's, we think."

"You think?"

"Or a man with small hands," Bloom said. "Either way, there's nothing on them anywhere, state or federal. The only other thing of interest is Corrington wasn't killed where we found his body, on the beach behind Mrs. Dob's house. Medical Examiner's Office says there would've been more bleeding on the spot, which there wasn't. He'd done most of his bleeding—almost all of it, in fact—somewhere else, we don't know where, and was only later transported to the beach and dumped there. So that's it for Corrington, that's all we've got so far," Bloom said, and nodded in dismissal. "And now we've got another one, only this time she's shot in the chest, God knows how many times, there's a lot of blood. What can you tell me about her? You must know *something* about her or you wouldn't have been ringing her doorbell, am I right?"

Matthew told him everything he knew about Holly Sinclair, *nee* Melanie Schwartz. Told him she'd been living with Jack Lawton up north and had studied acting in the same class with Ernest Corrington. Told him her drama teacher had indicated she was a lesbian . . .

"Who's the drama teacher?"

"Woman named Elena Lopez."

"Down here?"

"No. Up north."

"You spoke to her?"

"Detective named Carella did."

"I don't have any detectives named Carella."

"Not here. The Eighty-seventh Precinct," Matthew said. "Up north."

"Never heard of him *or* it," Bloom said. "The teacher told him the vic was lesbian?"

"That's right."

131

"Then what was she doing living with Lawton?" Bloom asked.

"She was bi," Toots said.

"Carella tell you this, too?"

"No, I talked with some friends of hers at Lizzie's tonight."

"Said she was AC/DC?"

"Yes."

"Okay, what else?"

Matthew told him Melanie was also seeing a man named Peter Donofrio, who was on parole following a dope violation.

"She's shaping up as a real sweetheart," Bloom said. "You get all *this* from Carella, too?"

"Well, in a roundabout way."

"He's been busy."

"Well, he's been very helpful," Matthew said.

"Looks that way," Bloom said. "Where's this Donofrio character live? He up north, too?"

"No, he's right here in Calusa."

"You spoke to him personally?"

"No . . ."

"Or did Carella?"

"Guthrie and Warren did."

"Donofrio the one gave you this address?"

"No, that was a man named Regan at the Surf and Sand Dinner Theater."

"Told you the vic was living here?"

"Last address he had for her," Matthew said.

"Jimmy!" Bloom yelled, and turned to where a short dark man was talking to one of the police photographers.

"Yeah?" the man said, and shambled over to where they were standing.

"You reach the landlord yet?"

"He's on his way."

"Good. Jimmy Falco," Bloom said, by way of introduction. "Matthew Hope, Toots Kiley."

Falco looked Toots over. "Haven't we met?" he asked.

"I don't think so," she said.

"Sorry, you look familiar," he said. "Nice to've met you both."

"When he gets here, bring him right over," Bloom said.

"Right," Falco said, and walked back to the photographer.

"Was she acting at this dinner theater?" Bloom asked Matthew.

"Waitressing."

"Was she acting anywhere? Up north, down here, *anywhere?*"

"I really don't know."

"Carella didn't tell you, huh?"

"Up there, she was taking acting classes," Matthew said. He had the sudden feeling that Bloom didn't appreciate the idea of a cop up north sticking his nose into any of his cases. "I doubt if she had an acting *job.* After she came back to Florida . . ."

"When was that?"

"December first. She spent some time with her mother in St. Pete, then came down here on the seventeenth of January."

"Who gave you this?"

"Both the mother *and* Donofrio."

"Excuse me, Morrie," Falco said, and trudged over to

them again. This time, he had in tow a short bald man in khaki Bermuda shorts and a short-sleeved, Hawaiian-print sports shirt. The man had eyeglasses and a long nose and a mustache. Matthew had the feeling that if the man took off the glasses, the nose and the mustache would come off with them. He *also* had the feeling he'd had this very same feeling before. Déjà vu all over again.

"Mr. Epworth," Falco said, "this is Detective Bloom, he's conducting the investigation. Morrie, this is Morris Epworth."

"How do you do, Mr. Epworth?" Bloom said.

The two Morrises shook hands. Morris Epworth looked uneasy. Morris Bloom was wearing a shirt, tie, and jacket and so was Matthew. Epworth seemed to be considering whether he, too, should have dressed a bit less casually for something as serious as a murder. But this was Florida, what the hell. Still, he seemed troubled. Maybe because the corpse had been found in one of his rental properties. Matthew raised an eyebrow slightly, asking Bloom whether it was okay for Toots and him to listen in on this. Bloom gave an imperceptible nod, but did not introduce them to Epworth. Better the little man with the eyeglasses and the nose and the mustache should believe they were somehow connected with the police.

"Terrible thing," Epworth said, trying to break the ice. His accent sounded British. Brits sometimes migrated to Calusa.

"Terrible," Bloom agreed.

Matthew figured that in his lifetime as a cop Bloom had merely seen ten thousand six hundred and thirty-eight gunshot victims.

"How long was she living here?" Bloom asked.

Epworth looked startled, as if he hadn't expected any questions to be asked so soon.

"She took the place the beginning of January," he said.

"January first?"

"The second. A Thursday."

"Through a rental agent, or what?"

"No. She came in off the street. Said she'd seen the sign."

"Walked in, rented the place."

"Yes."

"For how long?"

"Two months. I usually rent month to month, but she wanted it till the end of February, so who am I to argue?"

"How'd she pay? Check? Cash?"

"Cash."

"Isn't that unusual?"

Epworth shrugged. "Lots of young people pay cash," he said. "I'm not fussy, I'll accept cash."

Matthew gathered he meant this as a joke. Epworth didn't smile, but the corners of his eyes crinkled a little. Matthew kept waiting for him to take off the fake nose and mustache.

"She say why she wanted the place for two months?"

"It's the winter. I guess she wanted to be where it's sunny."

"Know if she was living here alone?"

"I can't help you there. Once I get the rent, I leave my tenants alone." He hesitated a moment, and then said, "I guess I can safely assume she won't be renewing for March, am I right?"

Matthew had the feeling this, too, was intended as a joke. Little dry British humor here.

135

"I guess you can safely assume that, yes," Bloom said. "Thank you, Mr. Epworth."

"When will you be out of here?" Epworth asked.

"Give us a day or so."

"Who'll clean up the mess?"

"We'll leave everything just the way we found it," Bloom said.

"That's not what I mean. I heard on television she bled a lot. Who'll wipe up after her?"

"I guess you'll have to find a cleaning service," Bloom said.

Epworth shook his head.

"Thanks for your help," Bloom said.

Epworth was still shaking his head.

"Is it something?" Bloom said.

"When can I go in there, see what kind of damage was done?"

"Right now, it's a crime scene," Bloom said. "We'll notify you when we're clear."

"Was there a lot of damage?" Epworth asked.

"Only to the young woman," Bloom said.

He called Matthew at home later that night, after he'd left the scene, and after he'd spoken to Peter Donofrio in his apartment on Pelican Way. For all his talk about the open relationship he and Melanie had shared, Donofrio seemed genuinely moved by her death.

"Guy actually burst into tears," Bloom said, "it was kind of surprising. I mean, you get somebody's a cheap thief, you don't expect tears. Anyway, the reason I'm calling . . ."

Matthew was wondering the same thing. It was now almost one o'clock in the morning.

"Ballistics called on the casings we recovered," Bloom said. "The gun killed her was a Walther. That mean anything to you?"

"Nothing at all."

"P38? Nine-millimeter Parabellum?"

"No."

"Four in the chest," Bloom said. "By the way, didn't you tell me she was here in Calusa on the seventeenth?"

"Yes, I did."

"Of *January*, right?"

"Yes."

"But Epworth said she rented the place on the second . . ."

"Yes?"

"Okay, if she was staying first with her mother in St. Pete, and next with her weepy boyfriend over the weekend of the seventeenth—why'd she need *another* place to stay?"

"Well . . ."

"Do you see my point, Matthew? Why'd she rent a dump on the beach when she's already got *two* places to stay?"

"I don't know why," Matthew said.

"It doesn't make sense."

"You're right, it doesn't."

"Yeah," Bloom said, and was silent for a moment. "No thoughts, huh?" he said.

"I'm sorry."

"No, *I'm* sorry I woke you up," Bloom said. "Good night, Matthew."

"Good night, Morrie."

One thing Carella didn't like was sloppy police work. What, for example, had happened to the gun one of the men was allegedly packing on the night Corrington and his good pal Lawton were arrested for a drunken brawl? What kind of piece had it been, and which of the five combatants had been carrying it? True enough, the Yuletide spirit had been in the air on that cold Friday night, the twentieth of December. Easy to overlook minor matters when old St. Nick was poised to drop down the chimney. But a gun wasn't such a minor matter in a city where gunshot murders were common—though not quite as prevalent as they'd been *last* year, the new mayor was quick to point out. And a police officer, even an alleged police officer, should have been at least mildly interested in an alleged gun on the scene.

"What happened to the gun?" he asked Parker.

This sort of came out of the blue, so Parker was justified in looking a bit startled.

"What gun?" he asked. "The fuck you talking about?"

Both men had just relieved the shift at a quarter to eight that Tuesday morning, another frigid day to start the week, as if the below-zero temperatures *last* week hadn't been enough. The squadroom windows were covered with rime that made it impossible to see outside, good thing a riot wasn't happening in the street below. Something was wrong with the oil burner—*again*—and both men hadn't yet taken off their overcoats, though the shift was already a good fifteen minutes old.

"From what I understand, the cocktail waitress . . ."

"Would you mind telling me what the fuck you're talking about?" Parker said.

"Corrington. Lawton. The lawyer down in Florida."

"Him again? Why's he breaking our balls?"

"He's not. I was just wondering."

"Why don't he put us on retainer?"

"Was the gun ever located?"

"I did not find any gun on any of the perps."

"Did you look for one?"

"We searched all five of them right here in the squadroom."

"Who searched them in the *bar*?"

"I'm assuming five guys arrive here in handcuffs, they were already tossed by the arresting blues. Anyway, like I said, nobody was carrying."

"Who told you the cocktail waitress saw a gun at the scene?"

"One of the guys riding Adam Three."

"Said the cocktail waitress saw a gun?"

"Is what he said."

"What's her name?"

"The cocktail waitress? How should I know?"

"I had the impression you were the detective who signed off on this."

"Steve, go tell your friend down in Florida to go fuck himself, okay?"

Lanford M. Oberling was curator of the Ca D'Ped Museum, a garrulous seventy-year-old retiree from Baltimore, who favored bow ties, Brazilian cigars, and shapely legs, not necessarily in that order. At nine A.M. that Tuesday, Candace Knowles was in his mahogany-paneled office on the second floor of the museum building, sitting across from him at a heavy, ornately carved desk he said had belonged to an Indian Affairs agent when Florida was still a territory. Lighting a cigar, puffing the smoke in Candace's direction, he asked, "Do you smoke, Miss Howell? Lots of women have begun smoking cigars lately, you know."

"Thank you, no," she said.

She was thinking she would rather kiss a toilet-bowl mop than a man who smoked cigars. She was wondering what kind of man would kiss a *woman* who smoked cigars. Suddenly and unbiddenly, she wondered if Jack Lawton smoked cigars. And immediately put the thought out of her mind. Business was business.

She had called Oberling yesterday, told him her name was Georgina Howell, and that she was writing a freelance feature article for the *Calusa Herald-Tribune,* to run as a follow-up to the newspaper's regular coverage of the coming exhibition. The event, of course, was the unveiling of the target cup right here in little old Calusa, Florida. Oberling welcomed the further publicity the museum would be getting. Candace didn't know it, but his job was a tenuous one; the Board of Trustees was already considering replacing him with a younger man.

So here they were now, in his mahogany-paneled office, Oberling lighting up a cigar, Candace crossing her legs to better distract him. The one thing she didn't want him to realize was that she was here to talk about security. Toward that end, she began the interview by asking him what sort of attendance he expected on opening weekend.

"It should be tremendous," Oberling said. "When they showed the cup in Atlanta, they broke all records at the High. Well, there's a *story* to the cup, you see. People love stories. You show them a terra-cotta medicine bottle, you tell them it's an example of Greek art from the fifth century B.C., they go mm-huh, that's nice. But you tell them this is the actual cup Socrates drank the hemlock from—well, that's what it's *also* called, you know, the Hemlock Cup, it's either the Socrates Cup or the Hemlock Cup, they're one and the same. The point is people like to think they're look-ing at actual *history* here. They look at that cup, they visual-ize it in Socrates' hands, visualize him sniffing at the potion, bringing the cup to his lips, saying his last words, whatever they were, and then taking that fatal swallow. That's very dramatic. People like a little *drama* in their lives. Don't you enjoy a little drama in *your* life, Miss Howell?"

Puffing out a cloud of smoke, directing his gaze down-ward toward her splendid legs (she had to admit) for just a grazing second, letting her know he appreciated her femi-ninity and sexuality and wouldn't at all mind sharing a bit of drama with her himself, if she was so inclined.

For today's visit, she was wearing a black wig cut in

bangs on her forehead, trimmed straight at the sides and back to fall in a clean shoulder-length line. She fancied she rather resembled Cleopatra, don't you know? Except for the eyeglasses, which she thought gave her a journalistic look. The wheat-colored suit was a bit more expensive than any freelance writer might afford, but she didn't own anything cheaper. A nubby linen with a tailored skirt and double-breasted jacket, she wore it with no blouse under it, the lapels lazily falling slack over her bosom. Nothing quite so distracting, she always felt, as a hint of breast and a flash of leg. No stockings. Wearing just a pair of panties and a sun-tan under the crisp linen suit, high-heeled, sling-backed, open-toed pumps, bright red polish on her toes, jiggle the foot a little, distract the old gent further, there you go.

"You don't have to volunteer a number," she said. "We can get that after the opening, from actual attendance figures. But could you give me some sort of estimate? A ball-park figure? Of how many people you think'll be here that weekend?"

"Well, the only big attraction we've ever had of a similar nature was the Tutankhamen exhibition back in 1979. We never expected to get it, I must tell you the truth. Calusa? The Ca D'Ped? Of all the art museums in Florida? Why not Jacksonville or Miami? We were thrilled! But I think we may attract a big crowd for this one as well, although admittedly the other Greek jewelry and artifacts in the exhibit compare in no way to the Egyptian treasures. They're museum quality, of course, and of the same period as the Hemlock Cup, but there's no question which piece is the star of *this* show, no question at all."

"You'll be exhibiting the cup separate and apart, of course."

"Oh, of course. In fact, it'll be in the center of what we call the Lavender Room, that's the Ped's name for this very secluded, silent chamber. The cup will be standing alone in the center of the room. Spotlighted, of course. Quite an array of lights, in fact. The visitors will come through the larger exhibition room, what we call the Terrace Room, where all the other period pieces will be displayed in cases around the room and here and there and in between. And then there'll be this gold rope running from a brass stanchion to the door of the Lavender Room, uniformed guard standing just beside the stanchion, smiling . . ."

"Armed?" she asked, her head bent, writing onto the lined yellow pad resting on her exposed knee, foot still jiggling.

"Hmmm? Oh. No, no. Serving more as a . . . what would you call him? A guide? A friendly presence? Indicating the way to where the *real* treasure is."

"The cup."

"Yes. The cup."

"How big *is* the Lavender Room?" she asked.

"Oh, it's quite ample," Oberling said, and directed a glance at the curve of her breast beneath the sweeping lapel of the jacket. "Quiet, secluded, but of ample size. Our thought is to regulate the traffic in and out of the room—there's a door leading in, you see, and another at the opposite end, leading out—pace the entrances and departures so that the visitors will have sufficient time to circle the case and have a good *look* at the cup. People often feel cheated when . . ."

"It'll be in a case, then?" she asked, writing.

"The cup? Yes."

"When you said standing alone . . ."

"I meant apart from the other pieces in the exhibit. It will be in a glass case, in the center of the room, lighted from above."

"There'll be guards in the room, of course."

"Two of them, yes."

"Armed?"

"No."

"You're not worried about anything like that?"

"No, no. Here in Calusa? No."

"Getting back . . ."

"Yes, I'm so sorry. You wanted to know how many visitors we're expecting. I may be proved absolutely wrong on this, of course, but you can always . . ."

"I *do* plan to check, yes. After the opening."

"Yes. There's a benefit showing on Saturday night, you know, but the true opening isn't until Sunday. I'm expecting six or seven thousand people, do I sound too optimistic?"

"Not at all."

"One must dream, you know," he said, and puffed on his cigar, and glanced at her legs again.

"The exhibit will be here for two full weeks, is that it?"

"Yes."

"I want to be sure to mention that in the piece," she said, writing.

"When will it appear?" he asked.

"The Monday after the opening."

"February third." .

"Yes."

"Good," he said. "The cup will be here through the sixteenth."

That's what *you* think, she almost said aloud.

"It travels again on the seventeenth," he said. "Back to Greece. The show's sponsors will come to pack it that Monday morning."

"Where do you keep it at night?" she asked. "I'm just curious."

"How do you mean?"

"Well . . . you don't just leave it there in the center of the room, do you? I mean . . . is the case alarmed or something?"

There it is, she thought. Please give me the answer.

"As a matter of fact, it isn't," he said.

Good, she thought.

"The museum *itself* is, of course . . ."

"Of course."

"But the cup . . ."

Yes?

". . . is secured in the vault when it's not on view."

Shit, she thought. A box to crack.

"A vault?" she said.

"Yes. The case is on ball-bearing casters. We simply wheel the whole shebang down to the vault."

Down *where*? she wondered.

Oberling was not elucidating.

"So tell me," she said, uncrossing her legs, and then crossing them again in the opposite direction, "do you think this really *is* the cup Socrates drank from?"

"Does it really matter?" he said. "What matters is the legend. A simple fifth-century medicine bottle tossed by a journeyman potter would have no particular monetary value. Hardly anything of artistic merit was being produced at that time, the golden age was during the preceding two centuries. It's the legend, the *story*—this is the cup Socrates actually *drank* from—that makes the Hemlock Cup worth a fortune. There are collectors who would *kill* to own this piece. Can you understand that, Miss Howell?"

For a moment, she'd forgotten the phony name she'd given him.

"Kill for it?" she asked, eyes wide.

"*Kill* for it, yes. Can you understand that, Miss Howell? A man wanting a particular piece so much he would *kill* for it?"

For a moment, she thought he might climb over the desk to demonstrate. She adjusted her eyeglasses, uncrossed her legs, crossed them, tried to appear flustered.

"Can you, Miss Howell?"

Puffing smoke like a volcano, eyes bright.

"Well . . . wouldn't such a man just break into your vault?" she asked innocently. "Wherever it is?"

"Vaults don't deter such men," he said.

"I'm assuming it's in a safe location . . ."

"Is that a pun?" he asked, and chuckled. "Vault? Safe?"

"Oh. Oh dear," she said, and uncrossed her legs again. "I didn't mean it as such." And crossed them again. "I meant . . . I hope with men out there who would *kill* for such a treasure . . ."

"Just to own it. Not even to *show* to anyone else. Just to keep for oneself alone, for one's own eyes . . ."

His own eyes roaming her legs from ankle to thigh.

"You'd better be careful then," she said.

"Had I?"

"With the cup. You'd better be sure the vault is in a very secure part of the building."

"The stainless-steel casing is embedded in four-foot-thick concrete walls," he said.

147

"It sounds impenetrable," she said.

"It is," he said. "Miss Howell, I don't wish to appear bold . . ."

"Oh my, look at the time," she said, and closed her pad, and rose abruptly, long legs flashing. "I have to be running, Mr. Oberling. Look for the article on the Monday after the opening. I hope I do justice to both you and the museum."

"I was wondering if I might call you sometime . . ."

"It was so nice to meet you," she said, cutting him off at the pass. "Thank you very much for your time, Mr. Oberling."

"My pleasure," he said, and bowed to kiss her hand.

She almost felt sorry for him.

Donofrio's landlady told Matthew that he went to the Strength 'N' Stamina Fitness Club to work out three times a week. Matthew drove there at ten o'clock that Tuesday morning. The club was upstairs over a bank overlooking the Trail. The day was suffocatingly hot but the spacious room was mildly air-conditioned to accommodate the people who came here to get fit or to stay fit. The club's director, a muscular individual who looked a bit like Bruce Willis, pointed Donofrio out to Matthew, and he thanked her politely and crossed the room to where he was climbing a set of moving stairs at the far end, near the windows. Everywhere around him were men and women in exercise clothes, exerting themselves. Matthew felt like a shmuck in his seersucker suit.

In all truth, he had never understood women who desired muscles. Nor men, for that matter. At least, not the kind of muscles you got from pitting yourself against machines that looked like they'd been beamed down from

Darth Vader's spaceship. Or from lifting weights, either, which he was always afraid would give him a hernia at the very least or else fall on his chest and crush it the way Giles Cory's chest was crushed in Salem Village when he refused to confess he was a witch.

Nor had Matthew ever understood people who claimed to *enjoy* working out. He himself enjoyed playing tennis, but tennis was a game. Straining oneself lifting weights or climbing stairs or running on a treadmill was *work,* which may be why all those activities were collectively called "*working* out" and not "*playing* out." Come to think of it, Matthew didn't much like men's locker rooms, either. They were smelly and sweaty and full of fat hairy guys running around naked with their precious jewels bobbing and bouncing. The only human beings in whose presence he enjoyed getting undressed were women. Then again, he'd been cranky ever since the coma.

Peter Donofrio looked exactly as Warren and Guthrie had described him. Matthew thought he might even be wearing the same clothes he'd had on the day they visited him. Short and squat, with curly black hair plastered to his forehead and skull, thick black eyebrows beetling over dark brown eyes, tangled chest hair above the neck of his white tank top shirt, heavy hairy thighs showing below the bottoms of his blue walking shorts, graying white socks showing above scuffed blue Reeboks, he struggled mightily to get to the hundred and second floor of the Empire State Building, climbing, climbing, climbing like King Kong, continuing to climb even after Matthew said, "Mr. Donofrio?"

He did not answer. Matthew had the feeling the man was silently counting inside his head, but he didn't know that people counted while they were climbing moving stairs. Donofrio was sweating like a warthog. His shirt was wet, his hair was wet, his shorts were wet, his entire body was wet, even the *stairs* were wet. Matthew prayed he wouldn't offer to shake hands with him. It seemed he had nothing to worry about; Donofrio was ignoring him completely.

"Mr. Donofrio?" he said again.

"Shut up, I'm singing," Donofrio said.

Matthew hadn't heard anything.

He waited.

At last, Donofrio allowed the steps to sink, taking him down to ground level again. Still ignoring Matthew, he reached over to a wall hook for a white towel the color of his graying socks, and began rubbing gingerly at his head and neck and shoulders, sending spray flying everywhere. Matthew backed away gingerly.

"I almost had it, too," Donofrio said, frowning, and began vigorously drying his arms.

Matthew kept his distance.

"What'd you almost have?" he asked.

"Who the hell are you?"

"Matthew Hope."

"That sounds familiar."

"My investigators spoke to you Sunday morning."

"Oh. Yeah. So what do you want now? It ain't enough Mel got killed?"

"I'm sorry about that," Matthew said.

"I catch the son of a bitch done it, it's the end of him, believe me."

"I know how you feel."

"Yeah? How? Your girl got killed, too?"

"No, but . . ."

"Then you *don't* know how I feel, so shut up. What do you want with me, anyway? I told them everything they wanted to know, I even gave them Mel's pictures, what the hell more do you want? She's *dead,* for Christ's sake!"

He put the towel over his face. Matthew waited. Donofrio turned his back to him when at last he removed the towel, and Matthew felt certain he'd been crying under it. Taking a bottle of blue Listerine from a small carrying bag on a bench against the wall, Donofrio uncapped it, rinsed out his mouth, and spit into the towel.

"I was singing when you came in," he said. "Inside my head. It's a trick I learned in the slammer. You sing inside your head, it blocks out all the other shit. I was working on *Evita.* That's very tricky music. I got the movie from the sound track at home, I play it all the time, I'd love to fuck Madonna, wouldn't you? I almost had it this time. All the words to 'I'd Be Good for You.' That's the song she sings when she meets Perón the first time, he's the dictator down there in Argentina. I almost had it, but naturally you had to interrupt."

"I'm sorry."

"Stop saying you're sorry all the time, I'm not a priest. What the hell do you want here, anyway?"

"You told my investigators . . ."

"Who remembers what I told them? They were bracing me. They seen I had a gun, they threatened to yell to my parole officer. I'll tell you something. I find the son of a bitch killed Melanie, the parol board'll *really* wanna see me."

"The police are working on it," Matthew said. "Let them handle it."

"How about you following your own advice?" he said.

"I'm not looking for Melanie's killer, Mr. Donofrio."

"No? Then what're you doing here? Never mind, I already know. You're looking for Jack *Lawton*. What's he got to do with Melanie, can you tell me that? He got something to do with her? Why does this Lawton shit keep coming back to me and Melanie?"

"She knew him up north," Matthew said.

"So I understand. Knew him *how*? Because if there was anything funny going on between them, I'm telling you, mister, you better find him before I do."

"Mr. Donofrio, you said Melanie came to your Pelican Way apartment on the seventeenth, a Friday. And left again on Monday, the twentieth, is that right?"

"That's my recollection, yes."

"Did you know she was here earlier in January?"

"No. When?"

"The beginning of the month."

"No, she was in St. Pete with her mother."

"She was here in Calusa on the second of January," Matthew said. "She rented an apartment here on the second."

"What are you talking about? Why would she need an apartment? Whenever she was in Calusa, she stayed with me."

"But she didn't stay with you on the second, is that right?"

"Who says she was in Calusa on the second?"

"The man who rented the apartment to her."

"He's mistaken."

"I don't think so. Did you speak to her at any time before the seventeenth, when she *did* stay with you?"

"We talked all the time. I saw her up in St. Pete the beginning of December, and then again on Christmas. She was my girl. Why's that so hard to understand?"

"I'm puzzled, Mr. Donofrio. Why'd she go to her mother's house if you have a place here?"

"Her mother was sick. Melanie came down to be with her."

"And you saw her several times in December . . ."

"Yes. Are you brain-dead?"

"And again on the seventeenth of January."

"Yes."

"But even though she was here on the second . . ."

"If she was here, she would've called me."

"But she didn't."

"Right, she didn't. And, anyway, why the hell would she have rented an apartment down here?"

Which was a good question.

Melanie waits until the third of December before she calls Jill. She expects rage, or at least a certain amount of frostiness, but Jill's voice is quite calm, almost gentle.

"Where have you been?" she asks.

Gone since June, she makes it sound as if Melanie's just gone down to the 7-Eleven for a pack of cigarettes and is late getting home.

"I'm sorry," she says. "Forgive me."

"Can you come here now?"

"I'm in St. Pete."

"Come when you can," Jill says, and hangs up.

Her mother's car is a dilapidated old Saab that clunks along like a tractor. It takes Melanie two and a half hours to make the trip from St. Pete to Calusa in horrendous traffic, even though the *real* season won't begin till after Christmas. Another forty minutes to Whisper Key, and she's pulling into the drive just before lunchtime. She has had only orange juice and coffee for breakfast and she is ravenously hungry. There is an unearthly stillness about the house, as if untold horrors await her within. She almost gets back into the car. But there is something exciting about the coming confrontation, and she steps boldly to the front door and presses the bell button and waits. She hears familiar chimes sounding within the house. Then there is silence.

She waits.

The sun at a little past noon is merciless.

Not a breeze is blowing anywhere on the key.

All is hushed, all is still.

She rings again.

The chimes again, and then more silence.

She is wearing a short navy-blue mini with a white T-shirt, no bra, white sandals with two-inch heels. Her red hair is cut in a sort of shag look, windblown and saucy, green eyes sparkling, lips touched with an orangey-red gloss. She feels she looks terrific. She hopes Jill will think she looks terrific.

She presses the buzzer again.

There is still no answer.

She tries the doorknob.

It turns easily under her hand. She steps into the coolness of the house, all of it familiar, this place she once shared so intimately, the potted palms and hibiscus in the entrance foyer, the cool dark slate underfoot, the floating steps leading to the bedroom wing upstairs, all of it so familiar.

"Jill?" she calls.

There is no answer.

For a moment, she is alarmed.

"Jill?" she calls again.

And becomes truly alarmed.

Her first instinct is to run.

She hesitates.

Something tells her to climb the stairs to the bedroom, that is where Jill will be, in the bedroom, on the big over-size bed in the bedroom streaming sunshine through the skylight, on the bed upstairs where the three of them first made love on a sultry August night seven years ago, upstairs on the bed is where Jill will be, she climbs the steps swiftly, long legs flashing, opens the door . . .

She is not in the bedroom, she is not on the bed.

And now Melanie becomes frightfully alarmed.

She runs downstairs to the door leading from the kitchen to the garage and opens the door and sees that Jill's car is there, the same Jaguar she owned seven years ago, the same Jag she's had forever, the same sleek green machine she owned when Melanie left late June to run up north to Jack, ran up north to live with Jill's husband, how can she ever be forgiven?

Well, the plan.

Melanie has a plan.

The plan will buy salvation.

But where *is* she?

She goes out back to the pool. The pool and the patio are both empty. A glass with perhaps an inch of watery tea in it, the ice melted, a lemon wedge resting on its bottom, sits on one of the patio tables, a copy of *Vogue* beside it. All is calm. The cry of a bird sounds like a gunshot. And suddenly she knows where Jill is.

Here in the attic there are musty volumes smelling of age and brine. Here in the attic there are velvet dresses hanging on sagging rods, laced garments from another age, corsets, satin dancing slippers. Here in the attic there are wooden steamer trunks with metal bands, brimming with browned and fading photographs. Here in the attic there are tin toys that play music and cast-iron toys that swallow coins. Here in the attic there is a wrought-iron French lieutenant's bed, with paisley mattress and cushions, and a headboard crest with the letters S and L and R intertwined.

Jill is lying on the bed naked.

She has powdered her face a ghostly white imprinted with red lipstick so dark it looks black. Her eyes are closed, the lids covered with a metallic-blue eye shadow. She looks dead. She is breathing shallowly, but she nonetheless resembles a beautiful corpse in a fairy tale, her long blond hair fanned against the paisley, her arms folded across her breasts, the nipples showing puckered and rouged. Melanie suddenly wants to kiss her on the lips, hoping her lips will be cold to the touch, hoping to wake her from the dead with a passionate kiss.

Jill's eyes pop open.

A mischievous smile cracks across the pale white face.

"You're late," she says, and Melanie's heart leaps.

They sit naked on the patio in the sullen December night, smoking, sipping cognac. There are insect sounds in the bushes now, and a faint breeze is drifting in off the bayou. It almost feels pleasant.

"What's going to happen," Melanie says, "is Jack and this guy Corry are going to knock over the museum."

"Jack? Please."

"I'm serious. They have a sponsor and all."

"What do you mean, a sponsor?"

"This Greek tycoon willing to pay two and a half mil-

lion for this piece of terra-cotta shit supposed to be the cup
Socrates drank poison from."

Jill was looking at her skeptically.

"I mean it."

"There are people who'll actually *pay* that kind of
money?" she said.

"It's a done deal. They're meeting him down here next
month."

"Were you sleeping with him up north?" Jill asked.

One-track mind.

"Yes. Both of them. Jack and Corry both."

"Was it fun?"

"Oh yes."

"Tell me about Corry."

She tells her all about Corry, how they'd met at drama
school, how they'd done a scene together in class, the one
where Stanley Kowalski rapes Blanche, it was very exciting.

". . . which was when I got the idea, I suppose, of introducing them, you know, see if . . ."

"You stole my husband, you know," Jill says, and nudges
her playfully.

"No, come on."

"Well, you did."

"He went up north on his own," Melanie says.

"Yeah, but you went up after him."

"Yeah, well."

"Left *me* to go up after *him*."

"Well, he called me, you know."

"When was that?"

"June sometime. Said he wanted me up there."

"Called you where? Here?"

"No, no."

"Then where?"

"My mother's. One weekend I was in St. Pete."

"You didn't have to go, you know."

"I know."

"You could have told me, you know."

"I know, Jill. I'm sorry, really. I shouldn't have gone, I know."

"You shouldn't have. Not if you love me."

"I do love you."

"So why'd you go?"

"I don't know. I sometimes do things I don't know why I'm doing them."

They are both silent. Smoke from their cigarettes floats on the air, drifts away on the mild breeze. There is the sound of a solitary insistent insect.

"What kind of bugs make that noise?" Melanie asks.

"Bugs, who knows?" Jill says.

"Why do they do it?"

"They're mating."

"Really. All that racket?"

"Mm."

They are silent again.

"So why'd you come back?" Jill asks.

"I missed you," Melanie says.

"Gone six months, not even a postcard," Jill says, and nudges her again. "First Jack vanishes, and then you. I thought you were both dead."

"You should have realized."

"I should have."

"I'm sorry, really."

"It was really a bitchy thing to do, Mel."

"I know, I'm sorry."

"Good thing I love you so much."

"Me, too," Melanie says.

Their hands meet in the dark. Their fingers intertwine.

"Nice out here," Melanie says.

"Mm."

"It's very different up north."

"Mm."

"I actually missed Florida."

"I was very lonely without you," Jill says, and squeezes her hand hard.

"I'm sorry."

"You remember Lilith?"

"Yeah?"

"I almost called her."

"I'm glad you didn't."

"I almost did."

"I love you, Jill."

"I love you, too. But I almost did."

"I'm sorry."

"You were gone."

"But I'm back."

"I'm glad."

There is the sound of a bird somewhere, and the insect suddenly falls silent. On the bayou, a fish jumps. Then all is still again.

"They *really* plan to rob a museum?" Jill asks.

"Oh, yeah, really. Corry knows all these people who are skilled at that sort of thing. He used to do that for a living, you know."

"What, rob museums?"

"Well, no, not museums. But other places. He was, like, an armed robber, you know."

159

"Come on."

"I mean it. He went to jail and all."

"You went to bed with Jack and an ex-*con*?"

"Well . . . yeah."

"Jesus."

"Yeah, I know."

"I didn't think Jack had the guts."

"Well, he was afraid of that, actually."

"Of what?"

"Of, you know, getting buggered or something."

"I didn't mean that."

"What did you mean?"

"Robbing a museum. The Ca D'Ped, you mean?"

"Yeah. That's where the cup'll be. In February. They'll be setting it up next month, and they'll go in soon as the cup is here."

"I didn't think he had the guts."

"Well, Corry'll be with him, you know. And these other professionals. It's not as if Jack'll be doing it all alone."

"Mm."

"I'll tell you the truth, I think he's too stupid to do something like that on his own."

"I think I agree with you."

"Which is why I think we have a shot."

Jill looks at her.

"A shot at what?"

"Stealing the cup from both of them."

"Stealing the . . ."

"Yeah. After *they* steal it from the museum."

"You're kidding."

"No. That's *really* why I came down, Jill. I wanted to . . ."

"I thought you missed me."

"Well, sure, that, too. But I thought you and I could fig-ure out some way to get the cup from them. Maybe arrange a round-robin or something, get them so fuckin dizzy they won't know what's happening. Suck them both out of their minds, get them drunk, whatever, stoned, whatever, then grab the poison cup and disappear from the face of the earth."

"You *are* kidding," Jill says.

"I never kid about money," Melanie says.

Silence.

"*How* much money did you say?"

"Two and a half mil is what the Greek is paying them."

Silence.

"Disappear *where*?" Jill asks.

The crowd at the Silver Pony was noisy, brash and young when Carella got there at six-thirty that Tuesday evening. Well, young in that they seemed to range in age from their late twenties to their mid-thirties, which put them within striking distance of Carella's own thirtysomething, and therefore qualified them as mere callow Utes.

The walls of the place were black, decorated with cutout stainless-steel ponies prancing about in various stages of gallop, designed to create a sense of motion and speed. The effect was one of being on a carousel in a black-and-white movie. Even the cocktail waitresses, all three of them, were wearing short black skirts and white aprons like the ones French maids used to wear in the good old days. Black patent-leather high-heeled pumps. Seamed net stockings. White satin tank top blouses, no bras under them, all slip-pery and nippled. The Hays Office would have taken a censorship fit, but nobody here remembered what the Hays Office was, except Carella, who'd once read a book.

The bartender told him that a waitress named Jacqueline Raines had been working the shift on the night Corrington and Lawton had got into their misbegotten brawl. He pointed her out to Carella, who knew better than to interrupt her while she was juggling drinks for five tables. He waited until there seemed to be a lull in the ordering, and then walked over to the service bar where she was standing. A brunette in her early twenties, she wore her brief, low-cut costume with blowsy assurance, and flashed a welcoming smile as he approached.

"I'm Detective Carella," he said, "Eighty-seventh Squad," and discreetly flashed the tin. "If you can spare a few minutes, I'll wait till you're not so busy."

"Sure," she said. "What's this about?"

"Fight that happened here on December twentieth."

"Oh yeah." She looked around as if estimating the size and longevity of the crowd, and then said, "We usually thin out around seven, maybe we can talk then."

Her estimate was off by about fifteen minutes. She finally sat opposite him at one of the black marble-topped tables some five or six feet from the bar, and lighted a cigarette, which at this distance was legal under the code. On the wall almost directly over their heads, a steel pony was bucking like a wild bronco that badly needed breaking.

"So what about the fight?" he asked her.

"Yeah, I was here," she said, puffing on the cigarette, enjoying it enormously, totally unaware that to some people the habit marked her as hopelessly ignorant and lower class. Carella simply wished she wouldn't blow smoke in his direction.

"What time was this?"

"Must've been around ten o'clock, ten-thirty, in there," she said. "They always came in around that time."

"You knew them, then?"

"Oh sure. They were regulars. Usually came in with a cute little redhead, but that night they were alone."

"We're talking about Lawton and Corrington, is that right?"

"Corry and Jack, yeah. The girl's name was Holly. I think she was an actress. Corry, too, for that matter. An actor, that is. I think they maybe had a three-way going. But who am I to say?"

"The two men and Holly," Carella said, nodding.

"Yeah. I think so. Anyway, on the twentieth, she was already history. I think they said she went down to Florida. Or out to California. Someplace warm, anyway."

"How about the other three men?"

"The Three Stooges, yeah. They came in around eleven. Greeted their old pals, same as usual, gave them the high five, you know how these macho jackasses behave in a bar."

Her eyes flicked away from his, toward a man and a woman who'd just come in from the cold outside. She watched them until she was certain they'd be sitting at the bar rather than one of the tables, and then she dragged on the cigarette again, a long slow hit this time, eyes closed.

"Greeted their friends, you were saying."

"Yeah, their old drinking buddies."

"So how did the fight start?"

"Well, they were all sitting at the bar, drinking together, laughing it up, when Jack happened to mention . . ."

"Excuse me. *Who* was drinking together?"

"The five of them."

"Corry and Jack . . ."

"Yeah, and the Three Stooges."

"Are you saying they knew each other?"

"Oh sure."

"So when the three others came into the bar, it was Corry and Jack they were greeting, is that it?"

"You're quick," she said, and dragged on the cigarette again.

"Why do you call them the Three Stooges?"

"Cause one of them's named Larry. Also, they're all three of them stupid."

"Larry what?"

"Who knows? Don't *you* guys know? You're the ones busted all of them. Don't you have a record up the precinct?"

"So all five of them were friends," Carella said.

"Yeah."

"So what happened?"

"They got into a conversation about cheating women, what else? All these macho jackasses can talk about is how good football is and how rotten women are. And Jack tells Corry that he always suspected his wife was cheating on him, which was why he left her to come up here. And one of the Three Stooges says I thought *Holly* was your wife, and Jack says No, Holly is just someone I happen to like a great deal, and Larry—I'm sure it was Larry cause he's the only one of the stooges whose name I know—Larry says I'll bet *Corry* here likes her a great deal, too, which was sort of like laying the three-way on the table, which both Corry and Jack told him it was none of his effin' business. So naturally, the three of them get their feathers all ruffled. Macho men don't like to be told to butt out, not after they've had a few drinks. So now starts the shoving contest. You telling *me* to mind my own business? Shove. Who you *think* I'm talking to? Shove. Well, it can't be *me* cause *nobody* talks to *me* that way. Shove, shove, push, shove, *bam,* somebody throws a punch."

"Who threw the first punch?"

"One of the stooges."

"At whom?"

"*Whom?* Oh, la dee *dah!*" she said, and rolled her eyes and squashed out the cigarette. "Corry was the first one got hit. So Jack jumps into the fray, and then Larry, and then the third stooge, and they're knocking over barstools and tables and bottles and glasses and rolling all over the place until finally the fight spilled over onto the sidewalk outside, with the three of them stomping the living bejesus out of Corry, and Jack trying to stop them from killing him. That was when he pulled the gun."

"Who?"

"Corry."

"What kind of a gun?"

"I don't know guns."

"Was it a revolver or an automatic?"

"Didn't I just say I don't know guns?"

Carella pulled a cocktail napkin to him. He took his pen from where it was clipped to the inside pocket of his jacket, uncapped it, and sketched a rough drawing onto the napkin.

"Did it look like this?" he asked.

"No. Nothing like that."

"How about this? he asked, and made another drawing.

"No."

"This?"

"Yeah, that's more like it."

"What happened to it?" he asked.

"When he heard the sirens, Corry tossed it in the gutter."

"And?"

"And what? Everybody got carted off to the cop shop."

"How about the gun?"

"Nobody noticed it."

"So it was still in the gutter when they all went off."

"I guess."

"You guess?"

"Uh-huh."

"Any idea what might have happened to it?"

"None at all."

"Anybody else see him toss that gun in the gutter?"

"How would I know?"

He looked at her. She took a package of Virginia Slims from an apron pocket, shook one loose, fired it up, blew a cloud of smoke at him. He kept staring at her, through the smoke. Finally, he said, "What happened to the gun, Miss Raines?"

"I told you . . ."

"Miss Raines," he said.

"Okay," she said. "Okay." She blew out another cloud of smoke. "He came back for it the next day."

"Corrington?"

"Yes."

"And?"

"I gave it to him."

"How'd it happen to be in your possession?"

"When everybody left, I picked up the gun and carried it back inside here. I figured, a gun in the gutter, somebody could get hurt. I put it in my locker."

"And gave it to Corrington when he came back for it."

"It was his gun, wasn't it?"

So now he knew that the gun flashed on the night of the brawl had been a Walther belonging to none other than Ernest Corrington, Matthew Hope's corpse.

"Thank you," he said, and wondered if Hope could make any use at all of this information.

8

There was something inappropriate about being in a public library during the month of January with the temperature hovering at the eighty-degree mark and the sun shining on an emerald-green lawn rolling away to cobalt-blue waters under a chicory-blue sky. Perched like a stark white wading bird on the very edge of Calusa Bay, the new Calusa Public Library had been built at a cost of twenty million donated dollars, but it was virtually empty at nine-thirty that Wednesday morning, when most sensible citizens were either lolling by their own pools or basking on powdery white beaches.

Candace's own memories of public libraries were of a different sort. Born and raised in Minneapolis, she grew up with the winter siege mentality of all Minnesotans. A beautiful girl even back then, she'd learned early on to place comfort above vanity, wearing bulky layered sweaters and coats, mittens and boots, heavy woolen socks, insulated underwear. In Minnesota, you traveled from building to building either underground or on covered walkways high above the snowy streets. In a state where a snow-stranded automobile could cost a person her life, emergency supplies and an extra battery in the trunk were essential to survival.

Minnesota's wintertime library was a snug and comforting place. With snow falling beyond its tall windows, the leather-bound books lining the shelves, the green-shaded lamps over the long wooden tables seemed to offer sustenance and warmth. Candace was an avid reader. From October to sometimes as late as May, when winter gripped the city and froze the marrow, she spent hour upon hour in the library. Her fondest memories of the city she left when she was nineteen were of the library.

Now, in a city far away, in another January some thirteen years later, she sat at another long table, and gazed out at the bay beyond the arched windows, watching a sailboat fighting the wind. She glanced at her watch and then went back to the computer screen.

Lanford M. Oberling—

She wondered what the M stood for.

Martin? Morris? Mario?

Lanford M. Oberling, curator of the Ca D'Ped Museum, had graciously informed her that in 1979, the Tutankhamen treasures had briefly occupied his humble little exhibition hall. So she was now surfing through the index of newspapers the library stocked, searching for the year 1979, and hoping that the library hadn't thrown out its old papers when the place was rebuilt two years ago.

It had occurred to her after her little chat with Oberling . . .

Milton? Michael?

. . . that a treasure of such distinction might have necessitated more than the museum's routine security. Surely the Egyptian government would not have allowed such riches to travel to a second-rate museum in a presumptuous little town without first obtaining guarantees that they would be well protected during their stay. She felt certain that in a two-bit museum like the Ca D'Ped, security *before* the Tut visit would have been merely adequate at best. She further assumed that whatever was in place now, the various sophisticated alarm systems she'd detected, the vault . . .

Well, perhaps not the vault. Perhaps that had already existed before Tut came along, though she couldn't imagine what the hell the museum would have *put* in it. But even supposing the vault *had* already been there, wouldn't the Egyptians have insisted upon greater overall security than already existed?

Thunderheads were building on the horizon. There was a distant flash of lightning, the low rumble of faraway thunder. The day was suddenly turning gray, the library suddenly felt cozier. She was pleased when first she discovered that the collection of *Herald-Tribune*s went all the way back to 1963, and that the entire collection had been preserved on microfilm. She asked a reference librarian for the 1979 cassette, went to another machine, inserted the film and began searching. There'd been quite a bit of coverage preceding the Tut visit. This was not surprising; she knew that a traveling exhibit of such prominence would naturally have attracted a lot of local newsprint. She wasn't particularly interested in previews of what the exhibit would contain, which—she learned almost at once—were gushingly prepared for the *Calusa Herald-Tribune* by its self-styled art critic, a woman named Irene Helsinger. Candace expected the advance excitement to be high; Tutankhamen had knocked the socks off art reviewers and historians everywhere.

But she had grown up in Minneapolis, remember—and please don't send me letters, she thought—and so she knew all about small-town municipal pride. *If* Oberling . . .

Manny? Max? Moe?

. . . *had,* in fact, improved museum security to satisfy whatever dictates the Tut sponsors had laid down, then in true local-yokel fashion, might he not have *boasted* of the acquisition and the extraordinary security measures the Ped was taking to ensure the hoard's safety while it was here in lovely Calusa? Of course he would have.

She hoped.

The rain came suddenly and swiftly and harshly, the way it often did in Southwest Florida. She felt suddenly safe and secure inside the library, somewhat like the young Minnesota girl she once had been. She kept searching.

And there it was.

The front-page headline read:

PED BEEFS SECURITY FOR TUT

The story under it began with the words *Dr. Lanford Maxwell Oberling* . . .

Maxwell, she thought.

. . . *curator of the Ca D'Ped Museum, announced today that the Board of Trustees had approved an expenditure of two hundred and forty thousand dollars* . . .

Bingo, she thought.

When the two men spoke at ten o'clock that Wednesday morning, the sun was shining up north but down there in Florida, it was raining cats and dogs—as Carella's mother might have put it. Matthew Hope seemed unhappy to learn it was such a bright day up there, albeit a cold one. People down in Florida never wanted to hear that the weather up north was good.

He seemed even more unhappy to learn that Ernest Corrington had been seen toting a nine-millimeter Parabellum on the night he and Jack Lawton were arrested and later released for creating a disturbance in a public place. Carella couldn't understand this until Hope told him Melanie Schwartz had been killed the night before—and Ballistics had identified the murder weapon as a Walther.

"Wheels within wheels," Carella said.

"Turning," Hope said. "I hate mysteries, don't you?"

"Matter of fact, I do."

"So why'd you become a cop?"

"I wanted to be one of the good guys. Anyway, there aren't any mysteries in police work, not really."

"No? What do you call a dead woman shot with a pistol owned by a dead man she once knew?"

"That's a pair of murders that need to be solved. You've got to remember something, Mr. Hope . . ."

"Why don't you call me Matthew?"

"If you make it Steve."

"A deal."

"You've got to remember, Matthew, that in police work, there are only crimes and the people who commit them. Somebody killed Corrington, and now somebody killed the Schwartz girl. That's two crimes with maybe one killer or maybe not. The gun may be a link, but who knows? If it's Corrington's gun, we may be onto something. But we don't *have* the actual gun yet, do we? All we have is the same caliber and make. Could be a million guns like it out there."

"Which is why it's a mystery."

"Well, no. It's two *crimes*."

"Which, until we solve them, are mysteries."

"Not to the person or persons who committed them."

"Well, sure, once we find out the whys and where-
fores . . ."

"We may *never* find out, Matthew. We may eventually get
the perp, but that doesn't mean we'll learn what the actual
motivating circumstances were. Only the person or persons
involved will know that. One person, a handful of people,
who knows?"

"A privileged few."

"A privileged few. But if you think of it as a mystery,
you're into all that bullshit of the butler being in the pantry
while Uncle Archibald was in the potting shed and Aunt
Agatha was in the garden. That's not real life, Matthew."

"*None* of this is real life to *me,* Steve."

"How do you mean?"

"I'm a *lawyer.* How'd I get involved in all this crap all of
a sudden?"

"Maybe you wanted people to hate you," Carella said.

"People *do* hate lawyers, you're right."

He sounded enormously despondent. Maybe it's the rain
down there, Carella thought. Maybe it's the fact that his case
seemed to be going nowhere. Dead ends and blind alleys
could do that to a man. Whatever it was, Carella felt like
buying him a beer and telling him everything would work
out, just relax, the sun was shining up here, wasn't it?

"You know why people hate lawyers?" Hope asked.

"Why?"

"Because we charge too damn much."

"No, no . . ."

"Yes. Who the hell is worth three, four hundred bucks an hour? That's why people hate us."

"Cops, too," Carella said.

"No, people *like* cops."

"Do you know why people hate cops?"

"Do you know why lawyers charge so much?"

"Why?"

"Because we invented a language only we can understand. We're being paid to *translate*."

"Do you know why people hate cops?"

"People like cops."

"They hate us because we arrest them for speeding."

"No, no."

"I'm telling you, yes. How many times have you seen an oncoming car flash its lights at you?"

"Well . . ."

"That's to warn you, right?"

"Well, no . . ."

"That there's a cop up ahead, right?"

"Well . . ."

"Waiting in the bushes, right?"

Hope began laughing.

"That guy in the car is warning you there's a cop up ahead waiting to write a speeding ticket. Which means if you *are* speeding, which is against the law, the guy in the car is aiding and abetting a *criminal*."

Hope was still laughing.

"Sure, laugh," Carella said.

"I just thought of a profession that's hated even more than lawyers and cops."

"Tell me."

"Dentists."

"You ought to start drilling teeth," Carella said.

"I should."

"Be the hat trick for sure."

He had not seen Adele Dob since the night after Corrington's murder, and Guthrie was grateful now for the opportunity to visit her again. He got there at ten-forty that Wednesday morning, and found her sipping coffee and reading the paper at a little white table in a window overlooking the beach where Corrington's body had been found. She offered him a cup of coffee, and he sat opposite her. She was wearing the same green caftan she'd worn on the day he'd first met her. Hanging plants basked in brilliant sunshine, leaves shining like emeralds, echoing the green of the garment and her eyes.

"I missed you," she said.

"Busy chasing bad guys," he said.

"Famous detective."

"Sure."

They sipped coffee together. The water on the Gulf was calm today. It nudged the beach almost languidly. A faint dispirited breeze wafted through the open windows.

"About Corry," he said. "The night you spent with him."

"Who said I spent the night with him?"

Actually, *she* was the one who'd said so.

"Adele, I have to ask you this," he said. "Did he take off his clothes?"

"He was bleeding. He took off his shirt, as I recall."

"How about his pants?"

"Am I under oath?" she asked, and smiled.

"No, but I would appreciate an answer."

"He took off his pants, yes."

176

"Was he carrying a gun?"

She hesitated.

"Adele?"

"Yes, he was carrying a gun."

"You saw a gun?"

"He took it out of his belt and put it on the dresser top."

"What kind of gun was it?"

"I have no idea."

"Could it have been a Walther?"

"What's a Walter?"

"Not Walter, *Walther*. With a t-h."

"I thought maybe you lisped," she said.

"Remember the guns all the German officers carried in World War II movies?"

"Sort of."

"That's a Walther. How'd you feel about him carrying a gun?"

"Well, he told me he almost robbed a drugstore, so I figured if somebody once planned a holdup, he must have had a gun, don't you think? So here was the gun."

"Adele, did he at any time tell you what he was doing here in Florida?"

"No."

"Did he mention a man named Jack Lawton?"

"No."

"How about a woman named Holly Sinclair?"

"No."

"Or Melanie Schwartz."

"None of those names sound familiar."

"Did you discuss the gun at all?"

"Discuss it?"

"Did you ask him why he was carrying a gun? That was a *second* parole violation right there, you know."

"I didn't know he was on parole."

"Uh-huh."

"What was the first violation?"

"Leaving the state of California. If I showed you a picture of a Walther, do you think you might be able to identify it for me?"

"Where'd you get the picture?"

"Friend of mine in Ballistics."

He was reaching into his jacket pocket. The five-by-seven glossy print had been supplied by a Calusa P.D. detective named Oscar Pinelli who knew that Guthrie had once testified on behalf of a fellow detective named Harlow Winthrop. What goes around comes around. He showed her the picture:

"That's a Walther," he said. "Also known as a P38, or a nine-millimeter Parabellum."

"Gee," she said.

"Is that the gun Corry was carrying when he spent the night here?"

"Yes," she said.

★   ★   ★

Guthrie was the one who'd done the legwork, so Matthew let him carry the ball.

"Before now," he said, "we knew only two things. We knew that when Corrington got into a fight up north on the night of December twentieth, he had in his possession a Walther pistol, which he tossed and later recovered."

The four of them were sitting at tables outside a Chinese joint around the corner from Matthew's office, eating spareribs and spring rolls while they waited for the rest of the meal. Toots Kiley ate like a truck driver. Warren Chambers admired this. Matthew was trying to lose weight. He wondered why he was eating this stuff. He was thinking that deep-fried food could kill you as easily as a bullet from a Walther. Warren and Toots were licking their fingers. Matthew thought there might be sexual innuendo here, but he had enough trouble leading his own life without worrying about developing black-white relationships in the Deep South.

"Second thing we knew for sure," Guthrie said, "is that Melanie Schwartz, Holly Sinclair, whatever we choose to call her, was killed with four bullets from a pistol identified as a Walther. We didn't know *whose* Walther, we still don't. Could be any Walther in the world. But now we know something else. We know that *Corrington's* Walther, which was last seen up north in December, was seen again down here two nights before his murder. Which means that the gun that killed Melanie *could* possibly be Corrington's gun. I'm only saying possibly. We won't know for sure till we find the gun and make a ballistics comparison."

"We know a few other things," Matthew said.

Toots looked up from licking her fingers.

So did Warren.

179

Guthrie picked up a spring roll.

"We know that Melanie, Jack and Corry were living together up north. Most likely, all three of them had access to the gun."

They all nodded, virtually at the same time.

"Now two of them are dead," Matthew said.

He picked up another sparerib.

"Until now," he said, "we were looking for a missing husband. Now we may be looking for a double murderer."

Melanie was privy to the scheme while it was fomenting up north, so she knows that Charles Benson is the name Jack will be using down here in Calusa. And Corry will be Nathan Hedges. Which surnames they'd pilfered from a package of cigarettes. Still, it takes some doing to find out exactly *which* house they've rented *where.*

Up north, they had talked about Sabal being a good choice because it was the most desolate of Calusa's keys. But a check of real estate agents discloses no rentals on Sabal to either a Mr. Benson *or* a Mr. Hedges, so she figures they weren't able to find anything there at the height of the season, which is when they were supposed to come down. Directory assistance tells her there is indeed a Calusa County number for a Mr. Charles Benson, but it's unlisted, and the operator won't give Melanie an address.

So she starts dialing the real estate agents on Santa Lucia Island, sort of a sister key to Sabal, in the county just south and connected to it by a narrow two-lane bridge, and there you go! A woman named Sally Hirsh at an agency called Sun Realty tells her she rented a house on Santa Lucia to a man named Charles Benson for occupancy on the first day of January this year.

"Well, that certainly is a big relief to me, I can tell you," Melanie says.

"Why is that?" Sally asks.

"Charlie's my brother," Melanie says. "He left without telling me where he'd be staying, and here I am in a station wagon with two kids, not knowing where he's at. Can you give me the address on Santa Lucia?"

She's not so sure about how they're going to welcome her since she hasn't tried to make contact since she left early in December. Told them to call her at her mother's, which they did, but never got back to them. Eight times, they called, before figuring fuck it. This is now the tenth of January; the boys have been down here since the first, advancing their plans for the museum robbery, plans she is about to tamper with big-time. Provided they don't beat her brains out and toss her in the bay. She keeps reminding herself that Corry is an ex-con. A violent man. The thought is exciting. Melanie likes flirting with dangerous situations.

Which is why she has come to this rented house on Santa Lucia today. A big, white, low-lying, sprawling, ramshackle, clapboard structure at the end of the island. Steep dirt road leading in, lined with palmettos and scrub oak, house hugging a lagoon beyond. She cuts the engine at the top of the road and lets the rented Ford roll slowly down it, braking, easing up, braking again. There is the dry crunching sound of tires on parched earth. She wonders if the drought will ever end. She wonders if Corry will kill her the moment he sees her. Hi, guys, I'm back. She parks the car alongside a Jeep Cherokee baking in the hot sun. Gets out. Eases the door shut.

She hears murmuring voices from behind the house.

She treads slowly and gently on a path leading around

181

back. She is wearing shorts and sandals, a white cotton T-shirt without a bra. The boys are still talking together softly as she comes around the corner of the house. There's a good-sized pool back here, you wouldn't expect it, and a lagoon as still as glass, with a tethered dock floating on it some six feet out from the mangroves. Wooden planking some two feet wide leads from the shore to the dock. She stops dead, her heart pounding under the white cotton shirt. She can hear the brown sounds of their voices, muted, low.

The boys are sitting at a round umbrella-shaded table near the edge of the pool, drinking beer, eating sandwiches. This is a man thing here, both of them bare-chested and barefooted, shining with sweat in brief swimsuits, elbows on the table, eating their sandwiches and drinking their beer. She stands watching them. Corry reaches for a pickle spear, bites off the end of it. Jack lifts his beer can, drinks from it. Corry says something low, and both men laugh. A man thing here. She loves witnessing man things unaware. Men excite her more than women do, something she would never dare admit to Jill, but it happens to be the truth.

"Hi, boys, I'm back," she actually hears herself saying, and comes smiling around the corner of the house. Then, instead of walking to where they're sitting looking surprised if not totally flabbergasted, she walks directly to the lip of the pool and dives in with all her clothes on, sandals and all, no sense spoiling a dramatic moment by kicking off your shoes first, Elena Lopez would be proud of her.

She swims underwater to the shallow end of the pool. Her head breaks the surface, eyes closed, a rocket from a nuclear submarine. Here I am, boys, good old Melanie Schwartz, Holly Sinclair, whoever. She hoists herself up onto the patio, the wet shirt clinging to her, long wet red hair slick and streaming, sandals sopping wet. She swivels over to the table, nipples first.

"Mind if I join you?" she says, and picks up a pickle spear and bites into it.

The idea is to get Corry out of the picture because he is the violent one. On the day of the robbery, when she and Jill plan to steal the stolen cup from unsuspecting Jack here, they cannot risk having Mr. Experienced Thief on the scene, bulging his muscles and brandishing his Walther. It is one thing to seize a two-and-a-half-million-dollar treasure from an unemployed graphic designer. It is quite another to try snatching it from a muscular hunk who, while behind bars, undoubtedly had to protect the sanctity of his ass from assorted murderous thugs and villains, black, white or indifferent. There was no way Melanie or Jill could ever wish to tangle with Ernest Corrington, no way, sister. Melanie has already tangled with him in bed and that is frightening enough, thank you.

The opportunity for an immediate private word with Jack comes immediately after they've all made love together, a quaint euphemism for what they actually did to each other in the big back bedroom under the whirling ceiling fan. One thing Corry learned in prison was that there was nothing nicer than a smoke after a blow job or a butt-fuck. But here on Santa Lucia Island at three o'clock on the afternoon of January tenth, Mr. Hedges discovers that both he and Mr. Benson are plumb out of cigarettes, which creates a minor sort of crisis since Corry is the sort of man who doesn't like to be deprived of *any* pleasure, large or small. Having just had his way, so to speak, with Melanie in a manner reminiscent of the way he used to violate the little Hispanic bitch who'd had the misfortune to become his cellmate, he becomes close to furious when he discovers that Jack has allowed them to run out of smokes, and he suggests playfully that if Jack doesn't run over to the Way-Mart right this fuckin minute while Corry and Melanie shower, he will ram the barrel of his P38 up Jack's ass and pull the trigger. Melanie says "*I'll* go for the fuckin cigarettes, don't get your balls in an uproar," or words to that effect, and Jack says "I'll go with you," which is how they happen to be discussing murder at three-oh-seven P.M. on an arrow-straight empty road bubbling asphalt.

"I worry about him," Melanie says for openers.

Jack merely nods.

He is driving, she is sitting beside him, her knees propped up against the dash. Both of them are smoking because Melanie found a crumpled packet of Marlboros in the glove compartment not five minutes after they were on the way. Melanie thinks she has never enjoyed a cigarette more in her entire life. There is something poetically righteous about their sitting here smoking while Corry paces the house in fury. In the air-conditioned stillness of the car, she smiles wickedly.

"I'm afraid he'll lose it the night we do the job," she says.

"I didn't know you were still in this," Jack says.

"Come on, Jack."

"I mean, you disappear from sight . . ."

"My mother was sick."

"We called your mother a hundred times, she didn't sound sick to me."

"She got better."

"So why didn't you return the calls?"

"I got busy."

"Doing what?"

"Thinking about the job. Thinking about Corry chickening out in L.A. Only this isn't a drugstore, Jack. This is a museum with a piece worth two and a half mil in it."

"I know."

Thoughtfully.

As if he's been pondering the same thing.

"He's very volatile," she says.

Understatement of the century.

Jack thinks this one over, too.

"Have you met with the Greek yet?" Melanie asks.

"Corry has."

"Not you?"

"No."

"Has any money changed hands?"

"Not yet."

"Are you sure?"

"I feel certain. If Corry had got an advance payment, we'd already be buying our crew."

"When do you *plan* to get some money?"

"The Greek's on his way up from Grenada right this minute. Corry plans to see him as soon as he gets here. Time's running short. The Greek knows that."

"Does the Greek *care* who he deals with?"

Jack turns from the wheel.

"What do you mean?"

"Does he *care* who steals that bottle for him?"

"Why should he?"

Looks back to the road again.

"I mean, he isn't *married* to Corry, is he?"

"I doubt it."

"So it could be *anyone* who puts together a crew, am I right?"

Silence.

She watches him.

He is still staring through the windshield, hands gripping the wheel tight. Heat haze on the road. Black shining mirage puddles appearing and disappearing.

"It could be anyone, yes," he says at last.

"It could be us," she suggests.

Parker's D.D. report gave Carella the names, addresses, and telephone numbers of the three other participants in the bar fight, the ones the waitress had labeled the Three Stooges. One of them was, in fact, named Larry, as she'd remembered. The file gave his complete name as Lawrence Randolph Rodino, and his work address as Andriotti Meat Packing Company, at 1116 Hampton Street, all the way downtown in the Quarter.

This was a shlepp and a half from the 87th Precinct on Grover Avenue, but Carella made the drive downtown with relative ease. The plows had been out and the streets were as clean as they were going to get until some real sunshine showed. More than that, the forecasters had scared a lot of people into leaving their cars at home, and so the roads were deserted. He parked alongside a row of trucks unloading sides of beef onto a platform, and was heading toward a small entrance door with the numbers 1116 on it when someone wearing a white coat and white gloves yelled, "You can't park there, mister."

"Police," Carella said over his shoulder, and opened the door.

Another man in a white coat and white gloves stopped him just inside the door.

This was a James Bond movie.

"Help you?" the man said.

Carella flashed the tin.

"Police," he said. "I'm looking for Larry Rodino."

"It ain't us had the dirty meat," the man said.

"I'm not looking for dirty meat, I'm looking for Larry Rodino."

"Door the end of the hall," the man said. "Our meat's clean."

Carella went to the end of the hall and knocked on a door that had neither a name nor a number on it.

"Come in," a voice called.

Carella opened the door, stood hesitantly in the door frame. "Mr. Rodino?" he asked.

"Yeah. Who are you?"

"Police," Carella said, and closed the door behind him. He turned toward the desk again, extended his hand. "Detective Carella," he said. "Eighty-seventh Precinct."

"I thought the One-Oh was the precinct looking for maggots," Rodino said.

"This has nothing to do with infected meat," Carella said.

"Then how come you seem to know all about it?"

"I watch television. I want to ask you some questions about a fight that took place in a bar called the Silver Pony on December twentieth . . ."

Rodino was already shaking his head.

"The gun, right?" he said.

He was a burly man, quite tall, Carella guessed, although he was still sitting and it was difficult to estimate an exact

187

height. Thick curly brown hair, brown eyes, bushy brown mustache, strong cleft chin. Carella would not have enjoyed getting into a fistfight with him in a bar. Or anywhere else, for that matter.

"It was used to kill somebody, right?" Rodino asked.

Which happened to be right on the button.

Carella instantly wondered how he'd known this.

"What makes you think so?" he asked.

"You're not here about flies in our meat cause we ain't *got* any flies in our meat. So it has to be the gun. Either somebody got killed with it, or it was used in a holdup. Otherwise you wouldn't be asking about a two-bit fight, after which everybody went home happy, am I right?"

"On more than one score."

Rodino looked at him.

"How well did you know Ernest Corrington?"

"Oh, Jesus," Rodino said, "he killed himself."

"No."

"He killed somebody else?"

"No."

"He used the gun in a holdup?"

"No."

"What is this, Twenty Questions? Oh, Jesus, did somebody kill *him*?"

"Yes."

"With his own gun?"

"No. With a shotgun."

"Where? When?"

"Florida. Last Tuesday night."

"Jesus. But what's that got to do with the Walther?"

"You saw the Walther?"

"Of course I saw it. You ever have somebody stick a gun in *your* face?"

"Never," Carella said drily. "Tell me about it."

"It was a fight got out of hand, that's all."

"You knew Corry and Jack, is that right?"

"Oh sure. We all knew each other."

"How'd you happen to know them?"

"Met them at the Pony."

"Hadn't known Corry before then, huh?"

"No. But I knew he'd done time, if that's what you're asking."

"How'd you know that?"

"Well, he wasn't exactly shy about it. In fact, I think he was kind of proud of it, you know what I mean? Like it was a badge of honor or something. Having survived prison."

"Uh-huh."

Some badge of honor, Carella was thinking.

"Tell me how the fight started."

"Jack got pissed off."

"Why?"

"He was drunk."

"Yeah, but why'd he get angry?"

"I guess one of us must have mentioned something about the three of them."

"Which three do you mean?"

"Him and Corry and Holly. The redhead used to come in with them all the time."

"That was you, wasn't it?"

"How do you mean me?"

"Who made the remark about the three of them."

"What gives you that idea?"

"Jackie Raines gives me that idea."

"Who the fuck's Jackie Raines?"

"The waitress who was serving you that night."

"Oh, Jackie. The waitress, right. She told you that, huh?"

"She told me that, yes."

"Well, then, yes, I guess it could've been me who said it. Cause I'd seen them together before, you know."

"Seen who together?"

"The three of them. Not just in the Pony."

"When was this?"

"November sometime."

"Where?"

"Place you'd never expect."

"Where's that?"

"A museum."

"Which museum?" Carella asked.

"ISMA," Rodino said.

As he tells it, the Isola Museum of Art on that windy day last November is packed with schoolchildren from all over the city, there to see an exhibit from Athens. Rodino has come there because he's discovered during forty-two years of bachelorhood that a good place to pick up girls is in museums. There, and at crafts shows. In this city, in the month of November, there are no crafts shows in the streets, it being a somewhat shitty time of the year, and so he has chosen on this dismal, gray, and dreary Saturday to visit ISMA instead.

He has no interest in the Greek stuff that is on exhibit on the second floor of the museum. But he notices that a goodly number of college girls in their early twenties seem to be drifting up the steps and standing on line to see what a huge poster advertises as THE SOCRATES CUP EXHIBIT. A photograph on the poster shows what looks like a

190

double shot glass crusted with mud and tilted on its side to show the letters ΣOK scratched onto its bottom. Lettered under the cup in the same color as the headline are the words *The Agoran Trove—November 9–November 15.*

He follows a college girl in tweeds and a woolen hat pulled down over her ears and her golden curls, and maneuvers a place in line behind her. He notices that everyone is holding a ticket, and he figures that's as good an opening gambit as any, so he asks her where she bought her ticket. She tells him she doesn't have a ticket, this is a student pass, and he says Oh, where do you go to school, and she gives him the name of some all-girls Catholic college in Calm's Point, which makes her suddenly even more attractive to him, what with her pert little Irish nose and freckles all over her face. He asks her to please hold his place in line while he goes to look for a ticket, which it turns out costs four and a half bucks! In line behind her again, the girl—her name is Kathleen, oh come eat my scapular—tells him that the cup on exhibit is supposed to be the one Socrates drank the hemlock from, but that the rest of the exhibit is even more interesting in that it contains various gold *phialae,* whatever the hell *they* might be, and a lovely silver-gilt *rhyton* in the shape of a winged horse, not to mention some very fine examples of Attic black-figure vase painting. This is the last day of the exhibit, she tells him, it's only been here a week. Tomorrow, it moves on to Washington, D.C. He is thinking none of this is anywhere near as fascinating as her slightly bucked teeth and tented upper lip.

He discovers that she lives in the next state, but that she dorms at St. Mary's of Our Beloved Devotion College of Virgins, or whatever the school is called, which he thinks is very handy since he has a small apartment right here in the city, convenient for a tweedy young Irish college girl who might care to visit yet other museums on other occasional Saturdays.

By the time they enter the hall where the cup is on exhibit, it has begun to rain. The rain is a cold November drizzle that oozes the long panes of glass in the high-ceilinged room, turning the hall cheerless and drab, which makes it seem utterly credible that the cruddy little cup in the glass cube was actually the one Socrates, or some other Greek playwright, drank poison from.

He is about to ask Kathleen—God, that *name!*—if she would care to join him for a cup of tea on this dark, dank and doleful day when across the room, he spots three people he knows from the Silver Pony uptown, none other than Holly Sinclair, Corry Corrington, and Jack Lawton, who before now he has suspected of enjoying what was known during the War of the Roses as a *ménage à trois,* a surmise that seems indisputable now that he is privileged to witness them unobserved in an intimate *tête-à-tête.*

"They had their arms around each other, and they were studying some kind of sign on the wall."

"Sign?" Carella said.

"Well, some kind of notice, I guess."

"Like what? 'No Smoking'? Something like that?"

"No, no. Something about the cup."

"And you say they were *studying* it?"

"Well, they seemed very interested in it, let me put it that way."

"Did *you* read the sign?"

"No, but I could see it was about the cup. There were these big bold letters I could read from across the room. The Socrates Cup."

"But you didn't go over to the sign and actually read what was on it, did you?"

"No, I didn't. I was hitting on this college girl, you know. I'm forty-two years old, I didn't want that to get back to the Pony. Anyway, what I'm saying is this wasn't just them happening to be in the same bar every now and then, this was a regular thing with them. This was a three-way, you follow me? This was both of them fuckin her, to put it in plain English."

"So you figured it might be a good idea to mention this."

"I was drunk."

"But you mentioned it."

"What I did was suggest it."

"What prompted you to do that?"

"Well, he was telling Corry how he'd always suspected his wife was cheating on him, and Jimmy said . . ."

"Who's Jimmy?"

"Jimmy Nelson, one of the guys there that night. He said he thought *Holly* was Jack's wife. Because she used to come in with Corry and Jack all the time."

"Uh-huh."

"And Jack said, 'No, Holly's just somebody I *like* a lot,' something like that, and the fight started."

"Why?"

"Because I guess I said something about *Corry* liking her a lot, too."

"Uh-huh."

"And they told me to mind my own fuckin business."

"Uh-huh."

"So that's it."

"Ever see the Walther *before* that night?"

"Nope."

"Corry pulled it when the fight started going wrong, is that it?"

"That's what happened. I was lucky. Cause it was already too late by then, the cops were already on the way. They got there a few seconds later."

"When did he toss the gun?"

"Minute he heard the sirens."

"In the gutter, right?"

"Yeah."

"Did the responding blues look for it?"

"Why would they? They didn't know it existed."

"You didn't mention that Corry had pulled a gun on you, huh?"

"And get my head blown off *next* time? No way."

"Well, thanks for your time," Carella said, and rose and walked to the door.

"You like steak?" Rodino said. "Come on, I'll give you some nice thick sirloins to take home to your wife." He clapped Carella on the shoulder and opened the door for him. "No maggots in them," he said, and winked. "I promise."

Melanie enjoys the contrasts and similarities between the two men. Jack is a trained graphic designer, and he views ordinary things with an artist's eye. Very often he will hold out his hands to frame a picture the way a movie director does, palms out, thumbs touching, as if trying to lock the image in that way. His one disappointment is that he never became an oil painter, but opted for a more commercial aspect of art instead.

Corry, on the other hand, is untrained but enormously talented.

Well, *that* way, too, but Melanie is thinking of class and the way he really hurls himself into a role. That's the only word for it, he truly *hurls* himself at it, becoming the character, inhabiting the character's skin, it's really remarkable. She admires him a great deal for that. Just the idea of him even *daring* to take lessons, a man with his background, in prison twice already, remarkable. In his own way, he's really just as sensitive as Jack is.

But the men are so different otherwise.

Corry is a man of action. He thinks of something and then immediately puts the thought into motion. Melanie feels he must have been a very good robber, although certainly the evidence is all to the contrary, busted twice, sent away twice, how good could he have been? But if a person is capable of thinking, for example, I'll hold up that liquor store tonight, and then actually *does* hold it up that night, well, that's admirable, that's something to be appreciated.

Jack, on the other hand, takes forever to put any kind of plan in motion. She thinks the reason he hasn't found a job up here is not because he isn't a very good graphic designer, which he is, but only because he isn't alert to opportunities. Took forever to redo his portfolio after a top man in the field told him it didn't show his talents to best advantage. Didn't contact the man for another interview until the job had already been filled. Kicked himself in the ass afterward, but too late is too late. He's that way about everything. Well, not everything. In fact, he's pretty *quick* about some things. Too *damn* quick sometimes. Sometimes she's grateful she's got the two of them in bed with her.

She's not surprised when Corry agrees to come to the museum with them one Saturday in November. She knows how talented he is, and it's her belief that a person who shows talent in one field is probably just as talented in another, probably a false premise in most cases, but isn't Anthony Quinn a wonderful painter, for example? Or Tony Bennett? So maybe there is some truth to it, after all, who knows? Museum-going was a habit with her and Jack long before Corry moved in. In fact, they'd been on their way to the museum that day they ran into whatever her name was, a friend of the Lawtons, Claire Somebody, wheeling her baby carriage, looking them up and down, hey, isn't Jack supposed to be *married*? Good thing he introduced her as Holly Sinclair because sure as shit the woman would be on the pipe to Jill the minute she got home. Guess who *I* ran into today, Jill? With a redheaded *bimbo* on his arm!

Melanie and Jack see the Socrates Cup for the first time on Saturday afternoon, the sixteenth day of November. It is exhibited in a glass cube on the second floor of the museum. The cup is tilted, so that the underside is reflected first in a mirror that reverses the lettering and next in a second mirror that corrects it to read properly as ΣOK.

"I saw it at the Getty in Malibu," Corry tells them. "It's worth a fortune."

"What do you mean by a fortune?" Melanie asks.

"Two, three million."

"Looks like an ordinary clay bottle," Jack says.

"Hell of a lot more than that. You see the lettering on the bottom?"

"Yeah?"

"It stands for Socrates. The first letter is sigma, which is our S. And in Greek, Socrates is spelled with a K. That's the cup he actually drank the hemlock from."

"Come on," Melanie says.

"No, really. This is the only bottle they found with a

marking on it. They think either the potter or one of the jailers intended to keep it as a souvenir. Scratched the name on the bottom."

"Wow," Melanie says. "So what do they do? Move it from museum to museum?"

"It must be on loan," Jack says. "There should be something here that tells us."

They find the information printed on a Lucite-covered placard fastened to the wall. It informs them that the cup is part of the permanent collection at the Museum of the Ancient Agora in Athens, and that a grant from the Greek government has made it possible for the historic treasure to be viewed in museums all over the world. The tour started last June. The cup has since moved through twelve different cities and is scheduled to move southward from here to Washington, Atlanta, and . . .

"*Calusa?*" Jack says, astonished.

"All we've got down there is a dinky little museum," Melanie says. "They must mean another Calusa."

"No, it's Calusa, *Florida,*" Jack says. "The Ca D'Ped. Look."

They all look at the placard again.

Calusa, Florida, it reads. The Ca D'Ped, it reads.

"What do you mean, dinky?" Corry asks.

"Sleepy time down south," Melanie says.

"So let's rob it," he says.

9

The man sipping iced coffee with Jack and Candace was huge. Broad shoulders, a barrel chest, hands like a heavyweight boxer. This was all to the good. In Candace's own words, Harry Jergens would be the one who "nullified" the museum's security presence. Zaygo, another experienced thief, had called it "laying the guards down." That was another good euphemism. Jack liked the way these people talked.

This was the Thursday morning two days before the heist.

"Two guards, is that it?" Jergens asked.

"Yes," Candace said.

She was wearing a short navy-blue skirt with strappy white sandals and a white T-shirt. They were all sitting outside by the pool. This was now a few minutes past ten. The sun had not yet reached its zenith, but the thermometer already read eighty-six degrees. The spot here at the end of the island was isolated, hushed except for the occasional cry of a bird. Some fifty feet of lawn edged with mangroves separated the pool from the lagoon beyond. They'd be coming back to the house by boat on the night of the heist, another of Zaygo's words, which of course Jack knew because he'd seen one or two caper movies in his lifetime.

"They're the museum's normal security," Candace said. "They won't be adding any when the cup is on the premises."

"You know where they'll be? I mean, their precise location?"

"I do."

"Reliable?"

"The horse's mouth," she said. "They're both outside, patrolling the grounds."

"Where outside?"

"One of them keeps circling the museum itself."

"Shaking doorknobs?"

"I would guess not. That would set off the alarm."

"Then what?"

"He probably does a torch show. I'm guessing. Throws the light on the windows, maybe peeks in these big French doors they've got. These are square-shield hicks, Harry. Most they've ever had at the museum is vandals. Nobody's expecting any trouble."

"Where's the other one? You said there are two."

"He does the perimeter. There's a stone wall around the entire property, he . . ."

"How high?"

"Six feet. He patrols just inside the wall. He's got a dog."

"Oh, terrific. I just love fuckin dogs."

"A Doberman."

"Better yet. How about the one circling the museum? Does he have a dog, too?"

"No."

"Is he armed?"

"They're both armed."

"This is a terrific fuckin job, you know that?" Jergens said. "Is there anybody *inside* we have to worry about?"

"Nobody."

"There's no *need* for an inside guard," Jack said. "There's a motion alarm."

"Anybody walking around in there would set it off."

"Really terrific," Jergens said.

"There's much more than just a motion alarm," Candace said. "There's state-of-the-art security worth a quarter of a million bucks."

"At least state-of-the-art back in 1979," Jack said.

"Let me hear it," Jergens said.

Jack had already heard all this; she'd come here yesterday, the moment she'd left the library. She repeated it again now, hoping Jergens wouldn't spook and quit the premises altogether. She wanted this job to succeed. She had big plans for this job.

In anticipation of the then-impending visit of the Treasures of Tutankhamen, the museum had invested $240,000 in a wide variety of security systems designed to deter intrusion. This despite the Arts and Artifacts Indemnity Act signed into law by President Ford four years earlier, which provided full insurance coverage for these priceless works. Candace figured Calusa didn't want to go down in history as the hick town that had allowed the treasures to be swiped from their Tinkertoy museum. The newspaper piece, an odd admixture of small-town bragging and unmistakable warning, was deliberately explicit about the measures the Ca D'Ped would be taking to improve security. This is what the museum has purchased, it seemed to be saying, so don't even *dream* of violating the space. What the museum had purchased was:

Magnetic contacts on all the doors and door frames. In alignment, the magnets and contacts showed a so-called "good" circuit to the system's control panel . . .

"I don't know if I explained this to you, Jack," she said. "In any electronic system, there are three major components . . ."

Live and learn, Jack thought.

". . . the sensors, the control unit, and the warning device. There are two types of sensor switches, the normally *closed* switch, what's called an N.C. switch, and the normally *open* switch, which is called an N.O. switch."

"I know all this shit," Jergens said.

"I don't," Jack said.

Then get out of the fucking business, Jergens thought, but did not say.

"I'll try to keep it simple," Candace said calmly. "A doorbell is a good example of the N.O. switch. There's a gap in the wiring, you press the bell button, it closes the gap, and the bell rings. With an alarm system, you close the gap when you open a door or a window. Bam, the bell goes off. You beat an N.O system by cutting the wires so the current can't run to the control box. The N.C. system works in exactly the opposite . . ."

"I know all this shit," Jergens said again.

"So shut up and listen anyway," Candace snapped.

He glared at her.

She glared back.

Too fucking much at stake here, she thought.

She kept glaring at him till he turned away.

"In a closed-circuit system," she said, "a mild current runs through the wires at all times. If you open a window or a door, the current is broken and a relay jumps out and this triggers the alarm. Cut the wires in *this* system, it's the same thing as forcing entry. You break the current and the bell goes off. Way to beat it is to cross-contact the wires. Then you can open as many windows and doors as you like. The easy way to remember this . . ."

"Oh, shit, kindergarten," Jergens said.

She glared at him again. He glared back. But, again, he turned away.

"The easy way to remember this," she repeated, "is to think open and closed. For the bell to go off in an *open*-circuit system, you have to *close* the circuit. In a *closed*-circuit system, you have to *open* it. To beat either one of them, you simply make sure the open stays open . . ."

". . . and the closed stays closed," Jergens said, mimicking her.

"Come on," Jack said mildly, "cut it out."

"It's just I know all this stuff," Jergens said.

"I don't. So let her talk, okay?"

"Fine," Jergens said, "let her talk."

"To keep an open circuit open, you cut the wires. To keep a closed circuit closed, you cross-contact them. In a combination system, you cut one set of wires and cross-contact the others. All clear?" she asked.

"As clear as are the skies of England," Jack said.

"Okay," she said. "Any change in the open or closed status sends a 'break' report to the control box. The unit deciphers the report and determines whether or not to trigger the warning device. The museum invested all this money to buy . . ."

. . . first, the magnets and contacts that ensured any forced window or door would immediately report entrance. Next, the window bugs. The bug was an electronic device about the size of a half-dollar. Embodied in its plastic shell was a microphone calibrated to distinguish the sound frequency of shattering glass. Smash a window to which the bug was affixed and the control panel would immediately be alerted.

But the museum was taking no chances. Not for nothing was it spending such a huge sum of money on protection. In addition to the window bugs and magnetic contacts, the electronic security system included shock sensors to safeguard all perimeter doors and windows. No larger than a credit card, these devices sent out high-frequency shock waves whenever they detected a violent assault on window or door. In addition to these, the perimeter was protected by window foil and security screens. The foil, not particularly gorgeous since it looked like exactly what it was, would be installed on the museum's basement windows . . .

"My guess is that's where the vault is," Candace said.

"Your guess?" Jergens said. "What is this, a fuckin *game* show? Do you or don't you know where the box is?"

"Not precisely," Candace said. "I walked around the building and everything above the foundation is stucco. The only concrete I saw was below ground level. So I figure the basement's made of concrete. Okay, Oberling told me they lock the cup . . ."

"Who's Oberling?"

"The museum's curator."

"Okay."

"Told me they lock it at night in a stainless-steel vault en-cased in concrete. So that's where the vault has to be."

Jergens nodded.

"In a concrete room in the basement," Jack said, nodding with him.

"Anyway, that's where I spotted the foil on the windows," she said. "So that's our best bet for the vault. Also, there are security screens over *all* the windows. You know what *they* had to cost? Measuring and fitting all those screens to size? But cut any wire in them, or try to take them off a window, and the alarm yells."

"Sounds very tight," Jergens said sourly.

"It is," Candace said. "If they really went ahead with the plans . . ."

"I feel certain they did," Jack said.

"So do I," Candace said.

Jergens grunted.

"If so," Candace said, "then once the system is armed, it won't be safe to step anywhere or walk anywhere or move anywhere in that whole damn building. If the article was telling the truth, the place is now wired like a Cambodian minefield."

"How does the signal go out?" Jergens asked.

The weak spot in any alarm system. Jergens knew it, Can-dace knew it, and now Jack was learning all about it.

"No opportunity there," Candace said, shaking her head.

"How come? Even a leased line can be beat, you know."

"Not if it's got a backup."

"Like what?"

"Long-range radio," Candace said. "The museum can send a signal even if the phone line is breached."

"Well, that's why you're laying in," Jack said, smiling. "To beat the system *before* it can send a signal."

"No, I don't think that's possible," Candace said.

The smile dropped from his face.

"Once the system is armed, I'm dead in the closet. I so much as move . . ."

"You so much as *fart,*" Jergens corrected, shaking his head. "And I'll tell you something *else*. A dog and a pair of guns ain't good news on the outside. These all got to be put down before we go for the box, that's for sure, man *or* beast. What kind of box is it, anyway?"

"I don't know. But two-forty wouldn't have been enough to buy a new vault, so I'm pretty sure it's pre–seventy-nine. One thing the newspaper *did* say . . ."

"The fuckin newspaper again," Jergens said.

"This one I'll quote," Candace said, and took from her handbag the Xerox copy she'd made at the library. Putting on her glasses, she unfolded the sheet of paper and began reading:

"The museum vault will be shielded by a sophisticated sound-sensitive electronic protective system recommended by Lloyds of London as the most formidable grade of protection on the market today. The interior vault sensor will be equipped to transmit an alarm at the first sign of a drill or hammer attack on the vault walls. Torch, tool, or explosive attacks upon the vault door itself will be recognized by heat disclosing elements and intricate vault-door electrification. Control panel instrumentation and related power supply units will be wired to detect intrusion at any point between the vault, the control unit, and the signaling system."

Candace looked up.

"Period," she said.

"So how do we beat it?" Jergens asked.

"We don't even try," she said.

We are the only two people who will ever experience
what is about to happen, Melanie thinks. Even if we tell it to
someone else in excruciating detail, even if Paramount
makes a movie of it one day and it plays all over the world,
we will nonetheless remain the only two individuals who
actually experienced it. Jack and I. Who are about to kill a
man.

He is an exceedingly dangerous man, they know this.
They also know that if it were done when 'tis done, 'twere
well it were done quickly, so to speak. There can be no mis-
takes here. They cannot merely disable this enormously
strong man because then he will come at them like a bleeding water buffalo. He must be dispatched swiftly, efficiently
and decisively.

It is Melanie who suggests a shotgun, not because she's
had any experience with one, or with any sort of weapon for
that matter, but only because she's seen movies where virtual
amateurs pick up shotguns and use them as if they're expert
marksmen. In the movies, nobody ever *aims* a shotgun. It's
usually held waist-high and fired from that position. Nobody peers down a barrel with one eye squinted shut. Just
level the gun and *bam*! From the movies, she has gleaned the
impression that it takes no particular skill to load and fire a
shotgun. She has also come to believe, again from the
movies, that a shotgun does a very good job, judging from
the huge ragged holes left in chests, bellies, and heads.

So it is Melanie who makes the suggestion and Jack who
makes the actual purchase, a simple matter in the state of
Florida, which has firmly upheld by legislation the constitu-

tional right to keep and bear arms for lawful purposes. Killing a person might not be such a lawful purpose, Melanie supposes, but apparently this prospect never occurred to the legislators.

On the weekend before the murder, Corry is out catting around as usual. That's another thing that makes him so dangerous. They have no illusions that this relationship they share is a lasting one. Steal the cup, and Corry will disappear in a flash. She sometimes thinks that's what this is all about: disappearance. Years from now, months from now, weeks from now, he'll be in bed with some slut in Seattle and he'll tell her all about the terrific museum heist in Calusa, Florida, same way he told Melanie all about the botched drugstore holdup in L.A. He is truly far too dangerous.

On Monday afternoon, Jack shows her the shotgun he purchased in a shop named Bobby's Gun Exchange, on the Trail and West Cedar.

"It's a used one," he tells her, "but the man said it was in A-1 condition."

"I would trust the man," Melanie says, and smiles.

Corry does not come home until much later that afternoon. Plastered to his scalp is a patch the size of a silver dollar, which he chooses not to explain. They can only assume he's been in another barroom brawl. Altogether too volatile, this man. By now, the shotgun is locked in the pool shed that houses the filter system and the cleaning equipment and the citronella candles and the gardening tools. In the short while they've been living here, Corry has never once volunteered to vacuum the pool. He has the mentality of all thieves everywhere: you worked only if you couldn't find anything to steal. For Corry, stealing was something like performing in a play. The danger of it. The constant balancing act on a high wire. Applause if you succeeded, punishment if you failed. Melanie can remember one time, up north, when a kid in class told them he'd become an actor only because he didn't have the guts of a burglar. Corry never told the kid why he'd found this so hilarious.

Murder is a lot like acting.

Or so she is about to discover.

On Monday night, the twentieth of January, the three of them make love together for the very last time. Tomorrow night at this time, though he does not have the slightest suspicion of what's in store for him, Corry will be dead.

Tuesday dawns like molten gold.

She hates this city, the intolerable heat here, the insufferable people here, hates the entire state of Florida. She tells this to Jill on the phone that afternoon. This is just outside Calusa First, there's a row of pay phones outside the bank there in case you want to call home, ask if you should rob the bank or mug an old lady making an ATM withdrawal.

"I can't wait to get out of this fucking city," she says.

"Soon," Jill assures her.

There is a silence on the line. The bank is close to the Santa Lucia beach, so you can walk up in your swimming trunks to make a deposit or shoot a teller. Gulls scream overhead. It is such a clear bright hot rotten day.

"How'd it go with the lawyer?" Melanie asks.

"Fine. He's on the case."

"Looking for Jack, huh?"

"Looking for Jack." There is another silence. Then Jill asks, "Do you still feel up to this?"

"Such a question," Melanie says, sounding very much like her mother, Lucille Schwartz.

To make certain that Corry won't decide to go wandering again tonight in search of more cuts and bruises, Melanie tells him she is cooking her specialty, which happens to be chicken Kiev, served with fresh garden peas and mashed potatoes. To make certain that Corry won't decide to oil his prized Walther tonight, Jack filches it from the top dresser drawer where he keeps it under his rolled socks—he wears only white socks, which is another thing Melanie finds revolting about him—removes the gun from the drawer and carries it into the bathroom, where he places it in one of those plastic refrigerator bags that seal across the top so nothing will leak in or out, and lowers it gently into the toilet tank in the bathroom. He can only hope that Corry won't decide on a change of socks before they blow him away, but in that case they will have to do the job sooner than they anticipated.

Jack is the one who is supposed to shoot him.

But murder is a lot like acting.

To ensure the proper amount of concurrence on Corry's part—they are, after all, about to kill the poor son of a bitch, and they don't want him to go out kicking and screaming—Jack is mixing the drinks tonight. Corry the cowboy is drinking bourbon neat with a wedge of lime to add a touch of high society. Jack and Melanie are both drinking gin-tonics. Every time Corry calls for another bourbon, which is often, Jack brings out from the kitchen something very dark and evil-looking with a lime bobbing in it like a green buoy on Cimmerian seas. Before Melanie serves dinner at a little before nine, they have each consumed four drinks and are working on a fifth. Corry has been drinking straight bourbon. Melanie and Jack have been drinking straight tonic water, no gin in it at all, how clever. And whereas Corry has something of a hollow leg, he seems nonetheless to be feeling the effects of the booze, if a slight stagger as he walks to the table is any indication. Melanie lights a candle. Jack pulls the cork on a good California chardonnay. The area around the pool is cool and dark and cozy. They plan to kill him before dessert is served.

They have chosen to kill him out here by the pool because it will be easier to tidy up afterward. The patio is designed for easy cleaning, hose it down, sweep the water into the drains, goodbye unsightly blemishes and stains. Shoot him inside the house, you're liable to get blood and brain matter all over the carpets and drapes, entirely too messy. So out here by the pool is the murder scene of choice, kiddies, here in the still of the Florida night on an isolated tip of land bounded by mangroves and lagoon and scrub palms, where a single shotgun blast, or at worst two, will be forgiven by the nearest neighbor a quarter of a mile away—though this was not why the boys chose the house. They chose it because it was far from the museum, and it had a dock, and nobody would be popping in unexpectedly to borrow a cup of sugar. Certainly, that is why Corry voted for it, though in a half hour or so he will have reason to regret the house's lonely location.

Melanie goes out to the kitchen to fetch the sumptuous feast she's prepared. At the table, Corry is sampling the chardonnay, which he pronounces both fruity and smoky, a line he picked up while he was rehearsing a scene at Theater Place. Jack walks over to the pool shed where the padlock is hanging loose on its hasp, and he opens the door and goes inside ostensibly to turn on the pool lights, which he does with a single snap, but actually to lift the shotgun from where it is leaning against the wall alongside the coiled vacuum hose. He carries the gun outside with him, closes the door, rests it against the door away from Corry's line of sight. There is a twenty-gauge shell in each of the gun's barrels. The gun is ready. So is Jack. So is Melanie.

But murder is a lot like acting.

The idea is to get him in a totally unsuspecting frame of mind. Toward that end, Jack tells a joke he heard at the supermarket while he was picking up the chicken and potatoes and peas, and Melanie keeps pouring the wine, which—with three of them drinking it, or at least one of them drinking it pretty heavily and the other two taking a mere sip every now and then—doesn't last very long. Melanie goes out to the kitchen for another bottle. Jack looks at his watch. Corry wonders aloud if they shouldn't all go for a swim later on, and winks at Jack, which Jack takes to mean he wishes to ream Melanie again after dinner, but of course he doesn't yet know he will be dead after dinner. Melanie comes back with a more expensive bottle of chardonnay, from a different vineyard this time, and she asks Corry to tell her if he can detect any differences. She begins twisting the corkscrew into the cork. Her eyes graze Jack's over the bottle. He nods briefly. She dips her head over the bottle again, pulls the cork free.

"Tell me what you think," she says, and pours for Corry, who is now beginning to look like a besotted lord of the manor.

"We need a citronella candle," Jack says, slapping at an imaginary mosquito, and he shoves back his chair and goes to the pool shed, and picks up the shotgun and walks swiftly to where Corry is sitting with his back to him, and raises the shotgun, bracing it against his hip, leveling it at Corry's head. Corry is sipping the wine. Little sips. Rolling it around his mouth. Melanie sees the shotgun coming up and backs away a pace because she doesn't want to get all splashed with tissue and blood. But Jack isn't pulling the trigger.

There is a frozen moment in time.

No one will ever know about this moment.

Jack has forgotten his lines.

This is a performance and Jack has forgotten his lines.

He is standing behind Corry, who is obliviously tasting the new expensive wine, but he is not pulling the trigger. Melanie can't yell at him to pull the fucking *trigger*, Jack, so instead she takes a quick step around the table and grabs the gun out of his hands, improvising. This is a performance and she is improvising because the star has forgotten his lines and she must save the play, it is as simple as that, she must blow Corry out of that chair before he realizes what's going on here and becomes a snarling violent beast. Jack stands paralyzed. Melanie rams the stock of the gun against her hip, swings both barrels up and around toward Corry's head. Just then, he starts to turn in the chair, a puzzled look on his face, like hey, guys, what's going *on* here? And suddenly everything starts happening in slow motion.

There is on his face . . .

It is an extraordinarily handsome face, it's too bad he is going to be killed in the next thirty seconds or so because had he continued with acting lessons he might one day have made a brilliant leading man . . .

There is on his face . . .

Although, in truth, the features have been dulled by whiskey, and the handsomeness is more like a memory than an undeniable physical fact . . .

There is on his face a look of puzzlement struggling with recognition, head turning in slow motion and in huge close-up, jaw hanging slack, sharp blue eyes blunted by alcohol,

everything huge and in slow motion. His face fills the screen
of Melanie's mind while her index finger gropes inside the
unfamiliar trigger guard to find one of the two triggers.

His hand comes out in slow motion, reaching for the gun,
reaching for some affirmation that this is really happening,
this is a double-barreled shotgun pointing up at his head, this
is the girl he has been fucking to a fare-thee-well since Halloween last year when he was a cowboy all in black and she
was wearing a seductively brief wedding dress, *this* is that girl,
and *that* in her hands is cold steel, and he is rapidly becoming
sober though in ten seconds it will be absolutely too late. If he
does not manage to wrench that gun from her hands in eight
seconds, he will be a dead man, if he does not grab that gun
by the barrel in six seconds, he will be history, if he cannot
tear it from her grip in five seconds, four seconds, he is suddenly cold sober, two seconds, oh Jesus, the last thing he sees
on earth is the coldly determined look in her hard green eyes.

What she dreaded most actually happens.

His face explodes in a shower of gristle and tissue and yellow custard matter and blackish red blood that splashes toward her in agonizingly explicit slow motion, she can almost
see each repellent drop as it bursts toward her face. The clean
white apron she is wearing over shorts and T-shirt suddenly
turns color, the white cotton becoming a red and yellow
pus-colored polka-dot spatter. The slime is warm from his
body, it touches her flesh as if it is still alive. She screams
aloud, and keeps screaming until suddenly here is brave Mr.
Benson, aka Jack Lawton, taking her shoulders and telling
her to calm down, it's all over, calm down, Melanie, shaking
her, you're fucking *right* it's all over, *I'm* the one who made it
happen, you cowardly prick!

"Calm down," he says.

"I'm calm."

"Calm down now, it's all over."

"I'm calm."

But no, it's not quite over.

They have planned to cart the body to the stretch of beach behind the shacks on North Galley Road. Bind his ankles and wrists with wire hangers to make it look like a gay murder, then dump him on the beach not far from a fairy hangout called Timothy B's. It is interesting that Jack can use words like "fairy" or "queer" or "fruit" or even "homo" when describing men who perform the very same acts he and Corry perform—*used* to perform—together in the throes of three-way passion. But such are the ways of men, she supposes, though often she becomes extremely confused about which are the ways of men and which are the ways of women. For example, she would never have thought that she could cold-bloodedly pull the trigger of a shotgun and blow away a person's face. That was a man thing, wasn't it? Playing with guns? Wasn't that a man thing? Girls played with dolls. This bewilders her sometimes, the man-woman thing and which is which. Identity, she supposes you might call it. In short, she sometimes wonders exactly who or what she is.

While they are taking off Corry's clothes, the better to encourage a Gay Murder Theory they hope will enter the mind of some underpaid, overworked civil servant, Jack comes up with the idea that makes her think about identity all over again. Maybe she will have to add identity to the short list of what this is all about. Maybe when all is said and done, this is really all about disappearance and identity. Cause the cup to disappear from the museum, steal it from Jack later on, and then disappear from the face of the earth to find new identities. Nepal might be a good place to spend

215

the two and a half million dollars. Well, don't forget greed. When there's that much money in the equation, greed most certainly becomes a factor.

"What if he's me?" Jack says.

She doesn't understand. She blinks at him and yanks off Corry's undershorts. His cock looks all shriveled and tiny, such a waste. There is blood and shit all over the pool deck, they will really have to hose it down good once they get rid of the body. It is a little difficult to think of Corry as a body. But that's what he is, of course. That is what she herself caused him to become. This, too, is a matter of identity. And disappearance, when you think of it. Corry is no longer Corry, he has disappeared. He has exchanged his identity for that of a corpse. So long, it's been good to know you.

"Because sooner or later, you know, Jill will come looking for me."

She thinks for a moment that Jack the cowardly prick has become a mind reader. Because only this morning, and all according to plan, Jill went to see a Calusa attorney named Matthew Hope, with the end in mind of establishing an alibi should the police later come knocking when they find old Jack tangled in the mangroves in the bayou behind his rented house. That is the further plan. Kill Jack on the night of the museum robbery. Steal the cup. Deliver it to the Greek, take the big payoff, and vanish. Nepal might be a splendid place to go. Live like a pair of maharanis. Make love on tiger skins.

"She'll never find us," Melanie says.

This is almost amusing. She almost smiles. Jack is worried about his wife finding them, when of course he will never again have *anything* to worry about after the night of February first. Meanwhile, this morning Jill visited a dimwitted lawyer who'd achieved some measure of fame after getting

himself shot—there must be easier ways. And the entire purpose of that visit was to convince Mr. Hope that she truly
wished a divorce and would go to unimaginable extremes to
find the wayward bastard who'd left her. The police would
later ask themselves why a woman would have hired a
lawyer to find her husband if she already knew where he
was, which she'd *have* to have known if she'd killed him. Jill
would tell them the absolute truth, sure. She was glad someone had shot the bastard because he most certainly deserved
it, but she knew nothing about it, and besides she was planning to leave Calusa in the near future, so if they had no further questions, goodbye and good luck.

Case closed.

But now Jack is worried about *her* finding *him*.

It is to laugh.

"We could make Corry look like me," he says.

She considers this.

The man has no face. It's a possibility.

"Give him my wallet with a credit card and my driver's
license in it."

She weighs this.

Sure, why not?

Warn Jill ahead of time so that she can immediately tell
them Hey, this is not my husband, Jack has a bigger cock, or
whatever. Keep the search alive, strengthen the alibi. Why
not? Anything to confuse them. The more confusion the
better. Disappearance and identity, why not?

"Sounds like a good idea," she says.

"Yeah, I think so."

She is already wondering what kind of story Jill can tell
the police when they show her Corry's body. How can she

possibly know at a glance that this is not her husband? The man has no face.

She suddenly remembers her Uncle Abe. Abraham Schwartz, her father's brother. A gambler from Arizona, used to come east every Passover to visit. Told wild stories about the Wild West, most of them bullshit.

"See this, Melanie? That's my tattoo."

"That's not a tattoo, Uncle Abe. A tattoo isn't a blue dot. It's a heart or an eagle or a butterfly."

"This is a special tattoo, darling. This is from when I had radiation therapy on my throat."

It might fly.

And who would ever know the difference? On the first of February, Jack himself would be dead. Would some smart Calusa cop look for a blue tattoo the size of a pinhead? First thing, there *weren't* any smart Calusa cops. Second thing . . .

There *was* no second thing.

Identity and disappearance, she thinks again.

"We'll have to put his jeans back on," she says.

"Jeans?"

"So he'll have a pocket for your wallet."

In bed with Patricia late that Thursday night, Matthew asked her if she knew what the hat trick was.

"Is that a trick question?" she asked.

"No. It's a perfectly legitimate question. What's the hat trick?"

"Everybody knows what the hat trick is."

"Okay, so what is it?"

"First tell me the Swan joke."

"What are we doing here, plea bargaining?"

"Yes, the hat trick for the Swan joke."

"How do I even know you *know* what the hat trick is?"

"I'm a sworn officer of the court and a state attorney besides."

"All the more reason to distrust you. Did you know that people hate lawyers, cops, and dentists in equal measure?"

"Is this information somehow related to the hat trick?"

"Yes. What *is* the hat trick?"

"First the Swan joke."

"Can I trust you?"

"Implicitly," she said. "The Swan joke."

"Okay. This man is decapitated in an automobile accident . . ."

"Sounds funny already," she said.

". . . and the medical examiner calls both his wife and his mistress to identify him. It happens that there's a tattoo on his penis . . ."

"Oh, the old Tattoo-on-the-Penis joke."

". . . and the tattoo reads SWAN."

"Gets funnier every minute."

"Do you want to hear this joke, or don't you?"

"Sorry, sir, forgive me, sir," Patricia said, and saluted. The salute was comical only because she was so seriously naked.

"So the wife looks down at the man's penis and she says, 'That's my husband all right.' The mistress looks down at the tattooed penis and says, 'No, that's *not* him!' The medical examiner is puzzled. 'But you told me there was a tattoo on his penis,' he says. 'Yes,' she says, 'but it doesn't say SWAN.' The medical examiner looks at her. 'Then what *does* it say?' he asks. 'SASKATCHEWAN,' she says."

Patricia burst out laughing.

Matthew laughed with her.

"The hat trick," he said.

"Okay, the hat trick," she said. "If any single player scores three goals in any one game of cricket, or ice hockey, or soccer, or the like, that's the hat trick."

"Why?"

"Why what?"

"Why's it called the hat trick?"

"Because in cricket, where the term originated, if a player scored three goals he was rewarded with a new hat."

"I see."

"Yes."

"So *that's* what he meant."

"That's what who meant?"

"Carella."

"Who's Carella?"

"Cop up north."

"Meant about what?"

"The hat trick. A lawyer, a cop, and a dentist. Three most despised occupations."

"I don't get it."

"I guess you had to be there. How do you happen to know about hat tricks?"

"I read an Elmore Leonard novel."

"Elmore Leonard writes about cricket?"

"No, this particular reference was to sex. A guy scoring with three different women on the same night."

"Speaking of which," he said.

"Cricket?" she asked.

"Sex," he said.

"I just got my period," she said.

He looked at her.

"I'm sorry, Matthew," she said.

"At least it isn't a headache," he said.

10

The GTE truck had been stolen in the middle of the night from the parking lot behind the telephone company building, a large asphalt-topped space surrounded by a Cyclone fence. The thief had cut through the thick chain and padlock securing the sliding gate on rollers, and had probably jump-started the truck before driving it off the lot.

The Calusa P.D. thought the incident peculiar but not particularly suspicious. In a city where auto theft was a common crime, it didn't much matter whether the stolen item was a Caddy convertible or a Land Rover. They'd never had a General Telephone company truck stolen before, but then again, they'd never had a school bus stolen until last July, when some kids took one from behind the Akira Naoi Junior High School and drove it all the way to Tampa as a lark. Lots of crimes were peculiar, and some of them were bizarre, but not all of them were suspicious.

★   ★   ★

On Friday morning at nine, the security guard standing in front of the Ca D'Ped saw a big white truck with a GTE logo on its side pulling around the oval and parking just to the right of the massive entrance doors. He would have told the driver of any ordinary vehicle to go park the car in one of the museum parking lots, but you didn't tell that to someone making an obvious service call. A man wearing orange coveralls and high-topped workman's shoes stepped down out of the truck. He was carrying a clipboard, and one of those leather tool belts was hanging from his waist. A plastic-encased photo ID card was clipped to the flap of a pocket in the coveralls. He nodded to the guard and walked right in.

Harry Jergens had a motto he'd lifted from Henry Ford, who'd invented the automobile. The motto was Never Explain, Never Complain.

He explained nothing to the security guard, just breezed right on by him without even calling attention to the ID card he'd assembled at home yesterday, using a computer for the printed material, and a GTE logo he'd snipped from the front cover of a Calusa telephone directory, and mounting a passport photo onto it, and then photocopying the whole seamless montage before having it laminated at CopyQuik on the South Trail, thank you very much, kids, you do a nice job.

He did not complain when another security guard asked him to take off the tool belt before he went through the metal detector arch, just nodded, and unhooked it, and handed it on through, and then went through himself without any whistles or bells going off. He put the belt on again when he was safely on the other side, and then walked directly to the nearest stairwell without telling anyone where he was going, Never Explain, Never Complain. He walked right on downstairs, where Candace had said she was sure the box would be, but he wasn't looking for the box, didn't even care what kind of a box it was. At the big benefit ball tomorrow night, nobody or nothing was going into that box.

Never Explain, Never Complain.

But always carry a tool belt and a clipboard.

He began sketching the moment he entered the below-ground level of the building.

On his left were the doors to the men's room and women's room. On his immediate right, behind him now, on the same wall as the stairs he'd just negotiated, were the elevator doors; this was the state of Florida, where at least some of the population were on walkers or in wheelchairs. Dead ahead was a sort of parlor furnished with sofas and easy chairs and standing ashtrays. This lounge, he guessed you might call it, was where the populace who didn't yet have emphysema could smoke their brains out while waiting to use the rest rooms.

There was perhaps fifty feet between the rest room doors and a concrete wall opposite them that ran the width of the space. Candace had told him she suspected the vault was in a concrete room in the basement. He didn't suppose it would be anywhere near a public area such as this one. Probably on the other side of the basement someplace, accessible only from a locked and possibly wired door. Actually, he didn't care *where* it was. Tomorrow night, the museum people would lead them directly to it.

The concrete wall was painted white and hung with museum posters of past exhibitions. Two metal doors painted a muted blue to enhance the rough concrete were side by side on this wall. Both doors had locks on them, but one of them was standing wide open, and he could see into a supply closet with brooms and mops and pails and a sink. He could also see the lock on the door. A night latch, the simplest type of rim lock, designed more for display than for true security. A night latch simply warned KEEP OUT. It did not pretend to be safeguarding anything of value. From the outside, a key unlocked a spring bolt. From the inside, a knob unlocked it. To breach the door, all you had to do was slide back the bolt.

The second door on the wall was closed.

A glance at the lock told him it was another night latch. He suspected this was a utility closet and that inside it he would find electrical fuse boxes and telephone boxes and perhaps some cable television lines. He did not think the museum's sophisticated alarm system would shelter its control unit in a room with a simple rim lock. Besides, he didn't care. No one was going to try to beat the alarm system.

He went upstairs again, and told the nearest security guard he needed a custodian to open that door for him. The custodian came out of his office, apologized for the inconvenience, and then led Harry downstairs again. As he searched on his ring of keys for the right one, trying key after key, taking more time to find the damn key than it would have taken Harry to slip the bolt with a piece of celluloid or a credit card, Harry casually asked, "Any telephone company equipment behind that other door?"

"What other door?"

"One at the end of the hall there," he said, and gestured toward a metal door at the end of a narrow corridor that ran backward at a right angle to the concrete wall. Harry could see even from this distance that the lock on it was a Medeco.

"Reckon not," the custodian said.

Harry figured the vault room was behind that metal door.

"Here we go," the custodian said.

As Harry had guessed, the room was a twin to the supply closet, except that there was no sink in it. So what they had here was a couple of rooms some four feet wide by six feet long with Mickey Mouse locks on them.

"When you're done, just slam it shut behind you," the custodian said. "It'll lock itself."

And almost open itself, too, Harry thought.

The idea was to make this look like a little family outing. Guy and his wife, two friends with them, riding home from a wedding or something. Calusa was a town that lived on the water. More damn docks here than there were in Venice. *Italy*, not Florida. Venice, *Florida*, was a stone's throw away down U.S. 41, and it *also* had a lot of boats and boaters and docks, though Zaygo guessed not as many as here in Calusa.

The three men would be in tuxedos, of course, because the museum benefit was a black-tie affair, and Candace would be in a long gown, he could hardly wait to see her looking all slinky and sleek, probably slit high up the side so she could climb in and out of the boat, pretty wheels on that lady. So the cover story had to be they were heading home from a wedding or from one of the balls they were always holding down here. See you Friday night, the governor's holding one of his balls, har, har, har. Of course, they wouldn't *need* a cover story unless the Coast Guard or even a Calusa P.D. boat stopped them for one reason or another. Which was why Zaygo had rented this kind of rig.

Nothing to call too much attention to itself. No forty-eight-foot Ferretti with race-tuned gasoline engines, you opened her up, she could do eighty, eighty-five miles per. Put a boat like that on the water at night, she attracted patrol boats the way honey attracted bees or bears. Not that you could *rent* something like that, he was lucky even to find a boat wasn't a little putt-putt you tooted around the canals with, canvas top and a lawn-mower engine. Ferretti cost you half a mil new, he'd love to own a beauty like that one, but not for a job like the one tomorrow night.

Boat he'd rented wasn't designed to outrace the Coast Guard. It was supposed to look like a family pleasure boat, which it was, a high-priced little sweetheart some five years old, but in mint condition as the guy at the marina had told him, used to be owned by a Presbyterian minister with three virgin daughters, just kidding har, har, har, wanna rent a boat? Nothing too ostentatious, nothing too basic, just your garden-variety thirty-one-foot sport cruiser with a pair of bucket seats and a wraparound aft seat in the cockpit. Zaygo would be captain and his mate . . .

Well, if you wanted to know, the full name was Zane Gorman, abbreviated to Zaygo when he was in the sixth grade, thank you, Felicia Maxwell, who had first called him that, and it had stuck. Zane, of course—as who didn't know?—was a variant form of Zan, which came from the Italian word *zanni,* which meant "clown" and which in turn had evolved from the name Giovanni, which was the Italian equivalent of John. Actually, Zaygo's mother *hadn't* known all this when she'd named him Zane after her favorite writer in the entire world, namely Zane Grey. Then again, Hilda Gorman was living in Colorado when Zaygo was born. What this all got down to was that Zane meant John, which was perhaps the most common masculine name in the entire world, having variations like Jan, Johann, Sean, Ian, Ivan, and even Evan, the first name of yet another writer, though not one as well known as Zane Grey.

Zane Gorman would be captain of the boat tomorrow night, and sitting alongside him as first mate would be Harry Jergens, also in tuxedo. Lounging on the wraparound aft seat, perhaps sipping champagne to lend a note of authenticity to the wedding party theme, would be the plot's brilliant mastermind, none other than Jack Lawton himself, if that was his real name, and Candace Knowles, if that was *her* real name. But then again, who was to say what name was a *real* name? If Zaygo had his choice, people would be calling him Zane, and he would be wearing a big white cowboy hat, and riding a roan pony, whatever that was. Instead, he was Zaygo, and he was driving a boat with standard 330-horsepower engines and a nice easy feel to the controls.

Another boat he'd love to get his hands on was the Formula 419 FasTECH. Stepped hull and MerCruiser power got you up and out faster'n anything he knew, ran you something like $320,000. Well, save your pennies, he thought. Go home with fifteen grand for tomorrow night's work, find yourself another sweet little job like that one, add up all the paydays, one day you ended up with a forty-six-foot Bertram, eat my wake, man.

The dock was just ahead.

Right off the marker Candace had indicated.

He eased the cruiser to starboard, came in at an easy angle. Didn't want to attract the attention of any daytime security guards who might be roaming the grounds, espe-

cially one with a fuckin Doberman on a leash. That would
be Harry's job tomorrow night, taking out the Doberman
and the guard walking him around the perimeter. Other
guard would be closer to the museum, doing a light show
on the windows. *Son et lumière* if the alarm happened to go
off, which everyone assured him there was no chance of
happening because the alarm would never be turned *on*.
Not that he gave a rat's ass since he'd be safe out here on the
boat. First sign of any trouble, off he'd go into the night,
leave the kiddies to fry back at the ranch. Which would
mean no remainder of his fee, no seventy-five hundred
upon safe delivery of the crew and the terra-cotta cup to
Santa Lucia Island, easy come, easy go.

All Zaygo had to do tomorrow night was lay off the marker
until he got a flashlight signal from the museum. Then he
would idle in toward the dock. No lights. Pick up his pass-
engers. Carry them to Santa Lucia. Collect his seventy-five
hundred. So long, it's been nice to know you.

He ran past the dock now.

Good deep water, nice long dock, probably used to get
big yachts in here when the place was a private mansion.

Didn't pause for a moment.

Swung right on past like a sight-seeing tourist glomming
the museum in the distance, all pink walls and sun-washed
tiles. Made an easy arc back out to the channel again, and
then headed north for lunch at a little seafood joint he knew
on the water.

Duck soup, he thought.

This one would be duck soup.

"Your wife on six," Cynthia said.

Matthew was normally very polite and courteous to his

fellow employees, especially when they were as valuable as Cynthia Harding. But this morning, he snapped, "I *have* no wife!" and then immediately added, "Sorry," and stabbed at the six button, wondering if he was sorry he had no wife, or sorry he had yelled at Cynthia or merely sorry that his ex, Susan Fitch Hope, was on the line.

"Hello," he said.

"Matthew, it's Susan."

"Yes, Susan."

"Don't sound so weary."

"I'm not. It's Friday."

"Matthew, I'll ask you flat out. Will you take me to the Ped's benefit opening tomorrow night?"

"I'm sorry, I can't."

"Why not?"

"I'm going with someone else."

"The Demming woman?"

Matthew hated it when she referred to Patricia as "the Demming woman."

"Yes, the Demming woman," he said.

"Take us both," Susan said.

"Take . . ."

"I wouldn't ask, but Justin was called out of town, and I'm stranded. I can't go alone, Matthew, it would . . ."

"Why not?"

"Well, you know Calusa. They'd think it was odd."

"Who's they?"

"They," Susan said. "You know who *they* are."

"Think *what* was odd?"

"Justin not being with me."

"If he's out of town, he can't very well . . ."

"That's just it. He isn't."

"You just told me . . ."

"We split up," she said, and suddenly she was crying.

He was never very good at comforting crying women. Come to think of, he did not know many men who were. But once upon a time she'd been his wife.

"Please don't cry," he said.

"I'm sorry, Matthew. You're the only one I could think of calling. Forgive me, please. He told me this morning, walked out this morning, oh, Jesus, Matthew, what the fuck's wrong with me, why do men keep *leaving* me?"

"That isn't true."

"You left."

"I know, but . . ."

"Twice," she said.

"Susan, please don't cry."

She fell silent then, but she did not stop crying. He said nothing more, simply listened to her crying, knowing she knew he was there on the other end of the line, until finally the tears stopped and she said, "Thank you, Matthew," and hung up.

He sat quite still at his desk for several moments, and then he picked up the receiver again, and punched the speed dial button for Patricia's number, and listened to the phone ringing on the other end, and then her assistant's voice said, "State Attorney Demming's office," and he said, "Dave, this is Matthew, could you put her on, please?"

When Patricia came on, she said, "I told Charles the Swan story this morning." Charles Foster was the S.A. in the office next door to hers. He insisted on being called Charles. Never mind Charlie or Chuck. It was Charles or nothing. Like a French king.

"Did he laugh?" Matthew asked.

"Of course he laughed."

"I'm surprised."

"Why? It's a funny story."

"I just didn't think it was the sort of thing Charles would appreciate."

"Why not?"

"Well . . . he doesn't have much of a sense of humor, does he?"

"Charles has a *wonderful* sense of humor," Patricia said.

There was suddenly a slight edge to her voice. It reminded Matthew of the defensive tone in Bloom's voice when he'd learned about Carella up north. The night Melanie Schwartz was killed. The night Morris Epworth told them about her walking in off the street to rent a beach house from him.

"Anyway," Matthew said.

"Anyway," Patricia said, "I have a meeting in three minutes."

"Susan just called me."

"Oh?"

"Asked me to take her to the benefit tomorrow night. Justin walked out on her."

"Oh, God, that's awful."

"Yeah."

"Call her back," Patricia said at once. "Tell her we'd be happy to have her join us."

"You mean that?"

"Of course. I have to run. Talk to you later. Call her."

There was a click on the line, and then it went dead. He looked at the mouthpiece. He blinked. He put the receiver back on the cradle. He waited a moment, and then dialed Susan's number, surprised that he still knew it by heart. He

told her they'd be there to pick her up at six-thirty tomorrow night, and was grateful when she didn't burst into tears
again. "I'll wear red," she said. "Thank you, Matthew," and
hung up.

Sometimes, ever since the coma, he felt things went by
too fast for him.

He sat looking at the phone.

Then he picked up the receiver and dialed Morris Epworth's number.

As he had on the night of Melanie's murder, Matthew
now fully expected Epworth to take off the nose, mustache,
and eyeglasses. Instead, he blew his nose honkily and explained that he had a terrible cold . . .

"All the snowbirds down here," he said.

. . . which was why he was sitting in the sun in a
bathing suit at ten in the morning, instead of being at his
desk, where he should have been if it weren't for this rotten
cold.

Matthew was there because he was still wondering why
Melanie Schwartz had rented that beach house when she
had a mother to go to in St. Pete, and a boyfriend to go to
right here in Calusa.

"You told Detective Bloom that she walked in off the
street, is that correct?" Matthew asked.

"That's absolutely correct."

The pool area was behind the condo in which Epworth
lived. At this hour of the morning, it was sparsely popu-
lated. A fat elderly woman wearing a white bathrobe and
blue scuffs came out of the building, sniffed the air, and
went immediately to where a thermometer was hanging in
the water near one of the pool's ladders. With some effort,

she knelt, fished the thermometer out of the water, and studied it. "Eighty-two degrees," she said to no one in particular, and then shook her head in disapproval and went to take a towel from a pile neatly stacked on a poolside table.

"You said she'd seen the sign . . ."

"Every time that woman comes to the pool," Epworth whispered, "she complains about the water temperature. It could be a hundred and four, she announces the temperature to everybody—'a hundred and *four!*'—and shakes her head and puts on a sour face." He, too, was shaking his head in disapproval now. Matthew felt certain the glasses and the nose would fall right off his face.

"About Melanie Schwartz," he said.

"She rented the place under Holly Sinclair. I read in the papers her real name was Schwartz, but that's not the name she gave me when she took the house."

"Where was this, Mr. Epworth?"

"I have an office on Dune Road. She saw the For Rent sign outside the house, and drove over to the office."

"You don't use a real estate agent?"

"No. This is my work, this is what I do. I own these rental properties, and I look after them. It's just this small office, I have. No secretary, no receptionist, just me. It's what I do. She parked outside, came in, told me she'd seen the sign on Barrington and wanted to rent the house if it was still available. I told her it was, and she took it. Actually, it had just come free. Someone else had left a deposit on it, and then changed his plans about coming down. She was lucky." Epworth paused, and then said, "Well, maybe not so lucky, after all, huh?"

"Maybe not," Matthew said.

The fat lady had taken off the bathrobe and the scuffs.

She was wearing a flower-patterned maillot that made her look somewhat like a giant man-eating tropical plant. She waddled to the shallow end of the pool, came partially down the steps there, and dipped her toe in the water.

"Eighty-four," she called to Epworth. "Can you believe how cold!"

Epworth merely nodded.

"How much was she paying?" Matthew asked.

"Two thousand a month. I know that sounds like a lot, but it's on the beach, you know. And it's within walking distance of Sonny's. A lot of young people think that's a plus. Do you like rock music?"

"Some of it."

"I don't even think it's music," Epworth said.

"Some of it isn't."

"To me it sounds like they're practicing."

"You said she paid you in cash . . ."

"Yes. Hundred-dollar bills."

"You told Detective Bloom this wasn't unusual."

"That's right. Lots of young people don't have checking accounts. They work, they save their money, they hand it over when they're renting a place for a month or two. Not that she was that young."

"Too old for the rock crowd?" Matthew asked.

"In her mid-thirties, I'd say."

Peter Donofrio had told Guthrie and Warren that his girlfriend was twenty-six years old. The newspapers had corroborated this on the morning after her death.

"I think she was younger than that," Matthew said.

"Well, maybe so. But she didn't look it. Some of these bleached blondes, it makes them look older than they are."

Melanie changed her appearance a lot, you know. A blonde one day, a redhead the next.

What was she this time, Mr. Donofrio?

When she got here, she was a redhead.

And on Monday? When she left?

A blonde.

"This was when, Mr. Epworth?"

"This was when what? Look at her. It'll take her an hour to get in the water. A hundred and four, it could be, it'll still take her an hour to go down those steps."

"When she rented the house. When did you say that was?"

"January second. A Thursday."

"Are you sure she wasn't a redhead?"

"No. A redhead? No."

The woman had come to the bottom step now. Bending over, squeezing her eyes shut tight in anticipation, she splashed water onto her arms and her breasts.

"Go on," Epworth urged under his breath. "Go on."

The woman hesitated. The suspense was unbearable.

"Go!" Epworth whispered.

Like a luxury liner coming down the skids after a champagne launching, the woman floated off the bottom step and into the pool

"It's *freezing!*" she called to everyone.

Epworth turned to Matthew. "Eighty-four," he said, "it's freezing."

"Tell me what she looked like," Matthew said.

"Holly Sinclair? She was thirty-four, thirty-five years old. Blond hair to her shoulders. Blue eyes. Good suntan. Wearing a white cotton suit and white flats."

He had just described Jill Lawton.

*   *   *

Morris Epworth was still sitting at the pool when Toots found him at eleven that morning—his cold worse, he promptly told her, despite all the beneficial vitamin D he was absorbing from the goddamn sun. Matthew had supplied her with a black-and-white photo of Jill Lawton, and she showed that to Epworth now. The picture had appeared in the *Calusa Herald-Tribune* on the night after Ernest Corrington's body had been found. The caption read MISTAKEN WIDOW, such was the humor of newspaper headline writers. It showed a blonde with shoulder-length hair, rather casually dressed in jeans, sandals and a man's white tailored shirt. It had been taken outside the mortuary of Henley Hospital, where Jill Lawton had gone to identify the corpse of her then thought-to-be-dead husband. Matthew could have used the photo when he'd spoken to Epworth earlier this morning, but little had he known that another case of mistaken identity was just around the corner. Epworth studied the picture. Toots fully expected Jill Lawton to turn out to be missing twins or something, like a regular Shakespearean comedy. Some comedy, this one.

"Yep, that's her," Epworth said.

So there you were.

From where Warren Chambers was sitting in his battered blue Toyota, he could not see the Lawton house itself, but he could see the opening to the street on which it nestled among several other houses built in the late sixties, early seventies. He'd been informed by Matthew that Jill Lawton drove a white Dodge, and he had swung past the house before taking up position, ascertaining that her car was parked in the driveway. He then drove back to the end of the street, turned the corner, and planted himself facing the stop sign, where she'd have to brake before entering the main road. He'd have preferred parking right across the street from her house, but this was Southwest Florida, not the South Bronx. Even if the lady had never met him in her life, a sitting car was a sitting duck.

His car phone rang at a little past eleven.

He picked up at once, hit the SEND button.

"Hello?" he said.

"Warr? It's Toots."

"How'd it go?"

"She's the lady," Toots said.

"Okay, I'm here," Warren said.

The red Mercury did not appear at the crossroads until eleven thirty-five, heading west from the mainland, stopping to signal for a left-hand turn. The windshield was glossed with sunshine; Warren couldn't see the driver until he made the turn, and even then he wasn't sure. He started the Toyota at once and followed him up the street. The man was one of those drivers who kept an elbow halfway out the front window. He was wearing a pink shirt. The elbow beckoned like a flamingo. Even on this quiet private street, the man was driving fast. But Warren didn't think he'd lose him, so he kept a respectable distance behind him. When at last he pulled into the driveway alongside Jill Lawton's white Dodge, Warren hung back.

The man getting out of the car was Melanie Schwartz's no-good boyfriend, Peter Donofrio.

"It's nice of you to let me come here," he told Jill.

"I was curious," she said.

The man was wearing a polyester pink shirt and polyester

237

pink trousers. White shoes and pink socks. It was apparent he'd dressed up for the occasion. She wondered if she should offer him something to drink. It wasn't yet noon, but perhaps something light.

"Would you care for something to drink?" she asked. "A beer? A soda?"

"I'll have a beer, thanks," he said.

"Please sit down," she said, and went out to the kitchen. Opening the refrigerator door, lifting a bottle of beer from the rack above the vegetable tray, she wondered if there was anything to fear from Melanie's former boyfriend, who looked like a gorilla and dressed like an organ grinder's monkey.

She carried the bottle of beer and a glass out to him.

"Thank you," he said, and perched himself on the arm of an easy chair facing the sofa. He drank directly from the bottle, wiped the back of his hand across his mouth, and said, "You know Melanie, huh?"

"Yes," she said.

"I figured. I got my phone bill a few days ago. Somebody made six calls from my apartment to the number here between the seventeenth and the twentieth of this month. The somebody wasn't me. Then I remembered Melanie was down from St. Pete that weekend. So I called GTE, and they told me the number she called was listed to a person named Jill Lawton. That's why I got in touch with you."

"Why is that, Mr. Donofrio?"

"Cause apparently Melanie knew somebody named Jack Lawton, who everybody's been asking me about lately. You wouldn't happen to know anybody named Jack Lawton, would you?"

"Yes, he's my husband."

"Ah," Donofrio said.

He drank some more beer. The house went silent. In Florida, houses can become more still more suddenly than anywhere else on earth. In the silence, Jill waited.

"She met him up north, huh?" Donofrio said.

"If so, I know nothing about it."

"Well, your lawyer seems to think they knew each other up there. So I have to believe *somebody*, right?"

"Yes, but . . ."

"Matthew Hope *is* your lawyer, right?"

"Yes, he is."

"Well, his people came around to talk to me, and then he came around himself, and they all seem to think Melanie knew your husband up north. So why would they tell me she knew him if she didn't know him, am I right?"

"My husband and I have been separated for more than a year now," Jill said. "I don't know who he may have met up north. In fact, I've been trying to locate him so I can get a divorce."

"How'd *you* happen to meet her?" Donofrio asked.

"We met in a play-reading group."

Donofrio took another swallow of beer. "A good actress, right?" he said. "Melanie?"

"Very."

"Are you an actress, too?"

"No. I'm just interested in theater."

"She ever mention me?"

Careful, she thought.

"No, I don't recall her ever talking about you."

"Didn't say I was her boyfriend?"

"Didn't say anything at all about you."

"How well did you know her?"

239

"I told you. We were in a play-reading group together."

"Here? Or up north?"

"Here."

"Recently?"

"Fairly recently."

"When would that have been?"

"Earlier this month sometime."

"Must be why she called you that weekend, huh?"

"I really don't remember."

"Six times," he said. "You know she's dead, right?"

"Yes, I know she's dead."

"You know who *else* is gonna be dead?"

Jill said nothing.

"Whoever killed her. When I find him, he's gonna be dead. If you happen to see your husband one of these days . . ."

"I told you. I don't know where . . ."

"*If* you happen to see him. Tell him I'm gonna kill whoever killed Melanie. Will you tell him that for me? If you happen to see him?"

He drained the beer bottle, set it down emphatically on the end table beside the sofa. "Nice talking to you," he said, and went to the front door. He opened the door, hesitated with his hand on the doorknob, turned to her, and said, "By the way . . ." and then shook his head. "Never mind," he said, and walked out.

"What do *you* make of it?" Bloom asked.

"I'm not sure," Matthew said.

The two men were sitting in Bloom's corner office at the Calusa P.D. Building in what was familiarly known as Downtown Calusa, although in this city there was only

240

north, west, east and south with no proper uptown, downtown or crosstown as such. In strictest terms, Downtown
Calusa was in the northeast corner of the city, which in itself was in the south-southeastern angle of the three cities
that together formed the Calbrasa Triangle. Snowbirds
found it totally bewildering. Even the natives were sometimes confused.

This was three o'clock in the afternoon, and the air-
conditioning was going full blast, but both men were sitting
in their shirtsleeves.

"You say she's the one who rented the house in the dead
girl's name?"

"Positive ID," Matthew said.

"Who made it?"

"Morris Epworth. From a photo Toots showed him."

"And you say Mrs. Lawton was visited this morning by
the dead girl's boyfriend?"

"Peter Donofrio. Spent at least a half hour with her."

"So what the hell's going on here?"

"Donofrio's got a record, you know."

"You told me."

"And he had a gun in his possession when my investigators visited him."

"It wasn't a P38, was it?"

"No such luck," Matthew said, shaking his head. "A
Smith & Wesson. Chiefs Special."

"That's a parole violation right there. I can have him
picked up in a minute."

"But do you want to?"

"I don't know what I want to do," Bloom said. "Have
you brainstormed this with anyone else?"

"Guthrie thinks the two of them are in this together."

"Who? Donofrio and Mrs. Lawton?"

"Yes. He figures that's why he went to see her."

"He thinks they killed the girl together?"

"The girl *and* Corrington."

"Why? What's the motive? A penniless actress? An ex-con on parole in California? I don't see it, Matthew."

"Well, that's Guthrie's thinking."

"He must be getting old. What do Warren and Toots think?"

"That the husband's in it, too."

"The missing husband? Jack?"

"Yes."

"The *three* of them conspired to kill Corrington and the girl? Why?"

"I know it's weak."

"There's something we're not getting, Matthew."

"Maybe you ought to bring them both in."

"Donofrio's no problem, provided he's still got the piece. I can easily get a search warrant, and he's back in the slammer tomorrow morning. About the wife, I'm not so sure. I've got nothing tying her to either murder except her renting the house under the dead girl's name."

"There's another tie, Morrie."

"What's that?"

"Melanie was living with her husband."

"You know that for a fact?"

"Carella talked personally to the landlady . . ."

"Well, another police department in another city," Bloom said dismissively. "I go barging in, *he* doesn't have to answer to the state attorney down here."

"He also talked to people who knew the three of them

personally. This wasn't a tea party, Morrie. They were living together."

"*Which* three of them?"

"Jack, Corrington and Melanie."

"Donofrio know this?"

"He didn't seem to. Not when I spoke to him."

"The wife know it?"

"She told me she never met Melanie Schwartz."

"How about Holly Sinclair, whoever?"

"Her neither."

"But she rented the house in her name. And now the girl's dead."

"So's Corrington."

"For all we know, the husband's dead, too."

"That's a possibility."

"Which leaves only Jill Lawton."

"And Donofrio."

"Who happens to be the boyfriend of one of the victims."

"Yes."

"What the hell is missing, Matthew?"

"The P38," Matthew said. "Get a search warrant."

"No judge would grant it. I haven't got cause."

"She knew Melanie. She rented the house in her name."

"That doesn't mean she killed her. I'm telling you, Matthew, a petition will be denied."

"What have we got to lose?"

"Nothing but my reputation. Provided I can find a judge who isn't out on the golf course at four o'clock on a hot Friday afternoon. And provided he doesn't laugh in my face. Look, I'll try. If it doesn't work, I'll ask the captain for round-the-clock surveillance on her. Better than that, I can't do. But Matthew, my gut feeling is we're missing something in this thing, there's something big that ties this whole damn thing together, and we don't yet know what it is."

"We may *never* know," Matthew said, quoting a friend of his up north.

Bloom found a judge who wasn't on the golf course.

The judge said, "Nice try, Detective."

Candace was modeling the long blue gown she'd be wearing tomorrow night. Zaygo suggested she ought to wear a gold choker with it, but she told him the faux diamond earrings and necklace made a better statement. The three men were wearing tuxedos. Candace told them they all looked quite elegant. Even Harry, with his big hands and blocky body, looked better in a tuxedo than she might have expected.

Jack was the only one of the four who might possibly be recognized here in Calusa because he'd lived here for such a long time. Candace admitted that this might be a problem. She told him he should have grown a mustache or a beard or both, and he said he should have, but he hadn't thought of it, and it was too late now, the thing being tomorrow night and all. She suggested that he go buy a fake mustache at one of those places that sold costumes and theatrical makeup, there was one up on the North Trail, near the airport. He said he'd be scared to death the mustache would fall in his soup during the middle of dinner. She agreed that this, too, might be a problem. She was thinking she never should have got involved with a fucking amateur.

"How about coloring your hair?" she suggested. "I'll be happy to help you do that. If you think it might be a good idea."

"Yeah, that might work," he said.

"Be a blond," Zaygo said. "Blondes have more fun."

Harry agreed that would be an excellent idea.

This was now around nine o'clock on Friday night, the last day of the month. Tomorrow would be the first of February, the night of the benefit ball, the night of the heist. The men went upstairs to change out of their tuxedos and hang them up for tomorrow, and then sat around drinking while Candace drove over to the nearest Eckard's. She came back with a Clairol Hair Lightener Kit just as Zaygo and Harry were pulling out of the driveway.

"Aren't you going to stay for the big transformation?" she asked, but they both said they were tired, and tomorrow was a big day, and all that, and off they drove into the night.

She and Jack went into the upstairs bathroom, where she asked him to take off his shirt and then draped a towel over his shoulders. His natural hair color was what the chart on the side of the box identified as a Dark Brown. According to the instructions inside the box, in both English and Spanish, Jack would have to leave the lightener on for at least ninety minutes to achieve a soft and natural blond look. In the box, there were two plastic bottles, a plastic packet, and a plastic applicator tip. One of the bottles contained lightener developer. The other bottle contained creme lightener. The packet contained lightener activator. Candace had been here before. She poured the activator into the developer, added the creme to it, screwed on the applicator top, and pulled on a pair of plastic gloves.

"Say goodbye to dull, drab hair," she said, and began working on him.

An hour and a half later, he was in the shower. Ten minutes after that, he came out and looked at himself in the mirror. The wet hair looked darker than he had hoped. He wondered if they should have left the lightener mixture on longer. He blow-dried his hair and looked at himself again. It did indeed look blond and soft and natural. In fact, he felt like kissing himself. He looked rather like a young poet, he thought. He wondered if that was good. He put on a terry robe and went downstairs to where Candace was waiting.

"Beautiful," she said.

"I need eyeglasses," he said. "Eyeglasses will provide the finishing touch."

"Do you wear glasses?"

"No."

"We'll get some at the drugstore tomorrow."

"Yes, good," he said. "I don't look too faggoty, do I?"

"No, you look like a very handsome blond man."

"I'll drink to that," he said, and mixed a pitcher of martinis.

They were sitting outside on the patio, talking quietly, sipping their martinis when he told her this woman he'd known real well had been killed Monday night. "I hope it didn't have anything to do with the heist," he said.

"What do you mean?" she asked. Whenever he said anything like that, it reminded her that he was nothing but a rank amateur, and she started getting nervous. "How could it have anything to do with the heist?"

"Well, she knew about it," he said.

"You *told* her about it?"

"Well, we were close."

Candace controlled herself from yelling at this jackass. Instead, she patiently and quietly explained that the cardinal rule of stealing anything was you never told a soul about it, not even your mother. This applied whether the object or objects to be stolen were a blind man's pencils, or the cup the pencils came in, or even, as was the present case, the cup from which Socrates had drunk his fatal draught, so to speak. All very calmly, all very patiently. But inside she was thinking it was a good thing someone had killed the broad, whoever she was, because it meant one less loose tongue to wag.

"Also," Jack said, "the gun is missing."

"The gun? What gun?"

"Corry's gun. A P38 Walther."

"What's that got to do . . . ?"

"Well, the newspaper said she was killed with a Walther."

Candace nodded. Boy oh boy, she was thinking, how'd I get into *this* one?

"I told Melanie I hid it in the toilet tank . . ."

"You hid it in the toilet tank."

"Yes, but that doesn't mean it's the same gun. The gun that killed her could've been *any* Walther."

And I could be the Queen of Sheba, Candace thought.

Her plan tomorrow night was to wait till Zaygo and Harry were paid off and gone, share a little farewell nightcap with Mr. Lawton here, and then stick the Browning automatic in his face and ask him to please hand over the cup. She didn't think there'd be any problem with him. Amateurs were amateurs.

"Well," she said, "I'd better get along."

"Three bedrooms here, you know," he said.

She looked at him.

Smiled in faint recognition.

Shook her head.

"See you tomorrow," she said.

"Sleep well," he said, and raised his glass in a reluctant farewell.

★   ★   ★

Melanie and Jill have chosen the house here on Sabal for two reasons.

To begin with, they cannot meet at the house Jack and Jill used to share on Whisper Key. He'd lived there, he knew Jill was still living there, all he needed to discover was that the two girls, as he used to call them, were still seeing each other. Figure *that* out, and the next step is Hey, the girls are going to steal the cup from me after I go to all the trouble of taking it from the museum. So it's necessary to keep him in the dark until he is permanently in the dark.

(They still aren't quite accustomed to the idea that they are going to kill him on the night they nab the cup, and so they tend to think in terms of mild euphemisms like "out of the loop" or "no longer connected" or even, yes, the somewhat stronger "permanently in the dark," which is to tell the truth a bit morbid.)

Second thing is they need a place to stash the cup after Jack has checked out, another euphemism. There is no doubt in their minds that the first person the police will come to visit after they discover his body—

Well, there you are.

Body.

Meaning corpse.

Meaning dead man.

Some things just can't be escaped, can they?

On Saturday night, the first of February, the night of the benefit preceding the official opening of the exhibit, if all goes as planned that night, then Jack Lawton will be a dead man. And on that night, or certainly as soon as the body is found, the police will come knocking on Jill's door to ask all sorts of questions about her deceased spouse. And if perchance the police have somehow connected Mr. Lawton to the museum heist, they will undoubtedly search the Whisper Key premises for the stolen cup, which just might put a crimp in the girls' plans to turn it over to Miklos Panagos for a cool two million four the very next day.

Ergo the cup—*and* Melanie—have to be someplace else, and the rickety little rented house on Barrington Street is as good a place as any to be—or *not* to be, as the case will turn out to be, though neither of the women knows this at five P.M. this Monday afternoon, five days before the impending heist and intended murder. Jill is here to discuss the travel arrangements she's made for both of them. They plan to leave for Southeast Asia on February ninth. This is already the twenty-seventh of January, and the clock is ticking. Happily, their passports are in order—Melanie's still carries the Schwartz monicker but she hasn't yet legally changed her name to Holly Sinclair, so that won't be a problem—and luckily American Express allows Jill to charge unlimited amounts so long as she pays her bills on time. That's a nice thing about American Express, though in other ways they're as much a pain in the ass as all the other credit card companies.

After February second, when they turn the cup over to the Greek, each of the women will be independently wealthy, if you can consider a million and some change wealthy. The trip to Southeast Asia is going to cost a pretty penny, but the brochure makes it seem well worth the price. On February ninth, they fly to Tokyo, where they connect with a flight to Bangkok, arriving there on the eleventh, go figure international date lines. On the thirteenth, they will board the Eastern & Oriental Express for Malaysia, rolling luxuriously southward along the beautiful coastline of the

Gulf of Thailand, crossing the bridge on the River Kwai, having their fortunes told by an on-board astrologer, continuing steadily southward through mountain and rain forest to Hat Yai, an hour from the Malaysian border . . .

"Where noisy food vendors crowd the platform as trains pull to a halt," Jill quotes from the brochure, "and the pungent fragrances of dried fish, fruits, lemongrass and barbecued meats swirl through the station."

"Oh God," Melanie says, "I can't wait."

On Valentine's Day, they will board an evening flight to Singapore. And from there, in the days to follow, they will travel to Indonesia, stopping in Jakarta and Yogyakarta before moving on to Bali, where they will look for a house to rent . . .

"Why not *buy* one?" Melanie asks.

"Why not? We'll be *rich!*"

They had not yet discussed how they will 'cashier' old Jack Lawton, as the British Army might have put it when they were still running the show in Singapore.

Melanie shows her the gun at around, oh, it must be six o'clock or so, a little after six o'clock. It looks like every German pistol Jill has ever seen in every World War II movie on television, as sleek and as efficient-looking as a fucking storm trooper. It is the gun they will use to kill Jack. Melanie uses the word at last.

"It's Corry's gun," she says. "We'll use it to kill Jack."

The room goes silent. Melanie gets up to put another CD on the player, moving toward the wall unit. Jill is sitting directly in front of the unit. She watches Melanie as she approaches. She is wearing nothing but an ivory-colored silk slip. She looks young and fresh and eminently desirable. Jill suddenly wonders if they still make love together, Melanie and Jack, out there in the house he's renting on Santa Lucia Island. Now that Corry has bought the farm, so to speak, do Melanie and Jack . . .

Ravel's *Bolero* insinuates itself into the room.

"Who kills him?" Jill asks.

"It's your turn, isn't it?" Melanie says, and sits again, stretching her legs.

"I guess so."

They are sitting opposite each other. The gun is on an end table alongside Melanie's easy chair. "Let me see it," Jill says, and Melanie hands it to her. The polished blue finish gives it an extremely lethal appearance. The plastic grip feels cool to her touch. She aims it across the room at the lamp behind Melanie's chair, sighting along the barrel.

"Pa-*kuh,* pa-*kuh,* pa-*kuh,*" she goes, like a kid playing cops and robbers.

Melanie giggles, pulls up her knees, hugs herself.

The Ravel choruses are becoming imperceptibly louder.

"Are you still sleeping with him?" Jill asks.

"Who?"

"Jack. Who. Who do you think I mean who?"

"Yeah," Melanie says. "I love this. Don't you love this? Do you remember that movie where they play this in a big seduction scene?"

"Yes. Why are you still sleeping with him?"

"*10.* The movie. With Britt Ekland."

"Bo Derek."

"Right. Whatever happened to her?"

"Mel? Why are you still sleeping with him?"

"Because we're supposed to be in this together."

"We are in it together."

"I mean me and Jack. He still thinks we're in this together. We *killed* a man together, we . . ."

"*You're* the one killed Corry."

"I know, but we put him in the car together, we drove
him to the beach together, Jack still thinks we're in this *together.*"

"Are you?"

"Am I what?"

"In this with Jack? Together?"

"Of course not. I'm in it with you."

"Then why are you still sleeping with him?"

"What is this, can you please tell me?"

"I want to know why, when we're planning to kill him
six days from now . . ."

"Five days from now."

"How*ever* the fuck many days from now, you're still
sleeping with him. Why is that, Mel? We're going to kill
him and steal the fucking cup from him, and sell it to a
fucking crazy Greek and run off together to the fucking
end of the world and you are *still* fucking him, why is that,
Mel, can you tell me why that is?"

"Stop waving the gun around, okay?"

"Just tell me why."

"You're making me nervous, stop waving it around."

"First you steal him from me . . ."

"Hey, come on, Jill, I didn't steal . . ."

"You *stole* him from me!"

Ravel is very loud now. The music has somehow snuck
up on them, moving relentlessly from a quietly insistent
theme to what is now a relentlessly repetitive strain. And
suddenly, something goes wrong with the disc, or the
player, or both, and the riff becomes maddeningly repeti-

tious, clicking and repeating, clicking and repeating, and Melanie suddenly shoves herself out of the easy chair.

"Jesus!" she shouts, and angrily lunges for the wall unit, going for the player, wanting to stop the music, but Jill thinks she's coming for her, Jill thinks she's reaching for the gun. Melanie realizes this a moment too late, realizes that an irrevocable act is about to be committed here, and she yells "Don't!" at exactly the same moment Jill yells it, but Jill's "Don't!" means "Back off!" and Melanie's "Don't!" means "Don't *shoot!*" too late, too fucking late, the gun goes off.

Melanie flies back and away from where Jill still sits leaning forward in front of the wall unit and its maddeningly stuck player, red blooming in a frightening splash on the front of the slip. And then, as if she herself is a part of the rhythm, as insistent as the percussion and brass, Jill rises from where she is sitting, firing again as she comes toward Melanie, who has fallen back into the chair, hypnotized by the blood bursting onto the slip, brass casing flying, another squeeze of the trigger, again, and now there is only the sound of Ravel.

"Melanie?" she whispers.

Click. Riff.

"Mel?"

B̲ecause there were so many inconsiderate felons in the city for which Carella worked, he could not leave for the museum until the shift was relieved at a quarter to four that Saturday afternoon. And because it had begun snowing heavily again, and traffic was already snarled in the streets, he did not actually get to ISMA until a quarter to five. The woman he'd spoken to on the phone told him she'd be there until six. She was waiting for him when he arrived.

Her name was Polly Erdman. She reminded him of the girl who used to run the slide projector in his art appreciation class when he was still a gangly teenager at Andrew Jackson High School in Riverhead. Same dark hair, same narrow face with a rather sharp nose, same mischievous blue eyes and cryptic smile that hinted at all the secrets of the universe.

Back then at the Big A, as Jackson High was affectionately known, he'd thought he might become a painter one

255

day. Not a guy who did ceilings and walls, but a real . . .
well . . . artist. He'd also thought, back then when he was
seventeen, that he might be in love with Ruth Kaplan, for
such was the name of the girl throwing images of famous
paintings onto a beaded screen set up at the front of the auditorium. But Ruth explained that her parents were Ortho-
dox Jews who would never accept a Catholic like him in the
family. The irony, of course, was that while he was in the
service, he lost all faith in any God who could allow such
carnage, and decided at the same time that upholding the
laws of civilization—so contrary to the laws of warfare—
might be a higher calling than smearing paint on canvas or
shaping wet clay.

If Polly Erdman didn't know where the body was buried,
she certainly knew where the shovel was. "Here at the Isola
Museum of Art," she said. "we *pride* ourselves on our wide
variety of special exhibits. We get art on loan from all over
the world, and if I may be permitted to wallow in self-
flattery for a moment, we mount our exhibits more beautifully than any other museum in America."

Sounded like Ruth Kaplan, too.

Ruth in the Booth, the other guys used to call her. Because she worked the slide projector from a booth at the
back of the auditorium. Love to get Ruth alone in that
booth, they used to say, embarrassing him because he liked
her so much.

They were walking on white marble floors along corri-
dors hung with paintings Carella should have recognized
but didn't. Polly was wearing black low-heeled shoes with
laces, and a rather short black mini that contradicted the librarian image. Her heels clattered on the marble. She was a
fast walker. He almost had difficulty keeping up.

"We rarely get the police here, except when they're tracing a forgery," she said. "There are a great many art forgeries, you know."

"Yes," he said.

"But your request is a peculiar one, I must say. I can't imagine why you'd want to see the printed material that accompanied an exhibit."

"Well, as I told you on the phone," he said, "these people seemed attracted to this notice about the Socrates Cup, and I was wondering what caught their attention."

"The bio card," she said, and nodded.

"Sorry?"

"We call it a bio card. The information we post about the artist, or the exhibit, or anything we think will be of interest to the viewing public. But as I said earlier, with a traveling exhibit like the Agoran Trove, the sponsor usually supplies the printed matter that accompanies the show."

"Was that the case here?"

"If memory serves. Then again, it's a long, long way from Greece. Poster and placards can get soiled or damaged, and often need to be replaced along the tour. Perhaps that happened here. If so, if the material was ISMA-generated, we may have it stored downstairs. Here we are," she said, and stopped before a locked door, and began searching for a key on a ring.

Carella was thinking that two of the people who'd shared the information on that bio card were now dead. The other one was missing. He wanted to know what that information was.

Polly unlocked the door, swung it open, reached for a wall switch, and snapped on a light. "Be careful," she said, "the steps are rather steep."

The steps had open risers and iron rungs, like the ones that led to the upper floors of the station house. But these steps led below at a much sharper angle, and he gripped the railing tightly as he followed her down. She snapped another switch at the bottom of the stairs, illuminating a vast storage room defined by wooden divider racks into which had been slipped black portfolios of various sizes. These all had string ties on each of three sides, and were meticulously hand-labeled, as might have been expected in a museum.

"We keep the posters of every show we do. If any printed material was saved from the exhibit, it'll be in the same portfolio. They're supposed to be filed alphabetically, but good luck," she said, and smiled a smile so reminiscent of Ruth's he almost asked her to go down to the corner ice cream parlor for a banana split.

The S file started with racks labeled SA-SC and then continued into the next row with SE-SI and from there to SJ-SO, where he surfed past portfolios for subjects as varied as an artist named Lars Erik Sjövall and a show titled Slave Coast Sculpture and another titled Slovakian Woodcraft and yet another titled Socialist Party Propaganda Posters and one titled Society Island Pottery, another for an artist named Antonio Solovari—and thought he might have missed an SOC portfolio, but he hadn't, there was nothing labeled Socrates Cup.

Feeling like a man being shunted from pillar to post in the Yellow Pages, he walked to the A racks, Polly Erdman tapping along behind him in her short skirt and laced black shoes, and quickly found the AF-AK section of portfolios. A disappointingly slender one was labeled AGORAN TROVE.

"Okay to open this?" he asked.

"Go right ahead," she said.

He loosened the ties.

There was a large poster showing a terra-cotta cup tilted on its side to reveal the letters ΣΟΚ scratched into its bottom. Headlining the poster were the words THE SOCRATES CUP. Running along the bottom edge of the poster were the words THE AGORAN TROVE— NOVEMBER 9–15. A smaller version of the poster was in a separate plastic slipcase. Another slipcase contained commentary printed on a white board some twelve inches wide by eighteen inches long.

"The bio card," Polly said.

Carella read it:

THE SOCRATES CUP

In ancient Greece, those convicted of crimes were not usually sentenced to lengthy imprisonment. Instead, they were either put to death, exiled, or fined. Many important personages were held in the excavated building now generally accepted by scholars as the state prison. Socrates was one of them.

In the year 399 B.C., he met his death through execution by poison. During recent excavations, thirteen small clay medicine bottles were found in an abandoned cistern. One of them was marked with the letters ΣΟΚ, undoubtedly an abbreviation for Sokrates, as it was spelled in antiquity. A small statue of the philosopher was found elsewhere in the ruins.

The cup and accompanying treasures have been traveling extensively across the United States. When the exhibit leaves ISMA on November 16, it will move first to the Corcoran Gallery of Art in Washington, D.C., next to the High Museum of Art in Atlanta, Georgia, and then to the Ca D'Ped in Calusa, Florida.

"Calusa, Florida," Carella said aloud.

★   ★   ★

The windshield of his car was covered with ice and snow and shmutz. The plastic scraper snapped in two when he applied it too forcefully, and he was compelled to finish the job with the back of his gloved hand. It was the first day of February and there was already a foot of snow in the streets. He drove slowly and carefully and did not get to the house in Riverhead until ten minutes past six. The kids were watching television and Teddy was in the kitchen. He took her in his arms and kissed her and then grumbled into her hair about all the goddamn snow out there. He told her he had to make a call to Florida, kissed the kids on his way to the den, and immediately dialed Matthew's home number. The message on the machine asked any caller to please leave a message at the beep.

"Hi, this is Steve Carella up here in the frozen North," he said. "I don't know if this is of any use to you, but your three people seemed very interested in something called the Socrates Cup, which was moving down to the Ca D'Ped, if that's how you pronounce it, after museum stops in Washington and Atlanta. I'm sorry, but I don't have any dates. Anyway, let me know if it helps. Talk to you."

At that very moment, Matthew was twenty feet from the front door of his house, backing his car out of the driveway.

The Ca D'Ped was glittering with tiny white lights strung in the trees leading to the entrance door. To protect the delicate satin slippers of dainty maidens in long gowns, a literal red carpet, some four feet wide, stretched from the valet station to the massive entrance doors. This was where the Range Rovers and the Benzes and the Continentals and the Beemers and even one Rolls-Royce pulled up to disgorge a horde of dazzling bejeweled women and tuxedoed men—*black* tuxedos, mind you. This was still winter, albeit winter in Florida, and white dinner jackets would not reappear until May. Merry and anticipative, they were here tonight to sip and sup after viewing in advance the cruddy little cup from which Socrates had allegedly swallowed his last baneful dollop. The cup was valued at somewhere between two and three million dollars, a sum many of these people could bandy about with ease. They had each paid a thousand dollars a plate for the privilege of standing in the presence of the spotlighted cup, its bottom upended to reveal the letters ΣΟΚ scratched into the clay. Most of them ooohed and ahhed in wondrous delight and then wandered out into the museum's main exhibition hall, grandly named the Louis P. Landsman Salon, to order cocktails from the open bar and to visit with other similarly dazzling and bedazzled residents of this town besotted on its own cultural pretensions.

Frank Summerville was unimpressed.

He told this to Matthew the moment he walked through the door, a blonde on one arm, a brunette on the other. Upon closer inspection—Matthew's partner was a bit nearsighted—the women turned out to be the most beautiful state attorney in all Florida and the most beautiful former wife any man could choose to have, old lucky Pierre here.

"To me, the cup looks like something a kid might bring home from his first-grade clay-modeling class," Frank said.

Matthew hadn't yet seen the cup. Frank was drinking a martini. Matthew was thirsty. He was also uncomfortable. He did not enjoy escorting two women who held no particular fondness for each other. The conversation in the car on the way over had been strained at best. He could not un-

261

derstand why Patricia had suggested they invite Susan along. He could not understand why Susan had accepted. He could not understand why Frank's wife, Leona, was wearing an emerald-green gown that exposed virtually all of her left breast but the nipple. Maybe he did not understand women.

He certainly did not understand ancient Greek cups.

He could find nothing of beauty in the misshapen clay tumbler spotlighted behind thick glass, and he could find nothing of historical value in it, either, perhaps because he didn't believe for a single minute that this was the actual cup Socrates had held in his hand back then in 399 B.C., reduced from 400.

He was very happy to lead both ladies out to the salon and to order for Patricia a Tanqueray martini, straight up and very cold, and for Susan a rum-Coke (was she trying to recall for them their early courtship back in Chicago?) and for himself a Beefeater martini on the rocks with a pair of olives, please.

"Cheers," the women said, and looked each other dead in the eye and clinked glasses.

The night was young.

Jill Lawton knew where her husband was tonight because up until the moment of her death, Melanie had been part of the planning and part of the scheme. She knew old Jack the Big-Time Museum Thief was at the Ca D'Ped, ready to steal a priceless cup—well, priceless to one Miklos Panagos, anyway. Sometime between twelve-thirty and one A.M., a boat driven by someone with the improbable name of Zaygo would pick up Jack and his cohorts and take them by boat to the house he'd rented on Santa Lucia Island.

Jill planned to arrive at the house after all the others had left. 26 Land's End Road, thank you for that, too, Melanie, you should not have acted so impulsively. At gunpoint, she would relieve Jack of the cup and shoot him dead. She knew how to use the Walther. She had used it only once before, but if you truly loved someone, once was sufficient. Kill one dearly beloved and the next one was easy.

There was only one problem.

If she was not mistaken, the Chevrolet sedan parked just up the street had been there since dusk, and she felt certain the two men in it were watching her house.

Candace Knowles and Jack Lawton made a spectacularly handsome couple, if they did say so themselves. Candace looked ravishing in her long ice-blue gown with its daring bodice and snug hips, the skirt slit high on her left thigh to afford easy leggy access to the pickup boat later. High-heeled glittery blue pumps, long hair piled on her head in a seemingly careless upswept coif, faux diamond pendant earrings, a faux diamond necklace, oh my but she turned heads. Jack was no less resplendent in his sleek tuxedo with its black satin lapels and stripes and his black patent-leather dancing slippers, newly acquired blond hair swept boyishly across his forehead, plano eyeglasses purchased from a rack at the local drugstore giving him a thoughtful scholarly vulnerable look, oh how the girls lusted.

They viewed the cup without apparent interest, and then walked out into the Louis P. Landsman Salon, where at the bar they each ordered a Perrier and lime because clear heads made for clean thefts. In what had once been the mansion's ballroom, there now floated the sound of big band music. It was only seven-thirty. The night was still young.

"Cheers," she said.

"Cheers," he said, and they clinked glasses.

Apparently, no one had ever told them that toasting with nonalcoholic drinks was bad luck.

Out on the grounds, Harry Jergens walked about in his tuxedo, seemingly enjoying a cigarette, but actually checking out the location of the security guards.

As Candace had reported, there were only two of them. One had a Doberman on a leash. Both of them were carrying long torchlights. Each of them, like himself, was enjoying a cigarette here in the balmy Florida night under the moonlit palms.

The guards would not really go to work until everyone left and the museum was closed for the night.

By that time, they would both be dead.

The fuckin dog, too.

He would never understand what prompted Patricia to choose tonight to break this to him, but once she'd blurted it, he completely understood why she'd encouraged him to invite Susan along. They were circling the dance floor to the tune of "Dancing in the Dark," or "I'll Walk Alone" or "You Made Me Love You," or one of those ballads of the forties that all sounded alike to Matthew, whose meaningful songs came later. The rich old folk on the floor were doing what they called the "fox-trot" but what Matthew and Patricia called "close dancing," when all at once she started telling him how lovely Susan looked tonight and what a lovely person she was and how glad she was that Matthew had thought of inviting her along (which he hadn't, by the way) and then, out of the blue, she said, "Why do you think Charles doesn't have a sense of humor?"

"Charles who?" he asked.

"Charles Foster, you *know* Charles who."

"I'm sorry, I didn't. And he doesn't."

"He does."

"I've never seen a trace of it."

"I'm going to marry him," Patricia said.

"Dinner is served," someone announced.

Zaygo must have gone over the boat a hundred times, making sure the gas tank was full, making sure nothing was going to quit on them tonight after the cup was safe in their hands. All he wanted was a nice smooth run from the museum dock to Santa Lucia. Drop off the parties, pick up his pay, and adios.

This was the worst part of it.

The waiting.

He wasn't due at the dock until around twelve-thirty.

It was now only eight thirty-five.

It was going to be a long night.

From where Detective Hazlitt and his partner Detective Rawles sat in the Chevy up the street, they saw Jill Lawton coming out of her house and walking briskly toward the white Dodge parked in her driveway.

"She's moving," Rawles said.

"I see her."

They waited.

The Dodge started, backed out of the driveway and into the street. She was coming their way. They slid down deep into their seats, below the window line, waited till her headlights swept past. Rawles started the car, and they pulled out after her.

Sitting at the intersection in his red Mercury, Peter Donofrio saw first Jill Lawton's white Dodge stop at the corner and make a right turn and then, some three car lengths back, two guys who could be nothing but cops following her.

He joined the parade.

"Don't lose her," Hazlitt said.

"You want to drive?"

"Just don't lose her."

Jill was driving eastward, toward the mainland. The car was white, it was a simple thing to keep her in sight. She went over the south Whisper Key Bridge, made a right turn onto the Trail, and continued driving south toward Sarasota. At the traffic light on the corner of 41 and Raintree, she made a left turn and then a sharp right into the Raintree Mall. This was a busy parking lot. They stayed close.

"Parking," Hazlitt said.

"I see it," Rawles said.

They drove past her just as she cut the engine.

"Keep an eye on her," Rawles said.

"Got her," Hazlitt said.

Rawles parked the Chevy a few cars down. It normally took a woman driver longer to get out of a car than it took a man. After she'd cut the engine, she had to fix her lipstick, fluff up her hair, make herself ready for a grand exit. Both detectives were out of their car long before she emerged from the Dodge. She was wearing blue jeans and sneakers, a blue cotton sweater. Like the white car, her blond hair was a beacon. They followed her into the mall.

"Shit, she's catching a nine-thirty movie," Hazlitt said.

"So are we," Rawles said.

Matthew was drinking too much wine.

That was because it was very difficult to enjoy one's dinner when the woman on your right was studiously avoiding you after having told you she was going to marry a man singularly lacking in a sense of humor, who happened to be sitting opposite you at the same long table, grinning a goofy smile while on your left there was another woman who was telling you that you and she never should have divorced, that she enjoyed the best sex in the world with you even though at times you were a son of a bitch, it was exceedingly difficult. There were times when Matthew wished he had never come out of the coma.

On the other hand, it was now well past ten o'clock and this evening would eventually end, and tomorrow the sun was gonna come up, betcha bottom dollar. Or maybe not. Either way, the police were now handling this case, which was perhaps as it should have been from the beginning. And if Matthew played his cards right, he would get a good night's sleep tonight for the first time in a long time. And by the way, how come a lady who's going to ditch you laughs at a joke about an oversize penis while lying naked in bed with you shortly before she kisses you off?

He did not know, of course, that two people intent on stealing the Socrates Cup were at that very moment ensconcing themselves in the basement supply closet not twenty feet from the door to a room containing the museum's high-security vault.

He poured himself another glass of chardonnay.

In the small closet, the scent of her perfume was overwhelming.

It was very good perfume. Tomorrow, when the sun came up, you betcha, Lawton would exchange the poison goblet for the remainder of the two million five Panagos owed him, and from that moment on he would be able to afford all the aromatic oils of Araby.

To lull him into complacency in preparation for what was to come later tonight, Candace silkily rubbed herself against him a little.

Jack almost forgot he was here to steal a cup.

The dog's name was Helmutt, spelled with a double-t at the end, lest anyone think Germans did not have a fine sense of humor. Helmutt was a fine Nazi bastard of a Doberman dog, capable of ripping a man apart limb by limb at the slightest provocation or the merest kill command. The only danger he couldn't handle was a pistol with a silencer attached to its muzzle.

Harry Jergens took out the pooch in two seconds flat.

Phh, phh, like whispers on the night.

The security guard, whose name was Ernest, looked earnestly surprised, but perhaps that was because Harry went *phh, phh* twice again.

Insects rattled in the tall grass.

The reason Harry liked to shoot people dead was so they couldn't later give accurate testimony at a trial. He dragged both carcasses into the bushes, and went to look for the second security guard, who did not have the benefit of canine protection.

"She's leaving," Hazlitt whispered.

"So are we," Rawles whispered.

They were sitting some four or five rows behind Jill Lawton, and they rose in immediate response to her imminent departure, both of them working their way out to the aisle over the protests of many outraged moviegoers because Sylvester Stallone was just about to kill forty bad guys in a richly comic sequence.

They raced out to the lobby just in time to see the door to the ladies' room closing behind Jill

"Hell, she only has to pee," Hazlitt said.

Out on Calusa Bay, Zane Gorman, alias Zaygo, had to pee. He debated dropping anchor while he went below to the head, decided that would be too much trouble, unzipped and pissed over the side instead.

Luckily for him, the wind was blowing in the right direction.

So far.

Matthew Hope had to pee.

Susan was telling him he ought to come home with her tonight since it seemed obvious that the Demming woman was paying far more attention to the humorless guy with the mustache across the table than to Matthew himself who was, after all, her escort, or at least half her escort.

Matthew poured Susan some more chardonnay.

"What do you think?" she asked.

"The night is young," he said mysteriously, and poured himself another glass as well.

The second security guard was sixty-eight years old, and he had been an accountant in Michigan before he retired and came down to Florida. He had soon grown tired of hanging about in the sun all day, and had taken a series of meaningless part-time jobs until he landed *this* meaningless part-time job at the museum. Oliver Hong, for such was his name because he happened to be Chinese, had never fired a gun in his lifetime, and would not have known what to do if his torchlight perchance illuminated an intruder on the museum grounds.

In fact, he *did* not know what to do when this great big guy materialized out of the bushes and pointed a pistol at his head, which gun had a longer barrel than any gun Oliver had ever seen in his life, which only gun was the one in the holster at his hip.

"Hey," he said reasonably, and tilted the torch into the man's face.

This might have blinded Harry, but fortunately he was already squeezing the trigger. He dragged Oliver off the tree-shrouded path and into the bushes. Courteously, he snapped off the torchlight, and looked at the luminous dial of his watch.

My, how the time did fly.

The window in the ladies' room was painted shut.

Try as she might, Jill could not pry it open. In half an hour or so, Jack and his makeshift gang would be stealing the goddamn cup. It was a forty-minute drive out to the end of Santa Lucia Island. She wanted to get there shortly after Jack's crew left. But she didn't want to get there with a police escort. So what to do?

She was staring at herself in the mirror over the sink when a fat woman wearing a bright green dress, and an orange kerchief that tried vainly to cover the curlers in her hair, came plodding out of one of the stalls, pulling the back of her dress down over her bloomers.

"Is it over yet?" she asked. "I hate Sylvester Stallone."

In the closet, Jack whispered, "What time is it?"

The closet door was cracked a fraction of an inch so that they could monitor what was happening out there on the lounge level. Candace was wearing a delicate gold watch with a tiny dial, but in the narrow wedge of light the time showed clearly.

"Ten past eleven," she said.

"Shouldn't Harry be here by now?"

"Give him time."

"I mean, he's supposed to be our takee-outee man."

Takee-outee man, she thought.

If this thing went off as planned with a jackass like Jack leading the way, she would never again doubt there was a Santa Claus.

From where Hazlitt and Rawles stood near the candy counter, they saw a fat lady in a bright green dress and white sneakers come waddling out of the ladies' room. The woman wore an orange kerchief over her head, and she was blowing her nose as she went to the exit doors and shoved herself out into the night. They paid her scant attention.

They were beginning to think Jill Lawton had climbed out the bathroom window.

* * *

Peter Donofrio knew better than to follow anybody into a mall when two cops were tailing her. So he'd parked the red Mercury two rows back of Jill Lawton's white Dodge, and now he sat there waiting for her to come back.

At 11:15 by his digital dashboard clock—oops, 11:16 already—a fat lady in a green dress and an orange kerchief walked up to the Dodge, unlocked the door on the driver's side, and got in.

Donofrio thought it was hilarious that some fat broad was boosting the lady's wheels.

Then he saw her rip the orange kerchief from her head, and lo and behold, there was the blond and beauteous Jill Lawton, and the Dodge started, and so did the Mercury.

Matthew was bidding good night to Patricia and her someday groom Charles, while Susan stood by patiently in her red gown, which was his favorite color, a faint triumphant smile on her face, though he wasn't yet quite sure what would happen tonight except that he would drive her home since that was where he'd picked her up and he was, after all, a gentleman albeit one running several sheets to the wind, he recognized. Being a gentleman, and knowing when a love affair was over, he did not attempt to kiss Patricia good night. Being a gentleman, he shook hands with her, and said, "Good night, Patricia," not goodbye, and not Pat, which name he knew she despised.

"Good night, Matthew," she said, and he thought he detected a faint wistful note in her voice, a faint glimmer of nostalgia in her eyes, for what he could not imagine.

He had to pee, and he wanted to get downstairs before they locked up the men's room and turned out the lights.

★   ★   ★

There were three of them in the closet now.

Candace wasn't rubbing up against anyone anymore.

Instead, she was listening intently for the elevator that would be transporting downstairs the wheeled case containing the Socrates Cup. She was carrying in her little beaded blue purse a Browning .25-caliber automatic, but neither Jack nor Harry knew this, nor did she wish anyone to know it until she shoved the gun in Jack's face later tonight.

"Shhh," she said.

She had heard voices.

The party upstairs was breaking up.

People were coming down to use the rest rooms.

In just a short while, the Socrates Cup would be transported to its safe resting place for the night.

It appeared as if Jill Lawton was driving her white Dodge out onto the very end of Sabal Key, where a bridge connected it to Santa Lucia Island. Peter Donofrio didn't know why she was heading out there at this hour of the night, but he figured if a lady had a rendezvous someplace, the rendezvous might be with her husband, who in his heart of hearts Donofrio knew had killed his beloved Melanie Schwartz.

Donofrio wasn't quite the amateur either Jack or Jill was. He had, after all, taken two falls and was perhaps heading for a third if his parole officer ever found out he had purchased a .38 Smith & Wesson, with which he planned to *off* Mr. Jack-Off if ever he *found* the son of a bitch. Semiprofessional that he was, Donofrio was already thinking ahead to how he could make this look like the *wife* had done Jack.

273

Maybe do them both and press the gun into her hand like they did in the movies. He did not know that she, too, had a gun, or that she, too, planned to kill her husband. Such a blatantly amateur idea would never have occurred to him. Donofrio may have been unlucky in his life of crime, but he was nonetheless neither a beginner nor a dilettante.

Another thing he didn't know was that Jill Lawton had already committed murder, whereas he himself had never in his lifetime killed so much as a water rat. Had he known that the woman in the car ahead had not too long ago pumped four big ones into the chest of another woman, he might have gone home instead of continuing his relentless pursuit. On the other hand, had he known that her victim had been none other than Melanie Schwartz, sitting in a goddamn slip *he* himself had given her this Christmas past, he might have stepped on the gas even harder and done a fucking drive-by shooting, had he but known.

But he didn't.

On this balmy February night, there were a lot of people who knew nothing at all.

So Donofrio kept a good distance behind the Dodge because he didn't want her to pick up his headlights in her mirror and realize she was not alone on this pitch-black road leading straight into the bowels of Hell, God forgive me.

Matthew was standing at one of the urinals in the men's room when he heard the door opening and a museum guard shouting, "Anyone in here? Last call!"

"Out in a minute," he said.

"Hurry it up, please, sir, we're closing, sir."

"Be upstairs in a minute," Matthew said.

The door closed behind him.

★　　★　　★

Out on the water, Zaygo went past the dock yet another time, waiting for the flashlight signal that would tell him they had the cup and were heading across the lawn with it.

There was nothing.

There were two museum guards inside the Ca D'Ped. Neither of them was armed. This was Calusa, Florida, and this had been a benefit showing, and each guard had served "more as a . . . what would you call him?" Dr. Oberling had asked rhetorically. "A guide? A friendly presence?" The only *un*friendly presences, the armed guards outside on the grounds, were both dead. This would have been a different story here if either of the inside guards knew what the other one was doing, but on this night of a thousand nights, nobody knew nothing from nothing.

That is to say, the guard who advised Susan that the building was clear and that perhaps her husband had already gone out to the car did not know that the other guard had not minutes earlier spoken to Matthew in the men's room. The second guard, hearing the first guard telling the lady in the red dress that the building was clear, assumed that the gentleman he'd seen at the urinal downstairs had already come upstairs and left the building. Susan figured she must have somehow missed Matthew in the general exodus. Nobody knew nothing. The guards waited until Susan stepped outside onto the red carpet. In the distance, they could see the last of the departing automobiles making their turns onto U.S. 41.

"Good night, ma'am," one of the guards said, and locked the door behind her.

Dr. Lanford M. Oberling, beaming with success, said, "Let's put her away for the night, boys."

When a person has been drinking a little, time assumes strange dimensions. It seemed to Matthew that it took him only two or three seconds to zip up his fly, and step away from the urinal, and go over to the sinks to wash his hands. Instead, in his somewhat inebriated state, negotiating the strange zipper on the infrequently worn tuxedo took him a full thirty seconds, and staggering over to the sinks and fumbling with the faucet on one of them took yet another thirty or forty seconds. As he leisurely washed his hands, he soberly (it seemed to him) reflected upon the fact that at least sixty percent of the men who left men's rooms did so without first washing their hands, an observation worthy of at least ten minutes of in-depth investigation on *60 Minutes,* a keen perception that caused him to vow never again to shake hands with another man in his entire life.

Lathering his hands, he wondered again (and again and again and again, although all of this seemed to be ripping through his mind at warp speed) why Patricia Demming, whom he'd truly loved with all his heart, had chosen to exchange him for a lardass like Charles Foster, and then he wondered, again and again and again, when the relationship with him had started and why he hadn't noticed any change in her. Shaking his head slowly, he blamed it all on the goddamn coma, and morosely washed his hands over and over again.

Oberling and the two guards were just then wheeling the case on its ball-bearing casters toward the elevator.

In the closet, Candace, Harry and Jack were poised to spring.

★　　★　　★

There were only four cars left in the parking lot. Susan assumed that three of them belonged to museum personnel. The fourth one was Matthew's smoky-blue Acura.

Matthew was nowhere to be seen.

So where is he? she wondered.

The guard had seen him leaving the building.

Okay, he'd looked a little bit tipsy when he'd gone down to the men's room. Was it possible he was still somewhere on the museum grounds?

She decided to go look for him.

Jill Lawton was leading him to the ends of the earth.

Jill Lawton was leading him to where the state of Florida joined the state of Maine. He was certain she would realize that she was being followed. How could she *not* realize when they were the only two cars on an arrow-straight, pitch-black road that skewered Santa Lucia Island from end to end?

He decided to pass her.

This was a smart move, provided she didn't suddenly turn off the road behind him, in which case he'd lose her. He stepped on the accelerator, moving closer to the Dodge, and then—even though there was no one behind him—he signaled that he was moving out, and hit the gas hard, overtaking the Dodge, speeding by it, and then pulling back into the lane, ahead of her this time. He kept his foot on the pedal until he could just barely make out her headlights in the rearview mirror, and then he made a sharp right turn into the next driveway.

Reversing direction at once, he turned the car so that it was facing the road again, and immediately doused the lights. He hoped no fuckin redneck with a shotgun would come out of the house. He hoped no fuckin Cujo would come charging across the lawn dripping spit. Holding his breath, he waited in the dark until her car swept by. He counted the seconds till she was well past, and then he turned on his lights, and swung out onto the road again.

He was hoping she would think the *first* car hadn't been on her tail at all. He was hoping she'd think the headlights reflected in her mirror were from a new car, a different car, a *second* car that couldn't possibly be following her, how paranoid could you get?

Or how fuckin smart? he thought, grinning.

Because both outside guards were dead, there was no one to stop Susan from coming around the side of the museum and walking out onto the lawn that stretched down to the water, where she figured Matthew might have wandered if he thought he needed a breath of fresh air.

It was pitch-black back here.

She reached into her handbag for her key ring.

Jill was sure she was being followed.

Nor was this the two guys in the dun-colored car who'd followed her into the movie theater and who were standing there by the candy stand with their thumbs up their asses when she waddled by in the fat lady's dress with the legs of her blue jeans rolled up and five rolls of toilet paper stuffed under the dress to give her a belly. She wondered if the fat lady was conscious by now. The dress was on the backseat. She was still wearing jeans and the sneakers and blue cotton sweater she'd had on when she left the house tonight and the two cops—she was sure they'd been cops—joined her.

She didn't know *what* the guy behind her was.

278

She was sure he was alone because she'd caught a glimpse of him as he'd zipped by earlier, disappearing off the road ahead—smart ploy if you were dealing with a dope—and then reappearing behind her, she felt certain it was the same man in the same car, call it intuition.

She decided to force the issue.

She pulled over to the side of the road.

Took the P38 out of her handbag.

Got out of the car.

Stood in the middle of the road, the gun in her right hand, flat against her thigh.

From where Zaygo idled the boat in the middle of the Intracoastal, he saw a flashlight blink on.

At last, he thought, and swung the boat around and nosed it toward the museum dock.

The elevator doors slid open.

Oberling stepped into the corridor and the two museum guards came out after him, wheeling out the case. The cup looked rather insignificant now that there were no overhead spotlights proclaiming its importance. One of the guards began looking for the key to the Medeco lock on the metal door at the end of the corridor. Once that door was opened, they would be inside a concrete enclosure facing the stainless-steel door to the museum vault.

Oberling heard what sounded like a door opening behind him. He turned to see two men and a blond woman stepping out of the supply closet. One of the men had a gun in his hand.

"That's as far as we go, boys," Harry said.

★   ★   ★

Crazy broad was standing in the middle of the road.

He braked the car to a stop. Either that or run her over, he didn't have the stomach for that. He rolled down the window. Play this cool, he was thinking. Hi, Mrs. Lawton, how you doing? Nice night for a drive, ain't it? Coming toward the car now. He suddenly saw the gun in her right hand, and reached immediately for his own gun in the glove compartment. Closer now. Left hand shielding her eyes from the glare of his headlights, approaching the open window, stepping out of the beams and around them. The Smith & Wesson was in his lap, below the window line, out of sight. The gun in her hand looked like some kind of German pistol. It probed the night, pointing toward his head.

She leaned in closer to the window.

"You?" she said, surprised.

"Listen, don't get excited," he said.

"Why are you following me?"

"I'm looking for your husband."

"Why?"

"I want to kill him."

"So do I," Jill said.

"Good, let's do it together," Donofrio said at once.

Reasonable, right? We got something in common. So put up the gun, okay, lady? We're in this together, okay?

She considered this.

"Why not?" she said, at last. "Follow me."

Oberling kept thinking the blonde looked familiar. Working on the combination, twisting first one dial and then the other, he turned and said over his shoulder, "Don't I know you?"

"No," Candace said.

"Open the damn door!" Jack snapped.

"It's open, it's open!" Oberling said.

Had Matthew come out of the men's room that very moment he'd have been locked into the vault with Oberling and the two guards. Instead, he was rinsing his hands, and drying them under the wall blower, which had been invented he was sure by the same mad Nazi scientist who'd invented panty hose.

When he finally did emerge from the rest room into an already darkened lounge, Candace and Harry and Jack, carrying the cup, were coming through one of the museum's back doors, onto the lawn, home free they thought.

Zaygo saw a dark-haired woman in a red dress approaching the dock as he pulled the boat in. For a moment he thought Candace had changed her dress and put on a wig. The flashlight she held cast hardly any illumination at all, it was probably one of those teeny little things you attach to a key chain so you can see a lock's keyway in the dark. He didn't know who this lady was, but he hoped she wasn't a cop. Sometimes cops came with long dark hair and red gowns.

And then, suddenly, in the far distance, he saw another light signaling.

As Matthew came up the stairs into the silence of the empty museum, he wondered where the hell everybody was. He stubbed his toe on something in the dark, muttered "Shit!" and heard a scream somewhere in the night.

Not for nothing had he been married to Susan all those many years.

The scream was hers.

He was suddenly stone-cold sober.

Donofrio left his car in the public parking lot off Santa Lucia Beach, and they drove from there in Jill's white Dodge to Osprey Drive, a dead-end street from which they could observe any boat traffic on the lagoon.

"They'll be coming by boat," she told Donofrio.

"Okay," he said. "You mind if I smoke?"

"I'd rather you didn't," she said.

"Okay," he said.

They sat in the dark in the parked automobile. There was a full bright moon that silvered the lagoon. It was a perfect night for lovers. Killers, too, maybe.

"Why you want to kill him?" he asked.

"Something I want from him," she said. "Why do you want to kill him?"

"Cause he killed Melanie."

"You don't know that for sure."

"Oh, I know it, all right."

"Uh-huh," she said.

She was wondering how he might react to the truth. She was also wondering what Melanie possibly could have seen in this hulking brute.

"What is it you want from him?" he asked.

"Nothing important."

"Just important enough to kill for, huh?"

"Some things have to be done," she said.

He was wondering why she reminded him so much of Melanie. They didn't look at all alike, no one could ever mistake them for sisters, that was for sure. But there was something. He didn't know what. Something.

"You think your husband was boffing her?" he asked.

"Who?"

"Melanie."

"I don't think she knew him."

"Oh, she knew him, all right."

Jill shrugged.

"What time is this boat supposed to be coming up the river here?"

"The lagoon." She looked at her watch. "Should be leaving around now," she said.

"Leaving where?"

She didn't answer.

He was dying for a smoke. Pissed him off that some people got so terribly *offended* if you lit a cigarette in their presence. Sitting here in the dark at the end of nowhere, waiting for a boat to show up, water all rippling with silver, nothing would have been better than a smoke.

"What've you got against smoking?" he asked.

"Nothing."

"So why can't I have a cigarette?"

"Who said you couldn't?"

"I asked would you mind if I smoked and you said you rathered I didn't."

"I'm trying to quit. But you can smoke if you want to."

"Gee, thanks," he said, and immediately pulled a pack of Camels from his shirt pocket and clicked open a lighter. She watched his hands. Left hand hanging the cigarette on his lip, right thumb snapping the lighter into flame. Strong hands. Watched the crude outlines of his face as he sucked in on the cigarette. Watched smoke streaming from his nostrils. He clicked the lighter shut.

"Why you trying to quit?" he asked.

"Bad habit."

"*Everybody* should smoke," he said. "Then there wouldn't be no bullshit about it."

She remembered sitting in the dark and smoking with Melanie. Wondered if Melanie had ever smoked with him. Wondered what they had done together. Wondered how Melanie ever could have made love to a man like this one. She shrugged the thought aside.

"What?" he asked.

"Nothing."

"No, what? I just seen you shrug. What was it?"

"I was wondering how well you knew Melanie, that's all."

"Very well," he said.

She nodded.

"What does that mean, that nod?"

"It means Okay, you knew her very well."

"I did."

"Okay."

"*Very* well," he said.

He dragged on the cigarette, serenely exhaled a stream of smoke. The car windows were open, the smoke wafted out onto the cool night air.

Jill looked at her watch again.

"Is that your whole name? Jill?" he asked.

"Yes. Sure. Jill."

"Okay."

"Why?"

"It seems short, is all."

"It is short."

"But it ain't short for nothing else, right?"

"Jill is all it is."

"Mine is Peter. When I was a kid, they used to call me

Petie. I hated that name Petie. Pete ain't no great shakes, either. Peter is a dignified name, don't you think? I mean, what the hell, Peter was a friggin *saint,* am I right?"

She was thinking Peter also means penis.

She shrugged *this* thought aside, too.

"What?" he said.

"Nothing," she said.

"The shrug again," he said.

"I was thinking Peter also means prick," she said.

"It does?" he said.

"Sure. A man's penis. His Peter."

"I never heard that in my life."

"Well, I can't help that. But it happens to be a fact."

"I'd bust anybody's head he tells me my name means prick."

"Willie, too."

"What do you mean?"

"Willie. That's another name for a man's penis. In London, they sell Willie warmers."

"They don't."

"They do. Women knit them for Christmas."

Donofrio burst out laughing.

"How come you know so much about names for a man's cock?" he asked.

"Just lucky, I guess," she said.

"You want a cigarette?"

"Yes, I think I would."

He took the pack from his pocket, shook one loose. He thumbed the lighter into flame, held it to the tip of the cigarette. She dragged in deeply. He lighted one for himself. Smoke drifted through the open windows.

"Wish we had something to drink, too," he said.

"Mmm," she said.

"Too bad we ain't in *my* car. I got a pint of Scotch in the glove compartment."

"Too bad," she said.

"You like Scotch?"

"Yes."

"Me, too. Which Scotch?"

"Johnnie Black."

Jack had taught her to drink Johnnie Black.

"I prefer Dewar's," he said.

"I'll have to try it sometime."

"I wish you would. Sometime."

They both fell silent.

The night was so still.

"This is nice," he said. "Smoking. Talking. Ain't it nice?"

"Yes," she said, "it is," and glanced out at the lagoon. "I wonder what's keeping them."

"What time were you expecting them?"

"One-thirty, two o'clock?"

"It's way past that now."

"Mm."

They were silent again.

"I wonder if we should drive over to the house," she said.

"Your call," he said.

"I just don't want to walk in on a whole fucking *gang*."

"Oh, it's a *gang* here?"

He didn't tell her, but he found it very exciting that she had just used the F-word, as his mother called it. For that matter, all that earlier talk about peters and willies and pricks and cocks had also been very stimulating, you might say. He suddenly realized what it was that reminded him of Melanie. It was what you might call this *sensuality* about her. It was this look on her face that said Come fuck me, please, even though she was wearing sneakers and jeans and a sloppy cotton sweater. He suddenly wondered if she was wearing a bra under the sweater.

"Why *don't* we run by the house?" he said.

They left the Dodge at the top of the drive, and walked down to the house on the dirt road that led into the property. Donofrio was thinking there could be fuckin crocodiles in here.

The house was dark and silent.

They stood in the shadows, watching, listening.

"There's nobody here," he whispered.

"Either that, or they're asleep."

"How many are there supposed to be?"

"Jack and three others. But if they got here, the others should have left by now."

"So then he's alone, right?"

"If they left, yes. If he's here."

"If he's here, he's alone. Asleep."

"Presumably," Jill said.

They were standing very close, in the dark, whispering. A peculiarly pungent aroma clung to him, neither a deodorant nor one of those phony faintly medicinal scents bottled by brand-name designers. Instead, it was something thoroughly natural and frankly stimulating, a scent that was entirely masculine and completely his own. She suddenly wondered if Melanie had ever taught him the Wichita Weep.

"Let's go see he's in there," Donofrio suggested.

Guns in hand, they approached the front door.

Donofrio tried the knob. It turned easily under his hand. He exerted a little pressure on the door. It opened. He hesitated before entering. Jill gave a brief nod. Gun hand leading him, Donofrio stepped inside. Jill went in immediately behind him.

The house was still.

They stood in the entrance hall, hardly daring to breathe, listening. Nothing. Moonlight illuminated the furniture with a pallid spectral glow. And now they could hear the sounds any house made in the night, the boards creaking and snapping, the pipes pinging, a clock ticking noisily and steadily in another room. They kept listening. Not a human sound. Donofrio gestured with the gun toward a flight of stairs that led to the second story of the house. She nodded. He led the way.

The upstairs hallway doubled back past the stairwell. There were three bedrooms up there. Each of them was empty.

"I think we're alone," Donofrio said.

"What time is it?" she wondered aloud.

"Quarter to three."

"Something must have gone wrong."

"I think so."

"So what do we do now?"

"I'm kind of sleepy, aren't you?" he said.

"Well, I guess I am," she said.

"So why don't we go to sleep?"

She looked at him.

He shrugged.

"Or not," he said.

She kissed him full on the mouth, the way she had kissed Melanie in the pool all those years ago, the way Melanie might have kissed him whenever she was with him, and she guided the hand not holding the gun to her naked breast under the sloppy cotton sweater, and she said, "Let me take you to Bali," and he thought she meant it only figuratively, whatever that was.

12

Steve, I was never so scared in my life.

I'd had a bit too much to drink, I thought at first I was seeing things, these figures in silhouette down at the dock, three men in tuxedos, Susan and another woman in long evening gowns, it was like a Fellini movie, all of them on the lawn by the dock with the moon shining on the water and a boat idling, a Fellini movie, all it needed was a dog barking at the moon.

Then I saw the gun.

And from Fellini it suddenly went to Tarantino because the guy with the gun weighed two-fifty if he weighed an ounce, and he looked as if he drank the blood of Vikings for breakfast and he was advancing on Susan with his left hand poised for a backhanded swat to shut her up. I came running across the lawn, downhill all the way, gathering speed and momentum, rushing down toward the dock where this surreal scene was being played. The guy in tuxedo at the wheel of the boat looked amused by the fact that the big guy was preparing to knock Susan silly. A third guy, blond and bewildered, also in tuxedo, had both hands wrapped around some kind of object he was holding tight to his chest, as if he'd just won an Oscar and was getting ready to thank his mom for bringing him up properly. Standing alongside him was the blonde in the ice-blue gown whom I was sure I'd seen inside, dancing or drinking, observing all this with a look of patient expectation, as if *she'd* been nominated for an award, too, and was now waiting for the announcement of the winner.

I was too late to stop the big guy from hitting Susan. I was still maybe twenty, twenty-five feet from the dock when he cut loose with a backhanded swipe that could have felled Tyson. She staggered back, a sudden smear of red staining her lips and her teeth, and then her eyes rolled up into her head and she simply collapsed. It was as if her spine had turned liquid. She merely melted into the ground, red gown spreading against the green lawn as if it were suddenly Christmas.

I threw myself at the big guy.

I could have been hurling myself at a rhinoceros. He shook me off and then smashed his bunched fist full into my face.

"Enough of that, Harry," the blond man said, as if scolding a disobedient child.

I was on the ground now, bleeding from the nose. I figured that whatever else they might do, they would surely kill both Susan and me because we were witness to whatever the hell this was.

The guy at the wheel of the boat whispered, "Come on, come on."

There was, it seemed to me, a moment's hesitation. I knew I was already out of this, I knew there was nothing I could do to alter whatever was about to happen next. I was helpless in a situation I hadn't created and couldn't change.

I'm no hero, Steve, I never have been.

In a world of macho males with black patches over one eye, I'm the ninety-seven-pound weakling who gets sand kicked in his face, even though I weigh a hundred and eighty-five. I'm no champion, I wasn't meant to be. In a world of leading men, I'm a supporting player at best, a man afraid of cowboys, I once got nearly beaten to death by a pair of cowboys, Steve, I'm no hero.

But I remembered in detail all the dirty tricks a cop down here once taught me, and I figured this was my last best hope before Susan and I got killed here, so I reached out for Harry's ankles, trying to topple him to the ground, you know, so I could step on his balls, you know. He kicked me in the head. I thought I'd black out, I thought it was coma time all over again— I got shot real bad once, Steve, I was in coma once upon a time, have you ever been shot?

"Leave them be," the blond man said. "Let's get moving."

"They saw me," Harry said.

Never mind *us*. They saw *me*. Which made it personal. In Harry's mind, Susan and I were already dead. All he had to do was pull the trigger. It was as simple as that.

"I don't want any killing here," the blond man said.

"Little late for that," Harry said.

There was a heavy silence while this sank in.

"For Christ's sake, let's get out of here," the man on the boat said.

I remembered reading someplace that the five most used words in the movies were "Let's get out of here."

Susan said, "Matthew, *do* something." My head was ringing from Harry's kick. My nose kept spilling blood into my cupped hand. The blonde in the ice-blue gown said in an ice-blue voice, "Drop the gun, Harry." The night resonated with triteness. *"Now,"* she said, compounding the felony.

"Are you kidd—?" Harry started to say, but then he must have seen exactly what I was seeing, though mine was a worm's-eye view. He was seeing a small pistol in the lady's fist, pointing at his head. I thought, Welcome to America, folks. In America, even cool-looking blond ladies carry guns. Especially in the state of Florida.

There was another heavy silence.

"Hey, come on, guys," the blond man said.

He was beginning to look familiar.

"Come on."

Plaintively. Almost a whine.

I didn't know Harry from any other cheap thief in the world, but I was willing to bet he wasn't going to let either a woman or a wimp bluff him out of what he perceived to be a winning hand. The smirk on his face said, "I'm bigger, guys," the glow in his eyes said, "My *gun* is bigger, too," and I knew he was going to shoot at least the woman and perhaps the man, too, because this was a guy who took no prisoners.

The woman fired before he did. Her first shot took him in the forehead. He fell like a sequoia, crashing to the ground, lying still and silent. She walked up to him, nudged him with the toe of one glittering blue shoe, and then pumped two more shots into his chest. For a small gun, it made a lot of noise. I hoped the explosions would attract the police. Or somebody.

"The cup," she said.

Another silence. The night was sullen with silence tonight.

"Jack?" she said. "The cup, please."

Jack? I thought.

Lawton?

So here we are, I thought.

This is all about a *cup,* I thought.

Who gets shot for it next?

"Matthew," Susan said. "Do something."

"Shut up," the blonde said. And then, again, "The god-damn *cup,* Jack!" I struggled to my knees. "Don't move!" she shouted, whirling on me. I wondered how many other hackneyed expressions this little troupe of players could come up with in the next few minutes before somebody got shot again. I thought maybe the blonde might add, "I know how to use this, Jack," and Jack Lawton, if he *was* Jack Law-ton, might say, "You haven't got the nerve," or words to that effect, and she might answer, "Don't tempt me," and Susan might say, "I thought I married a *man,*" even though we were no longer married, which in itself was a cliché of sorts.

"Jack, I don't want to kill you," the blonde said, which song I'd also heard before, but it was a refrain Jack seemed to appreciate at last because he said at once, "Here, it isn't worth it," and carelessly tossed the cup into the air. In the movies, the blonde would have dropped the pistol so she could catch the cup with both hands and Jack would have rushed her and turned the tables, but this was real life. She made a one-handed catch, touched the barrel of the small gun to her head in a kind of farewell salute, grinned, and climbed onto the boat, long shapely legs showing in the high slit of the glare-ice gown.

"Move it," she said to the driver.

The boat shot out from the dock like a rocket.

I helped Susan to her feet. We watched the boat disappearing over the water, heading north, heading God only knew where. I turned to the blond man, who actually had tears in his eyes, and I said, "Mr. Lawton, I presume?"

"Well, at least you found your client's husband," Carella said.

"But not my client. She's nowhere in sight, Steve. Donofrio, either. They've both vanished."

"Maybe they ran off someplace together."

"Oh sure, I can just imagine that."

"We'll never know, I guess. What does Lawton have to say about all this?"

"They charged him with Burglary Two, which down here is punishable by not more than fifteen. He's claiming he had nothing to do with the theft of the cup, the others nabbed him as a hostage. Named all three of them. Bloom's got all-points out on the blonde and the driver."

"They'll surface. They always do."

"You want my guess about Lawton?"

"Sure, what's your guess?"

"He walks."

"I wouldn't be surprised."

"Maybe I ought to represent him. Come out of this a winner."

"Good idea."

"Anyway, thanks for your call."

"I'm just sorry . . ."

"The message was there when I got home."

"Too late."

"It would've helped," Matthew said, and hesitated. "Steve," he said, "I haven't told this to anyone else yet, but . . ."

There was a silence on the line.

"I'm quitting criminal law."

"Why?"

"Let's say I'm not well suited to it. In fact, the only murder case I ever tried, I *lost*."

Both men laughed.

The laughter trailed.

There was another silence.

"Steve," Matthew said, "I don't want to get shot again. I came this close to getting shot again last night. Never again. I don't like being that scared. It makes me feel like an amateur playing cops and robbers."

"I feel that way myself sometimes."

"I don't think so."

There was a longer silence.

"What'll you do?" Carella asked at last.

"Well, I'm not sure, exactly. Take a long vacation, I guess. Rest awhile. Think awhile. Smell the roses."

"And then?"

"I don't know. Maybe go back to general practice again. Real estate closings. Drawing wills. Boundary disputes. Stuff like that. No guns, Steve. No cops and robbers. That's your job, not mine."

"Maybe you ought to give it some thought."

"Oh, sure, there's plenty of time, no one's pushing me. I've even considered trying something entirely new."

"Like what?"

"Well, I don't know. A friend of mine started sculpting when he was forty-five. Made a go of it, too."

"I wanted to be a painter once," Carella said.

"I wanted to be an actor."

"Everybody wants to be an actor."

The line crackled over the distance separating the two men. For a moment, they each thought they'd been disconnected.

"Steve?"

"Matthew?"

"I'm still here."

Silence. Each seemed reluctant to hang up.

"So," Matthew said, and his voice caught. He hesitated a moment. Carella waited. "If ever you decide to buy any real estate down here . . ."

"I'll keep you in mind."

"You have my number."

"And listen," Carella said, "if ever you need *my* help on anything . . . give me a call, okay?"

"I will."

"I'll be here at the same old stand, okay? Just give me a call."

"I promise." Matthew said.

And gently replaced the phone on its cradle.